M000204311

ACROSS THE DIVIDE

THE COLLECTOR SERIES BOOK 3

STACEY MARIE BROWN

ALSO BY STACEY MARIE BROWN

Collector Series
City in Embers (#1)
The Barrier Between (#2)
Across the Divide (#3)
From Burning Ashes (#4)

Lightness Saga
The Crown of Light (#1)
Lightness Falling (#2)
The Fall of the King (#3)
Rise from the Embers (#4)

A Winterland Tale
Descending into Madness (#1)
Ascending from Madness (#2)
Beauty in Her Madness (#3)
Beast in His Madness (#4)

Savage Lands Series
Savage Lands (#1)
Wild Lands (#2)
Dead Lands (#3)
Bad Lands (#4)

DEDICATED TO HONEY TITS!

ONE

Welcome home, Zoey. The words bounced around in my head, trying to stick to anything that resembled logic.

How did I get back here? The truth didn't make sense. *This can't be happening.* I squeezed my lids closed. My heart slammed in my chest.

Jump, Zoey.

I knew it was impossible to jump from here. Rapava designed the Department of Molecular Genetics, a secret branch of the government, to make sure fae would not be able to use their glamour or powers to escape. But the sinkhole in my gut still widened with fear and disappointment.

Beep. Beep.

My heart monitor continued to chirp in my ears.

"It's good to have you back with us." Rapava's voice sounded automated. They were simply words he said without emotion behind them. "Where you belong."

Belong. I belonged with Ryker and Sprig. I gnashed my teeth together. Where were they? Were they all right?

"We have reduced the dosage of Propofol. You should begin to feel more alert. After two weeks of keeping you in a coma, it will take a little time for your body to adjust."

Two weeks? Coma?

Beep. Beep. Beep.

"Zoey." The doctor said my name like an order. I pried my lashes open. Standing before me peering down was a tall, lean man in his late fifties with silvering hair and sharp hazel eyes.

Dr. Boris Rapava. The man I had once considered a mentor, and a brilliant scientist and doctor. I had respected him. Now he represented only lies and betrayal.

He tilted his head. "Did you understand what I said to you? Do you know where you are?"

1

My eyes darted to him then back around the room. *Of course I know where I am.* This place used to be like a second home, where I found sanctuary, love, friendship. That was all gone. And most of it had been untrue.

"Nod your head if you understand." His gaze fixed on my heart monitor and IV drip.

Ignoring him, I took in the familiar walls of the DMG, coated in the monotonous white walls and plywood cupboards. A cornucopia of medical equipment lined the black counters and shelves. I had spent many years in these rooms, but now I occupied the single hospital bed in the room. A table stood cross the room, covered with syringes, tubes, and vials of liquid. My gaze drifted down my body. I was dressed in a hospital gown, and my only accessories were leather-and-metal cuffs on my ankles and wrists binding me to the bed.

Did I understand? Yes, I understood the one place I used to call my safe haven was now my prison cell.

Beep. Beep. Beep. Beep.

The monitor screamed out my emotions, displaying them for everyone to see and hear.

"Turn. It. Off," I grunted. My throat felt so raw; I flinched in pain.

Rapava reached over and shut off the screen, silencing the room. "I know you probably have a lot of questions."

I did. But all that came out was the blaring truth of my return. The only reason I could be in this bed now. "You work for Vadik," I said softly, the words breaking over my sore throat.

Vadik was wealthy, extremely dangerous, and powerful. A demon. He had hired Ryker to steal the Stone of Destiny, the most powerful chunk of rock in the Otherworld. Ryker told me in fae mythology there are four magical artifacts: a sword, spear, cauldron, and the stone. Lia Fáil, Stone of Destiny. These items are so powerful, they can destroy the world if put in the wrong hands. Ryker reneged on the deal with Vadik. Now Vadik would do anything and everything in his ability to get it back. Including selling me to the highest bidder.

Rapava shifted back, his lids narrowing. "I do not work *for him.* Or any other fae."

"Really?" I choked. "Then how did I get here?"

Rapava pressed his lips together so firmly they turned white. "We are in a war, Zoey. Human lives and our freedom are on the line. Sometimes you have to do bad things to get what you want. I see the bigger picture. Vadik had something I wanted." He turned away from me and grabbed a cup of water from the table next to my bed. "Here." He placed the plastic to my lips.

I wanted to refuse, to spit in his face, but the cool liquid lapping against my mouth was too tempting, alluring me to give myself over. I could not deny the draw. He tipped the cup and the water trickled down and dampened the parched sections of my throat.

"I am sorry we had to constrain you, but it was for your own protection." He set the glass back on the table.

"Or for yours?"

Rapava's head jerked back to me.

"Take them off." I held up my arms as far as they would go.

"I'm not sure that is wise. You've been through an ordeal. You are not quite yourself right now, are *you*?" He let the question tapper off, implying he knew the answer to his own question. "You're an incredible specimen, Zoey. We have learned much from testing you." He folded his arms in front of his doctor's coat, gazing at me with wonder. "Even your vitals are unprecedented. Every test indicates you are a healthy young lady. I don't know how or why, but you are completely clear of the defect in your DNA."

My lashes dipped briefly as I swallowed. Ryker's powers had cured me. Just as I suspected. Deep down I felt I was all right, but couldn't be sure. The confirmation did not come with glee.

If I lived, Ryker died.

"Is that why you put me in a coma for two weeks? To be your lab rat?" My fingers gripped the leather cuffs on either side of the bed. Trapped. My chest flinched, the sensation creeping into my lungs, closing them down. Drawing on my childhood memories of being locked in the closet, sweat dampened the back of my neck. Vulnerable and defenseless didn't sit well with me.

"Zoey…"

I took a deep breath, wiggling my arms. "Please? They're hurting me."

"There's nowhere you can go. Every way out has been sealed. Thanks to you, we learned our lesson. We saw the weaknesses of this place. A lot has changed." Dr. Rapava watched me, his critical eyes analyzing me. "I'm sure there is no reason to tell you these things... you are *home*," he emphasized. "It took a lot for us to get you here. Much sacrifice to get you back to us. I hope you can appreciate what I've done to bring you home

3

safely."

I couldn't get my mouth to respond, but my gaze never left his, holding up my shackled wrists.

Finally, he nodded, turned, and walked to the internal call system on the wall. "Can you come down? Yes. Now." Rapava hung up the phone and proceeded toward me. He withdrew a pair of keys from his pocket. "Do not cause me to regret this," he commented as he unlatched my cuffs.

I yanked my wrists free and sat up, rubbing my arms.

"The two weeks you were in a coma were instrumental to us here. I hope you can see the good you are doing. But much remains a mystery. I want you to assist with this, help me understand how the magic transferred to you. How it changed you." His eyes glinted with excitement. "When I find the coding, and I will, there will be nothing I can't construct. You and I are going to create great things together, Zoey."

"You mean your own Frankenstein army?" Words shot from my mouth before I could think. "I know all about your experiments. Manufacturing humans. Like me." My lids narrowed on him.

"I understand you are probably upset—"

"Probably?" I spat.

Rapava pressed his lips together. "I kept the truth about your birth from you and how you were created for your own good. Your growth outside these walls, unaware of the fae world, was extremely important."

His lack of understanding of the horrors he put me through in the name of science made me sick. Acid burned my esophagus, settling on my tongue with bitterness.

"You and Sera were my greatest achievements. With faults, yes, but still miraculous. You two developed seer powers greater than any before you and both outlived the others by years. But everything has changed, and I see how shortsighted I was. Look at what a unique specimen you are. Think about what I can create with your genetic material.

"For the first time, we really have a chance against the fae, to fight and take back our world. We no longer have to be helpless against them." He placed his hand on my arm, excitement emanating from him. "Don't you see, Zoey? *You* are the key to saving the human race. You and I are going to change everything. We will be the most important race. *They* will fear us."

My teeth gritted at the absence of emotion in his voice. There was much I wanted to ask, so much I needed to understand, but anger, stubbornness, and fear kept my lips pinned tight.

Disgust and rage crawled over my skin at the betrayal I felt, the realization of the lie I had been living, and what he allowed to happen to me. I blinked and looked away from him. The impulse to flee wrenched through me. The need to jump to escape overwhelmed me, but nothing happened. How was he able to keep fae from using their gifts? I never needed to wonder before. Now it was something I had to learn.

"You're able to keep fae locked in here. You have power over them." Stroking egos always helped in retrieving information. "How do you do it?"

"Curious?" An amused smile tipped up his mouth, understanding my hidden meaning. "I've been especially aware of goblin metal and iron's effects on fae since the beginning. Learning the weaknesses of your enemy is the only way you can defeat them. To humans it is completely undetected, but every inch of this place is covered with pure iron and goblin metal paints. All exits at the ground level are now sealed with it." He gave me a pointed look, and I knew I wouldn't be able to use the same escape route as last time. "We also give our patients daily injections with a formula I created to keep the subjects in line."

Goblin metal was extremely rare and even more expensive. That Rapava painted the walls with it, used it in all the medication, and commissioned handcuffs made with it told me there wasn't anything he wouldn't pay or do to fulfill his ambitions.

Anxiety was hopping in my veins like a bad drug. I had to escape and find Ryker and Sprig. Did Vadik have them? Kill them? Air choked in my airways, and my lungs fluttered to keep up. I couldn't think of the bad; I just had to find them.

The door opened, pulling my attention to the figure walking in. A tall, broad-shouldered African-American man sauntered in, his ripped chest displayed through his two-sizes-too-small T-shirt. A smug, cruel smile tugged at the corners of his mouth. His large, dark eyes, framed by even darker long eyelashes, centered on me. He was the kind of good looking which caused you to do a double take—hair cut to scalp, huge dazzling smile, and high cheekbones. But his ego, cruelty, and arrogance saturated his aura like rank cologne, turning him foul in my eyes.

Liam.

His gaze found mine, a superior smile on his lips. It was his usual expression, but now it brought Daniel back to my mind in a web of memories strung with Liam's smirk and his condescending taunts. He always had to one-up Daniel, trying to prove he was the better hunter.

Liam, along with Sera, had strived to make my life miserable at DMG since the day I was recruited.

A mix of disgust and loathing pinwheeled in my chest, putting me on guard. I slipped to the edge of the bed, needing to feel the ground under my feet.

The door slowly fell back into its hold, about to close me in with the two men. Air syphoned out of my lungs, anxiety clutching them. The walls felt like they were crushing in on me. Hatred seethed out my bones like heat the closer my ex-Collector comrade and nemesis came. My gaze went between Liam and Rapava.

Get out now, Zoey. Run! Instinct screamed at me, compelling me to act.

My feet hit the ground, slapping against the cool tile as I bolted for the door. Air drifted up my exposed backside, the gown fluttering with movement. With every step the muscles in my legs cramped and threatened to give way from weeks of inactivity.

No!

I gritted my teeth and slammed my shoulder into Liam, knocking him to the side. My sudden action was the only thing letting me slide past him. He quickly righted himself, reaching for my hair. I twisted and grabbed the doorknob, yanking the door back hard.

Thwack! The door struck Liam between his eyes. A roar of pain emanated from his mouth as he stumbled backward.

Rapava didn't move or speak as I slipped out the door and ran down the hall. His lack of concern triggered apprehension, but I pushed it back and forced my legs to stretch farther.

Even after Rapava told me there was no hope of using my powers, I couldn't help but dig deep, searching for them. Something was there, I could feel it. But it was like trying to hold water in a sieve; the powers seeped through my hands.

I sprinted down the passageway for the exit. I had no idea which level I was on. It was simple to get turned around here. Every floor, every hallway resembled the next one—a labyrinth of rights and lefts till you could no longer remember how you got here.

Voices emanated from the hallway in front of me.

Shit. A flood of *déjà vu* spiked more adrenaline into my blood, and desperation for an escape sank its teeth into my flesh. I went for the door closest to me. Locked. I slapped it in despair. I went down the line, shaking and twisting the handles wildly. All locked.

Sprig, I need you. He was able to get us out last time with his power of undoing locks. Something told me this time he would not be able to help.

Pounding feet vibrated the floor, sending more terror up my spine.

"We have her in sight," a man's voice spoke. The sound of a walkie-talkie crackled.

Fuck! I bounced in a circle, like a wild animal.

"Don't move," a man shouted, and this time I recognized the voice.

Peter. A fellow Collector, a hunter, and one of Daniel's oldest friends. They had been in special ops together. He blamed me for Daniel's death. I swiveled around to see the severe six-foot blond man running toward me, a gun pointed at my head.

It looked like he still blamed me.

"Put your hands up," he shouted.

Three others—Matt, Marv, and Hugo—flanked him. Men who had once been my friends, my fellow Collectors, now held guns on me.

My gaze shot around with desperation. I had to get out. The thought of not being able to get to Ryker or Sprig rattled me. A deep whine curled over my tongue as I began to pace frantically.

"Get on your knees." Peter motioned to the ground with the gun.

Another distressed whimper escaped my lungs, my hands shaking. *No. Not again.* I was always calm and composed when I fought, sure of myself and my situation. But I couldn't take this again, being locked in here, not knowing what happened to my best friend and the man I loved…

Something in me snapped. I slammed my fists into the walls and screamed.

"Zoey! Get on your knees now," Peter ordered as he inched closer.

"Jesus. She's like a wild animal. What did the fae do to her?" Matt shook his head.

"This is your last warning." Peter took another step. Then another.

It was one stride too close.

I slammed my fist into the side of his face. He stumbled to the side. My leg hooked behind the back of his knee, breaking his stance and toppling him to the ground. Marv, Hugo, and Matt came for me.

I punched Hugo in the throat, and he grabbed at his neck, hunching to the side, gasping for air. Jerking my elbow back from Hugo, I sent it into Matt's nose. A crack of cartilage sounded as my elbow struck his face. He huffed in pain, blood already running down his face. I bulldozed into Marv's slight frame, knocking him against the wall. I had always been a better fighter than all three of them.

Run, Zoey! I screamed at myself. My feet obeyed immediately, heading for where the men had entered. I saw the elevator down the corridor and made a break for it.

Arms came from behind me, pulling me off my feet. "Noooo!" I bellowed. Dark, muscular arms constricted me so tightly I could barely breathe.

"I got her," Liam said from behind me.

I snarled, thrashing against him.

"Stop fighting me, Zoey." Liam's arms compressed even more, crushing my lungs. My head dropped, and my teeth found the soft flesh of his hand.

"Ahhh!" He wrenched away, and I tore free. Deep down I knew there was no hope, but in my frantic mind I just needed to get out, and they were my obstacles. I made it another five feet before hands grabbed the back of my gown and yanked me backward.

The sound of my bare skin slapping the tile resonated down the long corridor before I felt the pain as my spine slammed onto the floor.

Bodies moved in my direction.

"Hold her!" Liam's voice bounded over. He shook his hand as though it still hurt. I didn't break the skin, but it would probably leave a bruise.

Peter jumped on me, his pale face flushed red. "Don't move." His fingers dug into my arms, pinning me to the floor. Fury lit Peter's eyes. "Daniel would be disgusted with how you turned out."

"How do you know what Daniel would feel? You know nothing. You are merely a follower. A minion to Rapava," I growled.

"Daniel believed in this cause. Wanted to save human lives. And you go and fuck the enemy."

Anger burst in my chest like lightning. How did he know what I did with Ryker? Shame and embarrassment of his awareness was overshadowed with vehemence. "Yes. I fucked him. Over and over. It was incredible." I grinned.

"You are revolt—"

"Enough, Peter." Rapava stepped through the other men, striding to us. "Zoey is going to be confused for a while."

"What?" Peter tore his gaze from me to look at the doctor.

"I was afraid of this. She is experiencing Stockholm syndrome."

"Stockholm syndrome?" Peter sneered. "You seriously believe in that crap?"

"It is not crap. It's a serious condition. In order to survive, a captive builds a relationship with and even may believe they care deeply for their captor." Rapava watched me the whole time with curiosity. "I have seen it happen several times."

It wasn't true, of course, but I kept my mouth shut.

Peter leaned back, glaring at me. "You think that's why she is acting like this?"

Rapava stared at Peter with a gape-mouthed expression, as though he couldn't believe anyone was questioning him. "Yes, I do."

"You were testing me." Realization hit me.

"Yes." He nodded then turned his attention to Peter. "I wanted to see what you would do given the opportunity. I don't blame you, Zoey. He brainwashed you. But I can't allow you freedom here until you are healthy again. Back to yourself."

"What does that mean?" Dread trickled down my throat, sending alarm spilling into my gut.

"I know you are strong. You will get through this." Rapava ignored my question. His hazel eyes bored into mine, conveying there was more to say, but perhaps he didn't want to say it in the presence of these men. "It won't take you long before you are back to normal."

Normal? I was the furthest thing from normal, and he knew it.

"Get her on her feet." Rapava motioned for Peter to get up. "Take Zoey to the detaining room where she will be properly watched and maintained until she is in her right state of mind again."

Peter grabbed my wrists and tugged me to my feet.

Maintained. I understood what that meant. Handcuffed and drugged.

Even when logic told me one thing, primal instinct to protect myself always won out. I slammed my head forward into Peter's nose. He grunted as blood pooled from his nostrils. I ripped my wrist from his hold and darted to the side.

A hand reached out and clamped around my neck. Air evaporated from my throat as Hugo's fingers compressed. I struggled to free myself as Liam and Peter came in, grabbing and pinning my arms.

"Hold her." Rapava came beside me. Out of the corner of my eye I saw a needle. A flash of pain stabbed my neck, followed immediately by heat. My mouth opened to speak, but nothing came out. The room seemed to tilt and sway like I was on a boat in high seas.

"This is for your own good." Rapava's faraway words emerged from

9

his blurry and distorted face.

I stumbled but felt Liam grab and pick me up. His arms stiffened under my legs and back as he tried to hold me away from his chest. My head bobbed as he carried me down a hallway.

"Let's take her to the other holding room. It's more secure for her safety." Liam followed the doctor's orders and swung around the corner. The hallway rolled in my vision as though I was inside a kaleidoscope. This area was different. A lot of the rooms had viewing windows through which I could see the patient inside. Different faces and species of fae peered out of the rooms. Their faces warped and blended like a carnival mirror. Each merged with the last.

In the sea of faces, I saw a pair of almond-shaped black eyes. It was the only thing my gaze clasped onto, anchoring me. I smiled, feeling a strange comfort and peace. "It's a pirate's life for me," I mumbled in song before my lids closed, the drug consuming me with one gulp.

TWO

My lashes parted and light pierced my eyes. I slammed them closed before I slowly pried one heavy lid open and then the other, adjusting my vision to the abundance of light. My throat constricted as I tried to lift my head. I shivered, huddling my body in a tight ball against the wall. The thin gown did little to protect me against the cold tile. My muscles were limp and unwilling to cooperate. Thick webs coated my head, making it hard to even form a full thought. Foggy memories tickled my brain—Rapava and other staff coming in, hands on me, needles in my neck and arms—before I slipped back into my unconscious world.

When I woke this time, I wasn't chained to a hospital bed. Actually, there was no bed in this room at all and nothing to give me any comfort or that I might use against anyone.

Realization of my circumstances struck me, and I pulled at the restraints of a straightjacket, my arms folded around me in a taut hug. Anxiety spiked, pinching my lungs, and I gasped. My heartbeat thumped loudly in my head. *Dark closet. Tied. Alone. Scared. Hungry.* It was like a reflex. The nightmares from my past bucked at my phobia. Fear gripped at my heart and squeezed my soul.

Rapava had talked of how a captor beat and broke down a captive till they were nothing. They rebuilt you with their beliefs and opinions. This was exactly what he was doing to me. I couldn't gauge if he really believed I was brainwashed by Ryker, or if he was trying for reverse psychology. Either way, everyone at DMG would agree breaking me down again was for the best.

Everyone except me.

I struggled against the rigid sleeves of the jacket, terror clawing my throat. Tears sprang under my lids as I thrashed against the unforgiving material. It was useless. I understood this, but anger and fear raged from deep in my soul.

11

"Calm down, Zoey," a voice came from behind me. I jerked at Rapava's voice. Straining my head to look over my shoulder, I saw the doctor at the door. Rage clogged my throat, and I turned back to the wall. Violence was always my first reaction, to strike out at what was hurting or threatening me. When I couldn't fight back, I felt untethered and lost as if a part of me drifted off into space unable to make sense of things. Now terror set in, wrapping around my bones like wires.

The sound of Rapava's steps on the tile gnawed against my eardrums. From the corner of my eye, I watched him move around behind me. "I'm sorry for what I had to do, but you will understand and thank me later... once your mind is cleared and you are back to being yourself."

I snarled in revulsion.

"You don't need to recognize now what I'm trying to do for you, Zoey. But everything I do is with you in mind. You are extremely important to me."

"To your mission, you mean," I spat.

He stood over me and glared down. "I won't deny it. You are special. Your current genetic makeup, both fae and human, is extraordinary."

"Fae. Exactly. Why do you think what I'm experiencing is merely some mindfuck? Peter is right; I'm one of them now and I will never help *you.*" The words frothed out of my mouth in a heated hiss.

"I *designed* you to think of Faes as the natural enemy. Your coding is far too strong to override." Rapava clasped his hands together. "Plus, you've seen too much. You know what the fae are capable of, and Daniel's death will eat at you until you get revenge."

"We both know how Daniel felt about you and this *mission.*"

"Daniel's betrayal was unfortunate, but I finally have what he and his late father hid from me for so many years."

A coil wrapped around my heart. "Late father?"

"Yes. Daniel Senior passed away recently." Dr. Rapava watched me intently, like he was waiting for my reaction to this news. "Very suddenly."

He knew I went to Dr. Holt at the clinic where they had put him. I got the information Rapava had been searching for. By giving it to me, Daniel Senior forfeited his life.

"You mean you killed him." Anger and sadness pressed my shoulders firmer to the wall. I wanted to attack, for him to feel the pain I was suffering inside. "Just like you murdered Daniel's brother and probably his mother, too."

Rapava shifted his weight. "Remember what I told you, you have to lose a few to save many."

My throat wouldn't even let me respond. Dr. Holt died because he was no longer useful to Rapava. Rapava got what he wanted. Daniel's whole family was lost because of me, what I was made of.

"Why did you need those papers so badly when you had me and Sera in your hands? You had the formula walking around in front of you."

"I wish it had been that easy." Rapava's lips thinned in a tight smile. "Holt was a brilliant man. One of the best. He also knew how to disguise your coding. He told me he did this because if either of you were ever in the hospital or had testing done by civilian doctors, they would never be able to detect you were different. Now, I wonder if it was his true reason."

"You have the information. What do you need to test on me? What are you planning?"

"You have opened my eyes to more. I thought earlier you were pregnant, but now I know you are much, much more."

"You're sick."

He frowned, squatting next to me. "I'd be careful who you call that. Simply because you turned out not to be pregnant..." Abhorrence flashed across his face. "Your examinations still showed you were sexually active recently... and the sperm was not human."

Horror ballooned in my chest. Violation, embarrassment, and fury stiffened my back. I hadn't had time to think about the fact he kept me drugged for two weeks so he could poke and prod me. I had lain bare and vulnerable under his needles and examinations.

"But I know if you were in your right mind, it wouldn't have happened. It is wrong, but it's not your fault. He tricked you, took advantage."

Once again I felt his words drench me like water, drowning my truth. I couldn't tell if he believed what he was saying, but this was his own type of brainwashing. Sympathize and shame the victim, then cause them to feel it wasn't their fault, but still something they should feel reprehensible about. Cause doubt.

Wrath pumped in my veins like blood. My body trembled with the loathing and rage I felt for the man in front of me. This information explained why Peter sounded so sure when he accused me of sleeping with Ryker. He was. They all knew. Maybe they had been in the room as Rapava examined me. Naked and exposed, inside and out.

"It was not the fae who took advantage." I lifted my eyebrow. "You had no right to examine me like that."

"I have every right, Zoey. I created you. I gave you life."

"Dr. Holt gave me *life*."

He bit down on his lip, his nose flaring. "He produced you in a dish, yes, came up with the formula, but it was *my* idea."

I never realized how egotistical and needy for acknowledgment he was. Everything was because of him. None of us could survive if it weren't for him.

"And thanks to Holt's papers and you, I can begin again."

"Begin again?" A rock thumped in my stomach.

"Yes. I needed Dr. Holt's formula, the one he stole from here. But with you and your DNA, I have new data to work with. You are not fae, but now you are more than human. The new human hybrid. With you, I can create more and establish a whole new race of beings. This next group is going to be faultless. Don't you want that for humanity, Zoey?"

Bile rushed up my throat and into my mouth, and I spit it in his face. He jerked back, shock widening his eyes. He took off his glasses, wiping them on his lab coat as he stood up.

"I see you are not ready." Disappointment shook his head back and forth. "You need some more time here."

"Fuck you!" I screeched. Sanity took a back seat as words propelled from my mouth. "You think fae are revolting and horrible? Look at yourself, *Doctor*. You have become the tyrannical leader your father wanted you to be. Sick and twisted. You dissect and torture animals and people for your own narcissistic ego. You create babies in labs, let them be beaten and raped, all in the name of science. Is that what you tell yourself so you can sleep at night?" I felt saliva drip down my chin, strands of my hair tumbled around my face. "You are the most vile and repulsive specimen in this building. I can't wait till I get free, because I will feed you to the fae... in pieces."

Silence took up where my words ended. No emotion resonated on his face as he stared at me. "We'll see how you feel in a week." He turned and moved to the door.

I stood, running after him, wanting my words to penetrate his soul. For him to recognize what he did. To feel pain.

The door slammed behind him, the lights in my room going off. Darkness shrouded me as I threw myself against the exit. Over and over I smashed against it. Physical pain helped take away the internal pain I felt.

I wailed and banged till my body collapsed, rolling into a ball.

The only way I knew how to deal with my past horror was to let my mind go, let it wander to the far reaches where it couldn't feel or experience pain. I wrapped up the bits of my soul I had left and carried them with me, leaving only the shell behind.

Fingers trailed down my spine, curving over my ass, stirring me awake. The masculine smell of woods and a storm over a field of vanilla clung to the T-shirt I was wearing. I burrowed into it and took in a deep, greedy breath, filling myself with him. I opened my eyes and turned my face to the man lying next to me. The white sheets wound softly around me. We were back in our room in Peru—the perfect bubble of happiness I had for a brief stretch of time.

"Thought it might wake you up." A smile glinted in his white eyes.

"Ryker," I whispered, emotion straining my vocal cords.

"Miss me?"

"Yes."

"Wow. You said that without the least bit of sarcasm."

Liquid surged under my lids.

"Hey." His hand came to my face, cupping my cheek. "Are you all right?"

I nuzzled against his hand.

"Zoey, you're freaking me out."

"I know you aren't real, but I need you. To get me through this."

Ryker drew me to him, his lips brushing my forehead. "You are strong. You can get through this. You don't need me, but I'll be here whenever you want."

"I wish you could tell me you are all right. That you got away from Vadik."

He let his hand drop, leaning back to look in my eyes, his voice low and husky. "If I were free or capable, I would have already found you."

Hell. Even in my imagination he could make me burn for him. I bit my bottom lip, drawing his gaze to my mouth. He grabbed my hips, pulling me forward till I straddled his lap. I inhaled sharply. The warmth of his solid body between my legs felt so real.

"Even without the oath, I would find you," he growled, bringing me closer to him.

Right. The promise I made him swear when Vadik had us. When I thought I was dying. If Ryker wasn't the one to kill me, his powers would be lost to him forever. I made him vow to be the one to kill me before I died from the weakness. Intuition had told me we were going to be separated. I hadn't thought about the consequences or where I would end up; I simply acted in the moment. If he made the oath, we would be connected. It would lead him to me, wherever I was. Ryker even said this kind of vow was more powerful than being in debt with someone. Sprig always found me, and Croygen seemed to be able to locate Ryker when he needed. This meant Ryker wasn't able to get to me.

"I wish the vow worked both ways. I want to be able to feel you and know you are still alive."

One blond eyebrow arched on Ryker's face. "You want to feel me, huh?" He surged up, flipping me. I fell back on the pillows. He crawled between my legs, and his eyes locked onto mine. He lifted my T-shirt up my body, his lips grazing my stomach, his stubble tickling as his mouth moved.

"Feel this?"

He tilted my hips up, my underwear slithered down my thighs, and his hands roamed freely over my exposed skin. I let a small groan escape. I wanted to reach out for him, to touch him, but my arms wouldn't move. I struggled, feeling a slight pressure against them holding them down. Reality scratched at my brain, pulling me back toward reality.

"Stop. Stay with me." Ryker clawed over me, placing his hands by my shoulders, his knees on either side of my hips. "Just a little longer." He inclined, his lips finding mine.

It felt like home. Emotion surged through me, igniting my desire for him.

"I've done some interesting things, but this might be hitting a new level," he mumbled against my mouth.

"Why? You're not even real. This is all in my head."

Ryker lifted his head, his intense gaze burning into me. "Zoey, I will make you another promise. I am going to bury myself into you so deeply and fiercely we are both going to feel it in reality."

THREE

Time continued on, divided only by intervals in which researchers or Rapava entered the room. I was left alone in the darkness curled in a ball in the corner with only my fears and memories.

Ryker's presence in my dreams was the only dash of strength I felt that kept me from revolting against Rapava. But even those spikes were lessening. I wanted to believe I had endless strength to fight, but I didn't.

Some days no one came in, leaving me alone with my dreams of Ryker, memories of Sprig, and happy times with my sister or Daniel, anything which kept me sane. Other days it was an endless stream of tests and medical staff, treating me like a specimen.

I now lay coiled up, my head on my knees, humming a song to myself I used to sing Lexie to help her sleep. Sanity oozed from me like a sliced milk carton.

Something flickered above me. My eyes squinted against the sudden blaze of light, and I lurched away from it, digging myself into the corner, hiding. Lights meant people coming in: needles, drugs, exams, forced food and pills through tubes when I denied them.

Filthy, tangled strands of hair fell into my face, guarding me from the onslaught of rays burning my pupils. The sound of the squeaking metal door curled my back into a tighter ball. My arms still wrapped around me. I had lost feeling in them days ago. I had stopped talking and eating. Only my thoughts let time pass, and I indulged in them.

Footsteps sounded at the doorway, heading for me. Already I knew this person was not my usual visitor. Most of the staff had clipped, determined steps. Rapava's sounded the most pronounced. His ego making sure every step resonated in my bones.

A floral perfume scent hit my nose, and I peeked through the gaps of my locks. The plum color of my hair had become only a hint of lavender coating my brown tresses. Just like my hope, it was fading with each passing

Stacey Marie Brown

day.

The short, curvy figure of a woman appeared in my line of vision. Long snowy-white hair cascaded around her shoulders, and her side-swept bangs were pinned back by the reading glasses perched on her head. She stopped, sadness filling her soft brown eyes as she took me in.

I used to consider Kate Grier an aunt, a crazy aunt who was scattered and talked your ear off. But I loved her because of those things and because she was warm and caring. Kate's hugs could cause any bad day to become better. She had a nurturing presence, making me want to curl into her warm embrace and forget all my worries.

Her betrayal hurt the most.

She glanced over her shoulder at the door and then climbed down on the floor in front of me. "Oh, Zoey." Her hand reached out to touch me.

A growl rose in my throat.

Her hand stopped and dropped back on her lap. "I don't have much time," she whispered so low I barely heard her.

I kept my eyes on the wall.

"I'm sorry I haven't visited before," she muttered. "They are always watching and listening." Then she cleared her throat, her voice escalating an octave. "Please stop fighting us." Kate's hand brushed the hair away from my face. "We are only trying to help you. We. Want. You. To. Get. Better." Her round, brown eyes willed her determination into mine.

I glared at her then returned to staring at the wall.

Kate could be clueless and absentminded but was never cruel or acted like she had a god complex. She had compassion for the fae. Although her love was truly for science and helping humans. Was she that blind? Could she not see what Dr. Rapava's true intentions were? Did she agree with them if she did know?

"Daniel would not want to see you this way, Zoey." Her warm hand cupped my cheek. I pulled away, turning my head from her. "He'd want you to *fight*. But not like *this*." Her tone caught my attention. She tilted closer to me, her words tickling my ear. "Don't let all his hard work be in vain. You can stop it."

My head jerked over to her, for the first time really taking her in. Her face was expressionless, but I still couldn't fight the feeling she was trying to tell me something through her eyes. Did she know Daniel was secretly investigating and finding information to take DMG down?

"What?" My dry throat crackled, not used to speaking, and my eyes scrutinized every inch of her face.

18

"We want you to get better," she repeated.

I watched her a few moments more before I faced the wall again.

"You have family who care about you here." She leaned in to kiss me on the temple, her voice low, snaking into my ear. "Daniel didn't die for you to give up. Play the game, Zoey."

She then stood and walked out of the room, the door clicking behind her. The light went off several minutes later, surrounding me in darkness. A blanket of fear and loneliness clenched my chest, leaving me with Kate's words to mull over.

"Play the game, Zoey." The sentence rolled over and over in my head. It was hard for me to trust anyone here, but a feeling in my gut told me Kate was on my side trying to help me.

"Play the game," I mumbled to myself, taking in the deeper meaning. I suddenly felt I had never seen Kate before today. We all brushed her off as sweet and flaky, the absentminded professor. What if there was more to her? Was she more aware of what Dr. Rapava was really doing far below her office? I hoped she was against it.

I wasn't ready to fully trust my theory, but if Kate was sympathetic to my side, she would be a great ally.

She was right about one thing; I needed to play the game. I would not beat Rapava the way I was going. Standing by my ethics would only leave me locked in a closet till I was no longer useful. He was smart, so I couldn't do it half-assed. This was as dangerous as a cop going undercover to spy on the mafia. My life depended on him believing I changed. The old Zoey had to come back.

I couldn't slip up. The line I would have to walk was thin, but if I took it slow, let them believe I had reformed, eventually they might begin to trust me and let me out of this room.

It was all or nothing.

Game on.

I had to be subtle and proceed much slower than I would have liked. But if Rapava came in one day, and I was suddenly "cured" he would never buy it. The depths I had to dig inside myself to keep patient and determined bit at me like a mosquito—constant and relentless.

It took eleven excruciating days.

I focused on the small things: acknowledging the people who came in the room, taking more bites of food and thanking them for it, answering questions when they asked. I could see it in their faces that my deception was working. Their interactions with me were energized, and they spoke to me like a timid child they were trying to encourage, instead of a lab rat.

Adapting to the pace of a sloth was painful. The straightjacket seemed to grow tighter around my chest with every moment. A couple of times I almost broke, but I dug deeper, knowing the strength was somewhere in there.

By the fifth day things started to change. With every visit after, my treatment improved slightly. They took off my jacket when Rapava deemed me "no longer a threat to myself or others." I was given more substantial meals and even a blanket and pillow.

As my advancement progressed, Rapava's visits increased. Those were the hardest to get through. But Kate's words kept coming back to me.

Play the game.

And I did. Each day feeling like years.

FOUR

"I am proud of your progress, Zoey." Rapava had come in after lunch on the twelfth day. Right away I felt something was different in his demeanor with me. "I think you have made such incredible strides this week, I want to reward your headway."

I straightened against the wall, standing almost like at command. "Sir?"

"We are going to get you cleaned up, fresh clothes, even a new room. How would you like that, Zoey?"

His condescending tone drove my nails into my palms.

"I would like it very much, sir."

"Good." He nodded. "After you get cleaned up, I'd like to reveal all the positive things we are doing here. I'll have Nurse Delaney take you to the showers and get you situated in your room. Then I will show you around." He stalked to the door. "I hope this trust we are building between us will continue, and you will return to your old self again."

He wanted me back to the time before I knew the truth and thought he was a gift to the medical world. When I believed he truly wanted to help people like my sister. He'd like me even more if he could brainwash me—have another minion to control.

"Yes, sir." I nodded. Throwing in a lot of "sirs" seemed to make him happy.

He tilted his head in a goodbye and left.

Even after he left, I did not move or let any true feeling show on my face. Kate's statement, *They are always watching and listening,* was a constant warning in my head

A woman about my height entered the room soon after. She was one of the main researchers who had come in to give me shots and food, but she never did the tests. She had dark blonde hair tied back in a ponytail and brown eyes. She wore no makeup except a little mascara and was

21

dressed in baggy, green scrubs, hiding her body, but she appeared to be thin. Her pink-and-black sneakers were the only thing she wore that showed her personality.

"Hi, Zoey. I'm Delaney." She had an open, compassionate aura about her. Someone who immediately calmed me, like a nurse in a pediatrician's office.

I was never a person who trusted, no matter how kind a person was. It was not how you survived on the streets. You always needed to be watching out for yourself and skeptical of everyone.

"Come with me. I'm going to take you to the showers so you can get cleaned up." She motioned me to follow her out of the room.

I silently obeyed. My bare feet shuffled across the cold floor. I still wore the hospital gown I woke up in weeks ago, my hair knotted and filthy, and my dirty skin bruised from the shots. The last time I had a shower was in Peru... that I was aware of. Who knows what they did to me unconscious?

The moment we left the room, I noticed Liam following behind us. *So Delaney was not my only babysitter.* He didn't hide the fact he was there to guard me, and he sighed and huffed to let me know how he felt about it.

Delaney took me to a shower stall and sat outside the curtain. Liam stayed outside the door. They weren't ready to leave me alone, especially when handing me a razor. The hot water gushed down my skin, massaging my stiff muscles and washing away the grime of the prior weeks. It took two washes and double conditioner to untangle my hair. Finally I emerged from the stream when the warm water faded and turned to icy liquid.

"Here are your clothes and undergarments." Delaney patted the fabric folded on the counter. Gray scrub-style pants and top, white underwear, socks, and a sports bra. I didn't miss the slight to me. The staff here wore blue or green scrubs. Fae wore gray. Rapava was making it clear I was not one of them.

Under the counter, on the floor, sat a pair of worn black boots. Boots DMG issued to me six months earlier when my last ones fell apart. Emotion came out of nowhere, blinding and blurring my eyes.

"My boots." I dropped to the ground, touching them like long-lost friends.

"Uh. Yeah." Delaney seemed unsure why I was getting weepy over a pair of boots. She had no idea what these shoes meant to me. What they had been through. They were the only thing I had left. The dirt and scuffs were like a timeline of the past events of my life. Ryker. Sprig. Croygen. Even that bitch, Amara.

"Dr. Rapava thought you might like something of yours. Also, they were still in okay condition, and even though Seattle's getting a lot better, it's still tough to get certain items."

Right. Seattle was trying to recover from the big electrical storm.

"It's getting better?" I turned to Delaney.

"Slowly, but yes. I'm one of the lucky ones. My house actually has water and electricity most of the time now. Downtown is still a mess and gangs have gotten worse, but it's better than it was." She shrugged. "I will let you get dressed."

Delaney picked up my shower stuff, cleared the room of anything I could use as a weapon, and exited the small bathroom. She left a disposable toothbrush and cheap comb.

I quickly got dressed but took my time lacing my boots. They felt good on my feet. Like they had come home. Maybe I had been in the dark by myself too long, but I felt this strange connection to them, like they really were old friends. I brushed my teeth and hair then went out to where Delaney and Liam waited for me.

As we walked down the corridor, I kept scanning my surroundings, taking in anything helpful. Every room we passed that I could see into, a fae was curled on a cot, sleeping.

I was also fighting a sluggish, lethargic sensation. Paint laced with goblin metal and iron coated everything down here. I hated it, but I couldn't deny it was ingenious. Along with being surrounded by poison, they were also injecting us with small doses—robbing fae of their will to fight or the ability to control their magic. A perfect weapon.

Liam and Delaney led me down a network of hallways, where the rooms didn't have windows, and it grew more and more silent.

"Rapava thought it best for you to be separate from the fae." Delaney keyed a door, opened it, and flicked on the lights. "And to have a little more privacy."

I stepped in. The room was no bigger than fifteen by twenty. It was painted the typical sterile white. A cot was placed against one wall, a table, cupboards and a sink on the opposite wall. Otherwise it was empty. Not even a toilet.

"There is a bathroom you can use down the hall in the mornings and before you go to bed." Delaney picked up on my train of thought. "I will store your toothbrush and personal effects there."

They purposely didn't want me to have a bathroom. They could control me better this way by keeping all items that could be used as weapons away from me and only used with supervision.

"Well, since I don't have to unpack or anything." I turned to leave the room.

"You don't want a moment to settle?" Delaney asked.

"Settle?" I lifted an eyebrow. "As comfy as the thin cot mattress looks, I think I'm good."

Liam snorted from the doorway and stepped aside to let me pass. Delaney nodded and followed me out. "Okay, we'll take you to Dr. Rapava. I think he wanted to show you around." She sounded relieved to be getting rid of me. She was acting pleasant and professional but was probably nervous as hell to be around me—a tainted human—one who was not totally stable and could kick her ass in ten seconds. Hence Liam. His ego would never allow him to doubt for a moment he could handle me.

The pair led me to the elevator. Liam slid a card into a slot and pushed the button for the level above mine. I subtly glanced at the card in his hand before he shoved it into his pocket. All the cards I had seen before were white with a black DMG symbol on it. This card's symbol was red.

A key card was needed to obtain access to anything below the first three levels. I had never thought much about access, as I never needed to go below the third level. I figured it was for security reasons to protect it from outsiders. Now I knew it was to keep people in, not out.

Anything below the first few levels of DMG were designed to hold or study fae. The more dangerous you were, the farther down you were held, becoming harder and harder for one to escape. I was detained one level below the middle, teetering on the fence between dangerous and a medium security risk. I needed to keep my behavior in check, stay on script, and gain their trust. Then I might have a chance to move up and be closer to freedom.

Liam nudged me out when the doors opened and herded me down the hall.

I spotted a camera at the end of the hall. Delaney saw the focus of my attention. "They don't work." Delaney swished her hand at it. "Been out ever since the storm. They utilize too much energy so we've kept them off."

"Hey." Liam clicked his tongue, shaking his head at Delaney. "They work fine." Liam's voice held a threatening tone to it. Her face turned red and she dropped her gaze to the floor. This was definitely something she wasn't supposed to tell me. Cameras weren't working here. Good to know.

They took me into a room where Rapava was mixing vials of colored liquid between tubes.

"Ah, Ms. Daniels." He took off his protective glasses and came around the table. He hadn't called me that since before everything happened. The name coming from his mouth was like a slap in the face. I was named after Dr. Daniel Holt, "Daniel's kids." This whole time Rapava knew my true origin and how I got my name.

Bastard.

"Come with me, I want to show you what we are doing. How we are helping the human race."

Delaney and Liam left. Rapava took me around the different lab rooms, showing me the studies and the "progress" into fighting diseases and birth defects. He showed me nothing I could use against him. I felt he was giving me the tour he would do for the head of the FBI or government official checking on what he was doing here. It only displayed him in a good light, emphasizing the achievements and greatness he was doing to help mankind.

I wanted to vomit on my boots, but I liked them too much.

He strutted around, full of one-sided facts and praise for what DMG did. And I kept nodding and saying, "Wow, that's incredible." A lot.

Finally we returned to the lower level where I was housed, but we came out the elevators on the opposite side of building. Rapava led me down the corridor, and I figured we were heading back to my room. Instead, he turned another way, stopping at one of the doors.

"This might be of interest to you, Zoey." Rapava grabbed the handle. "I think this may cement your direction here with us and see what we are really fighting for."

A nervous sensation curled around my esophagus like a leash. He opened the door and moved aside, letting me go first.

I stepped in.

FIVE

A small, young girl lay in a hospital bed. She was so thin the bed dwarfed her tiny frame. A ventilator tube thrust into each nostril pushed air in and out of her lungs continuously.

The girl shifted her head, her dark eyes finding mine. My chest clenched and my feet went rigid on the floor. *Oh... no... no.*

She was not a little girl.

It was Sera.

I stood at the door, not able to move.

Sera turned her face to the ceiling, the bones in her cheeks so thin and sharp they cast shadows on her pallid complexion. Her body stirred under the blankets, and she closed her eyes as though that minuscule movement was exhausting.

"How are you feeling today, Sera?" Rapava moved around me, walking to her bedside. He never once looked at her but kept his focus on the monitors around her.

She didn't respond or reopen her eyes.

Rapava glanced over his shoulder at me then returned to his charts. "When we first tested you, it wasn't long before we realized you were cured of the blemish in your DNA. We tried to inject her with your blood. It did not take." He lifted her wrist, taking her vitals. "Another thing I need to understand. Why you are changed, but the same blood did not alter Sera."

I opened my mouth to respond, but quickly slammed it shut. It was not blood which altered me but a fae-induced storm. Electricity so powerful and intense it dragged Ryker's powers from his body into mine.

For a long time I was merely a carrier of them, a duffel bag, until they started to adapt to their new home. Now they were fully mine, and the only way Ryker could get them back was to kill me. If I died by another hand or in an accident, they would forever stay locked inside me.

26

The doctor was not aware of this knowledge. If I told him the truth, what would happen? Would he be able to save Sera's life? Or would having that information only destroy thousands of others? Whatever decision I made, lives were on the line. And no answer was right.

I took a step into the room, my gaze tethered to Sera. We had never gotten along. Actually we couldn't stand each other, but now all I saw was the connection between us. She was the only one still alive like me. The link went beyond sisters or family.

I dragged to the side of her bed, like a magnet. I wanted to flee, to walk away from the dying girl, but I couldn't. My hand reached down and touched the blanket over her legs. Sera tilted her head to look at me.

Sadness and fear formed a block in my throat. I could not speak. Selfish or not, I didn't want her to die and leave me all alone. Without her it would only be me, the only experiment left, the last living freak who had been designed and concocted in the lab.

"Does she know?" My question came out before I could think.

"As much as she needs to." A frown creased the doctor's forehead. "I guess you put some questions in her head the night they tried to capture you on the roof."

I saw Sera's lids narrow, her black eyes spark with anger.

"She knows she was an experiment and that she's dying." Rapava patted her shoulder. "I will be sad to lose this one. She would have made a great fighter if the blood had worked."

My stomach rolled at his blunt, cold demeanor.

"You think I'm callous about her demise?" He turned his head, watching me.

"Yes." I swallowed, knowing the truth was probably written on my face. "Sera was one of us. A seer. You created her."

"And you don't think I care if she lives or dies?"

"I'm not sure."

"I do. Very much. But death is something I had to grow accustomed to at an incredibly young age. I've experienced loss you could not even fathom." He looked back on Sera's form. "I grew up near the Soviet Union in the slums. Death, disease, and starvation was a daily struggle. Detachment was the only way we could survive. I lost my mother and an infant sister in a bombing. My mother used her body to cover us. But the baby didn't live. I survived under my mother's corpse for three days before they could dig me out of the wreckage. My brother was born disfigured and was killed because of it. Another brother died of disease."

He paused, sliding his hands in his coat pockets. "Even then, my father was a true believer in Stalin and moved us north, to the heart of the Soviet Union. Stalin was dead, but my father was devoted to his beliefs and got a job as a janitor for the government. I was put to work at eight. My father's position allowed me to attend school. But it was there I acquired the most knowledge. I learned about the existence of fae. The government was aware of them. I uncovered dozens of files containing truths most would never know, but I did. They started wars to feed off our suffering, greed, and violence. They caused the war which killed my mother and sister." Rapava's brow furrowed, his words sharp and angry.

I stood stock-still, taking in every word. I was not sure why he was telling me this, but it was more than I ever knew about him. He was an exceedingly private person. Showing emotion was rare for him, and it captured my attention like I was under a spell.

"My father's iron fist pushed me to achieve greatness. To be the next Stalin. I ran away when I could from his grasp, but I vowed I would do something with my studies and awareness of the fae. Use them, like they use us. Help people like my brothers." His neck whipped back to me, his eyes narrowing in like an eagle sighting its prey. "And I have. I have achieved more than my father's small brain could ever dream of. I will keep going till I have accomplished my goals. Sera's death will be merely another causality in this war. But the research means everything to me and the human race. Leaders have to look at the bigger picture. Not one life, but thousands."

Oh. Wow.

Frightening as his speech was Rapava made more sense to me now with his past and how and why he became the man he was today. The harsh world he lived in, all the death and sadness, pushed so far down, he no longer felt it.

Someone cleared their throat at the door, and I spun around to see Liam filling the doorway.

Rapava straightened, shaking off his past, and returning to the composed doctor. "Come in, Liam. Spend some time with her." He indicated the empty seat next to Sera.

Liam nodded, heading for her bedside. "Thank you, sir."

"Come, Zoey. There is something else I would like you to see." Rapava grabbed my bicep, clapping down with ownership. Fury burned through my limbs at his touch. And I wiggled free of his grip. No matter his past, he still had become rotten to the soul. He could convince himself

28

he was doing good things, but he was no longer doing what he set out to do. He had lost his way a long time ago.

He turned for the door, his distinct steps ramming in my ears. I swallowed, about to turn and follow him, when Sera's fingers wrapped around mine. Startled, I jerked my head to look back at her. She was frail, but her gaze drilled into me. Her eyes were filled with desperation and unspoken words.

I didn't know what she was trying to tell me, but it seemed important. Whatever it was, it would have to wait. Somehow I would get back here. Alone.

I squeezed her hand.

Relief fluttered her lashes. Her fingers slid from mine, her eyes drifting closed.

"Zoey?" The doctor said my name from the doorway.

I circled around the bed and moved to the exit. As the door drew closed, I saw Liam sit, taking Sera's hand in his. Pain and adoration filtered over his features, an expression I had never seen on him before. Emotion twitched the muscles at his jaw.

I never knew for sure if anything happened between them, but the bond between hunter and seer was enough. It broke my heart to see his pain, no matter how much of a jackass he was. Sera was his partner. When you trusted someone with your life and could understand them without a word, the relationship went beyond love or friendship. I had it with Daniel. I didn't want to tell Liam the loss he was going to feel when Sera passed would be unbearable.

The door clicked and Rapava moved down the hall.

"How long does she have?" I asked, keeping in step with him.

"Not long. Days. Maybe a week."

I took in a deep breath, rolling my shoulders back. Guilt congealed in my gut. No matter what kinship I felt for her now, I kept silent.

I followed him to the next level. There were at least two more below. The last one was restricted, needing a different card and a thumbprint to get access. I needed entry to that floor, where Dr. Boris Rapava kept all the things which would bring this place down.

I will do it, Daniel. I promise.

The doctor's long legs strode along the hallway, veering down the same passage where they had locked me up. I clenched my jaw.

29

"You are not the only thing that came back to us that night." He cut down another corridor. A rush of air escaped through my teeth. The use of the word *thing* to describe me was like a thousand needles. At one time, he treated me with respect. Maybe even liked me.

"What do you mean?" I kept my voice even and unemotional.

Rapava stopped in front of a windowed room, nodding his head toward what was inside. I took a step to the glass, my eyes latching onto the little figure on the hospital bed, fast asleep.

Sprig!

My heart cried out. It took everything I had to hold the reaction under an indifferent facade. My lids flickered, hiding the emotion at seeing my best friend. I didn't know if I was more relieved to see him alive or upset he was back in DMG's hands, subject to their torture and experiments.

"Was he part of the trade?"

"Yes. He is our first successful animal-fae case study. This specimen is ground zero in our work here at the lab. The two of you are especially important to our continued research here, Zoey, and I hope you understand the good you are doing for mankind."

What a bunch of bullshit. I used to believe his notions and think we really were doing something valuable. Now who was to say one life was worth more than another? Did all those fae who had families, people who loved them, deserve to be kidnapped, dissected, and tested for the benefit of humans? Once upon a time I would have said yes.

Looking at Sprig now, his little body coiled in a ball, defenseless and powerless to what the researchers would do to him, all I wanted was to wrap him in my arms, burrow him close to my chest, and protect him with everything I had.

Sprig's arm twitched, and he stirred in his sleep, coiling himself into a smaller ball. He looked scared. The entire time I'd known him, he slept sprawled on his back or curled around either Ryker's or my head or Pam. Now his pose was defensive.

"What are you planning to do to him?" I kept my gaze locked on my buddy. Everything in me wanted to tear through the door and snatch him up into my arms.

Rapava cleared his throat, taking a step next to me. "Like with you, I need to understand why he worked when many didn't. As I told you, he is the base of our research. It should not only be humans who can be used in our battle against fae."

My head snapped to look at the doctor. "So, this is only about your army? You're going to torture thousands of animals and fae to breed smarter animals?"

"Not all animals. Mostly primates. They are quite similar to humans and exceptionally smart."

If he wanted an army of intelligent animals able to understand orders and be able to communicate and fight, primates were the leading animals to try the theory on.

"Babies and animals. You like when they don't have a voice and can't stand up and fight against what you are doing to them." Anger tossed the words from my mouth before I could stop them. I knew I went too far.

Rapava's back stiffened, his eyes stared at me, lids narrowing. "I don't think you *understand* the true severity of the situation. This is for our survival. The human race is in jeopardy, Zoey. Our world is being stolen from us. Whatever it takes, we need to learn how to survive and fight against them." His critical blue eyes roamed over me. "I thought *you* of all people would understand the most. You were held captive by them for almost four months and saw what they are capable of doing."

I held his gaze, my nails digging into my palms as opposing words came out of my mouth. "No. You're right. We need to do whatever it takes."

He watched me, trying to decipher the truth in my words. I forced myself not to swallow back the knot in my esophagus. Sweat beaded at the base of my neck. Finally he nodded. "I hoped you felt that way. You are strong, Zoey, and will be a skillful warrior. Even though the fae took your body, I hoped it hadn't taken your soul."

I forced liquid to brim at my lids. "He tried, sir. But no matter what he did or said, I knew the truth deep down."

Pride curved his mouth up. "Your dedication and knowledge to our cause is crucial to us. You are fundamental to our survival." I used to strive for his praise, to crave it. To get any recognition out of him was a feat. Now I was finally bestowed with his approval, and I felt sick to my stomach. All I saw was a demented man, high on his own self-importance and superiority.

Time only enhanced his narcissism, paranoia, and God complex, narrowing his mind to see only what he wanted. He no longer saw fae as anything more than meat or subjects to be used. Even humans were not important to him compared to his vision. He would sacrifice us all if he

31

felt it would fulfill his theories. It was hard to imagine him a small boy, weeping over his mother's dead body or crying when his father struck him. It was almost impossible to feel *he* was human anymore.

"Thank you." I turned away, no longer able to look at him. "I will do what I can for you."

"Yes, you will."

My nails dug deeper into my palms. We stayed silent for a few moments before I spoke. I needed to be careful. This was a high-wire act from which I could easily fall.

"Sir." I cleared my throat and nodded to the sleeping figure on the bed. "Would you consider leaving this specimen in my care?"

Rapava turned; his frame always so stiff it appeared to move as one unit.

"He knows me, sir." I rushed to continue before he stopped me. "He grew an attachment to me. He listens to me, follows me. At first it bothered me, but now I see it could be useful." I shifted my gaze to the doctor and kept my voice in a questioning tone.

Rapava inspected me, his mouth clamped in a solid line. I felt heat swirl up my spine, and my heart thumped a little faster.

A slow, cruel smile arched his mouth.

I went too far. He sees through me.

"I had not thought of that."

"Of what, sir?" I gulped.

"Both animal and sub fae seek a master, someone to command them…" He drifted off, lost in his own thoughts.

Hell. That wasn't where I was going with this, and by Dr. Rapava's expression, his mind was going nowhere good. But right then all I could worry about was getting Sprig.

"I will allow you to supervise him. It will be an interesting case study."

Whatever idea existed in his mind frightened me, but it allowed access to Sprig. It was the only important thing right now.

SIX

Rigid and terrified I walked toward Sprig's prison. Muscles along my shoulders and back constricted under Rapava's gaze. He was egotistical but incredibly smart and extremely manipulative. Every moment was a test. And failure probably meant death.

Please don't wake up, I chanted in my head. If Sprig woke and saw me, I knew he would give away our true relationship in a matter of seconds. The sprite didn't have a filter in his body. Food, feelings, thoughts—he held nothing back.

I walked to the bed where he slept. The metal box they kept him last time sat on the table next to the bed, as if it were threatening him to behave.

He stirred, smacking his lips, his hands tugging his tail in tighter. Tears pricked at my eyes, and I bit down to keep them back. My best friend was here in this hell, but he was all right. My muscles strained against the need to grab for him.

My fingers brushed his soft brown fur as I scooted my hands gently underneath him, picking him up. Highly aware of Dr. Rapava on the other side of the window, his watchful eyes felt like they were drilling holes through the glass.

"Deal, chipmunk," Sprig mumbled, wiggling restlessly in my palms. I froze.

Shit.

"No. No. The troll has to strip... that's the rules," Sprig yelled, his lids fluttering open. He glanced around, then twisted his head to peer at me and blinked. I could see recognition setting in. My stomach sank, breath catching in my throat. I dropped him back on the bed.

"Bhean?" His eyes widened into saucers, filling with joy.

What I had to do now was going to destroy me, but with Rapava watching my every nuance, it was the only thing I could. Even if Sprig didn't know it, I was keeping him safe.

"*Bhe—*"

"Shut up, sprite," I snapped. "I told you not to call me that." Sprig's mouth opened then shut.

"For so long I had to pretend I was sympathetic to you. I'm finally back where I can be myself again."

"What?" He sat up, frowning at me.

"You heard me. I don't have to suffer any more crap from you, fae. I only pretended to care, so I could get away." The lies crossing my lips felt like battery acid.

Hurt filled Sprig's gaze, stabbing my heart.

"Now if you want those *banana chips,* I know you like so much, you will do what I say."

"Banana chips?" Sprig frowned. "You know—"

"Yes, banana chips." I cut him off. *Please understand.* Sprig hated bananas. I was hoping he'd get I was acting.

"What the hell, *Bhean*? Are you drunk?"

I grabbed him and thrust him into the cage, slamming the lid closed. The bang of the metal was like putting my heart in a panini presser.

He will understand, I told myself. *He will forgive you.*

Sprig, for everything he had been put through, had the biggest, most sincere heart. He didn't love in halves. He wasn't capable of cruelty or manipulation. He was himself. A genuine, pure, open heart. And mouth. The verbal diarrhea off Sprig's tongue was what I was deathly afraid of at the moment.

"It would be wise to stay silent. I have a short temper for your antics today." I latched the cage and picked it up.

A brown eye appeared in one of the holes, watching me. "Crumpet munchers. This is *bad.*"

"What did I just say?"

"You are in desperate need of food and a certain Viking club?" Sprig replied. "Oh sorry, that's what I heard."

Fear was running too high in my system to find his response funny, as true as it might have been.

Rapava shifted and clicked his tongue from the doorway behind me, expressing that his patience was running thin.

"Not another word," I ordered and pivoted toward the door, following Rapava, and taking Sprig with me. Sprig thankfully did as I instructed and stayed quiet.

The walk back to my room felt like an endless tunnel of doom, where at any moment a trap door would open and plummet us to the dungeon below. Every square tile was either safe or a snare. And Sprig's mouth was the trigger.

Rapava deposited me back in my room. At the sound of the lock on my door clicking, barring me in, I ran to the table by my cot, setting the cage down.

My fingers fumbled at the latch, my eyes studying the room for any hidden surveillance.

"Oh god, Sprig. I'm so sorry," I whispered as I lifted the cover off the crate. He sat in the corner, his fingers wrapped around his tail, stroking the end, soothing himself.

I would have taken a thousand needles to the heart than see the hurt and pain etched on his face.

"Sprig, I had to say those things. I didn't mean any of it," I whispered hoarsely.

He stayed silent.

"Please, talk to me," I pleaded. "Tell me you're not talking to me. I don't care. Something."

"*Obviously*, I'm not talking to you," he huffed. "Thought by *not* talking it was evident."

I let out a relieved chuckle. "I've been worried about you." He shifted, peering over his shoulder at me. "I hate that you're here, but damn it's good to see you. I've missed you like crazy."

"Like how crazy?"

I grinned. "Like honey-dipped-in-sugar-rolled-in-honey-and-fried-in-honey kind of crazy."

Sprig's eyes widened, fully turning to me. "Fried honey?" He licked his lips. "Sounds crazy good."

I nodded. "I missed you that much."

A smile lighted his eyes. "I missed you too, *Bhean*."

I felt the impulse from both of us to reach out for each other. I wanted nothing more than to hug the little bugger. "We need to be careful, Sprig. Delaney told me the cameras don't work in the rooms, but we need to be careful. I need to keep you protected. Rapava can't know the truth of our friendship, okay? If he does, he will separate us. I can't handle it. Not

35

again."

Sprig nodded. He still clung to his tail like a security blanket.

"Are you okay? They haven't hurt you, have they?" I asked. A cold fury roared through me at the thought of someone hurting him. I clenched my teeth.

"They took Pam from me." His expression filled with sorrow.

"Buddy, I'm sorry." Pam was a tiny stuffed goat I had bought Daniel as a funny birthday present, teasing him about his Capricorn sign. Sprig found it when we were investigating Daniel's apartment and claimed the goat as his own. It became his companion and security. Pam, the goat, had been through a lot with us. It reminded me how I felt seeing my boots again. It was an anchor, a connection and comfort.

"If they've done anything to her," he huffed, "I swear I will go apeshit." His eyebrow lifted up and down.

I snickered. "Good to see you haven't lost your bad puns."

"Bad as in badass, right?"

"Right."

"So, do you know where the Viking is?" Sprig asked.

"No." I shook my head. "But most likely Vadik has him." My lids squeezed shut with images of Ryker being tortured and beaten. Like Rapava, Vadik had no limit as to what he would do to get what he wanted.

Vadik wanted the stone. For some reason though, I felt it was more than that. He seemed to want Ryker almost as much.

"After I passed out, did you see or hear anything else?"

Sprig wobbled his head back and forth. "No. They knocked me out right after you. Woke up here."

"Yeah," I sighed.

I didn't doubt they had been treating him like a walking pincushion as well. We both seemed to be the foundation for all experiments here.

"Lots of needles and no honey. It's inhumane."

"The lack of honey, not the needles?" I winked.

"Well, yeah, of course." He stomped his foot. "It's cruel. I'd like to file a complaint."

"Yeah. Me too," I snorted. "Let me know how it goes for you."

"We need to do something, *Bhean*. I can't live in these conditions. They don't even let me have those granola bars. The nurse laughed at me when I mentioned I'd settle for churros."

A grin settled on my mouth. It was so good to have Sprig back, to smile and laugh again. A happiness I hadn't felt for a month filled me with light. He brought me a peace only a friend and loved one could give.

"You're right. We have to come up with a plan." My smile slipped, the seriousness of our situation returning. "Do you remember the girl, Sera? She was the other seer and Collector?"

"The one I threw a brick at on the rooftop?"

"Yes, her."

"I should have thrown poo."

Sprig had helped Ryker and me escape from a building where we'd been hiding when the Collectors hunted me. That night felt long ago.

"She's dying."

"Oh. Does that mean no poo?"

"No poo," I confirmed. "I need to sneak into her room tonight. When I saw her today, she was trying to tell me something, I could feel it. I have to see her."

"Oh, a night full of danger, mystery, intrigue, action." Sprig inched forward, excitement glowing on his face. "And food."

"When did food become part of our evening?"

"Because I only do the other stuff if food is involved."

That was true.

"Who knows, maybe there's a drive-through on our way."

"Really?"

I tilted my head to the side, lifting an eyebrow.

"What did I tell you about teasing and food?" He folded his arms.

"I should never tease about food."

"And what did you just do?" he scolded.

"Teased about food."

"See. I get grumpy."

"Sorry. I promise I won't do it again."

"Not talking to you right now." He stuck his tongue out at me. I knew from the many times before, this would only last about thirty seconds. I needed to use the silence to think of a plan.

I drifted from the table, trying to figure out how to get to Sera. I sat on my cot and lay back, my gaze going to the ceiling. We were locked in, and probably deadbolted. No lock picking there.

I popped back up instantly. The panels along the top were in perfect squares. All made of a foam, cardboard type of material, and all moveable. It was how Sprig and I escaped this place before. The vents. Rapava said they secured all the escapes out of the building. But I wasn't trying to escape. I was only trying to get to another room—a room on the same level as mine. It was a couple corridors over and a few lefts and rights, and the vents went to every room.

"What?" Sprig jumped on the top edge of the cage, watching me.

Twenty seconds.

It was too early for me to check things out; the lights in my room still blazed brightly. Until this place shut down for the night, I wouldn't feel safe to check out my idea. Sprig's size, sensitivity to fae magic, love of danger, and agility made him the perfect candidate.

"I need you to do something for me." I lowered my voice even more. "I want you to check out the access to the vents, and find out if there are any alarms or triggers on this level."

He nodded with eagerness.

"But only go as far as you feel comfortable. If you feel or see anything wrong, come back. Okay? Your safety is priority to me."

He saluted me and leaped to the top of a cupboard. Not wanting to focus on him in case we were being watched, I paced and fiddled around the room, watching him through my lashes. He pushed at a ceiling panel, lifting it enough to slip through.

I waited. My nerves were so severely strung I could only inhale the smallest bit of air. Every creak or sound I heard caused me to jump, dampening the back of my neck with sweat.

Trying to act "natural" when you wanted to lose your shit was a feat in itself. My hands fidgeted and twisted around each other. The hum of the fluorescent lights grew louder, ticking like a clock as time passed, filled the strained silence.

"Hell," I mumbled to myself. Something was wrong. I could feel the panicked scream building in my chest. *What if he got caught or hurt?* Why did I put this on him? What did I make him do?

A thump sounded above me. I jumped, covering my mouth to stop the cry waiting to escape.

Sprig crawled out, leaping on the cupboard.

"Oh, thank god." My words rushed out, allowing me to take the first real breath.

Sprig climbed down. "First, there are rats up there. Big ones." He crinkled his nose. "I think they thought I was fast-food delivery... or they were trying to mate with me."

Knowing Sprig was safe and no one had broken down the door to take either one of us away, I let myself laugh.

"I tell you, *Bhean*. It's always sex or food." He sat back on his hind legs by his cage. "Hey, you and rats have something in common. Speaking of—"

"Sprig," I interrupted. "What did you see?"

"The vents are clear if you stay on this level. When I tried to climb up, like we did last time, I saw sensory triggers and everything has now been bolted down with goblin metal."

Rapava was not lying. He did block the exits to leave, but moving around internally was feasible.

"How far did you go?"

"All the way to the end of this floor. They don't seem to care if we crawl around the vents like rats in a maze. But the maze is of their making. We can't get anywhere good... oh, unless there's a cafeteria on this floor?"

"Let's try finding Sera first, before we venture out."

"Eye-Matty." He saluted me.

I fell back on my bed with an amused groan.

Now all we had to do was wait till lights out.

SEVEN

Metal rubbed against the fabric of my pants, sending electric shocks into my knees and shins as I slid slowly through the vent. The space was smaller and thinner than the one I escaped through last time, and my weight created an unnerving pinging sound through the flue. It was a succession of moving through a series of mazes and climbing over ceiling beams like a gymnast.

Sprig was not wrong about the rats. Several of them scurried over my hands as I blindly made my way through. Rats didn't bother me normally, but the feel of their fur and claws scraping over my skin created chills down my arms, causing me to shake them off in disgust. I had to rely on my memory to get to where I thought Sera's room was located. Sprig's sharp night vision helped steer me. After a while, my sight adjusted and my senses heightened. But my stomach was still tense with fear.

I was putting us in an insane amount of danger. But I would not be a victim. If fighting meant playing their game while secretly obtaining information to take them down, that's what I'd do.

Sprig yelped. A rat squeaked.

"Stop, fooling around up there. Leave the rats alone," I whispered.

"Le-leave the rats alone?" he exclaimed in a hoarse whisper. "Tell them to leave me alone. Beady-eyed bastards."

"If you stopped flirting with them," I whispered as we came to another vent exit.

"Flirting?" He scoffed. "They want to *eat* me, *Bhean*... and yes, in that way too."

"Okay, didn't need that visual." I unhooked the vent door, crawling down to check if this was Sera's room. The last four rooms had been empty.

My fingernails dug into the plaster around the vent, and I lifted the panel. The soft beeps of a heart monitor and the rhythmic pumping of air wafted up. My heart jumped into my throat. *I think I found her.* I leaned over, poking my head down the hole. One dim light was turned on Sera's motionless body in the deep shadows. From this distance I couldn't see her breathing, but the machines reassured me she was still alive. If only barely.

"Is it her?" Sprig climbed on my back, trying to peer with me.

"Yeah." I pushed myself back up. This was harder than I thought, being alone with her. What would I say? *Sorry you're dying? Or, there is a chance I could cure you, but I don't want Rapava to know the truth about how I got Ryker's powers... my bad.*

"Hello? You go on holiday?" A tiny finger tapped against my head. "You going down there or did we simply sneak over here for the rush? I could see this is all getting boring. No hot Viking to pummel all night."

"Sprig!" Heat crawled up my cheeks. His jab hit a little too close to home. One of several dreams I had lately flashed through my mind. Ryker's lips skating up my inner thigh, his hands...

Zoey, stop! I rubbed my face fiercely.

"What?"

"Shut up," I hissed.

"Not getting any is making someone grumpy."

"Like you and food."

"Exactly. Ryker is your honey stick." His face scrunched up.

"Ugh." I shook my head. "Let's not ever use that reference again."

"I think I might even have ruined honey for me with that comparison."

I raised a dubious eyebrow at him.

"Yeah, you're right." Sprig grabbed his stomach, laughing. "That could *ne-ver* happen."

I shook my head, a smile curling on my face. No matter what, Sprig could make me laugh, even in difficult times.

"You know, all this talk of honey—"

"If they ever allow me beyond my room, I will try and find you some."

"This is why we should never part ways."

"Because I supply your addiction?"

"Pretty much." He nodded.

"That's what I thought." I sighed. "My role in life." I stared back down the gap in the ceiling. "Okay, let's do this."

41

"Great!" Sprig bobbed on my shoulder then stopped. "What are we doing again?"

I reached over and grabbed Sprig. "This." I lowered myself into the opening and held him over the bed. "Jump."

He easily leaped on the bed as I turned myself around in the vent and slid through the opening feet first. I dropped to the ground, my knees bending with the impact. I barely made a noise. I was exceptional at several things and being stealthy was one. Robbing homes, starting at the age of nine, taught me early how to move so I could break into places undetected.

I crept over to Sera's bed, her frail form disappearing in the mattress. My gaze roamed over her face and hair. We didn't come from the same parental DNA, but we came from the same formula Dr. Holt designed. I guess I still hoped to find something visual connecting us—a trait, a birthmark, something tangible. But we were only related on the inside. A unique coding in our DNA linked us.

Without realizing it, I reached for her hand. It was small and cold in mine. Sweat beaded at her hairline and a shadow of blood crusted the base of her nose.

"I'm sorry," I whispered, my voice startling me. Emotion struck my heart. "I am so, so sorry."

Sera's lids quivered and slowly they lifted. Adrenaline sent spikes of energy through my limbs. What if I read her wrong earlier? What if she cried out for help or hit a button to get the nurses in here? All my work to obtain Rapava's trust would be down the drain.

I stiffened and glanced nervously at Sprig. He had moved to the opposite nightstand as me, hiding behind a jug of water.

Sera's head bowed toward me, her gaze taking me in. I was half expecting anger or even fear to flash in her eyes, but instead liquid filled them as she squeezed my hand.

Air I didn't even know I was holding slipped over my tongue.

Sera took back her hand and tried to push herself up.

"Here." I adjusted the pillows so she could sit up. She struggled to move, and after repositioning a little she laid back on the pillows, her eyes closing with fatigue.

I felt helpless and guilty. My conscience kept stabbing me. *What kind of person are you? You could save her. Do something.* And the shame only thickened with the knowledge I wouldn't; I was going to let her die.

She licked her lips as she opened her eyes. "You. Came." Her voice was soft and every syllable struggled to come out.

"Sera, I—" She grabbed my hand, halting my words.

"I should have believed you." She huffed slowly, sucking in deep gulps. The tube in her nose wheezing with strain. "I'm sorry."

"I don't think I would have believed me either."

"Dr. Ra—Rapa—va." Sera coughed.

"I know. I know what he's done to us, what he wants to do." I tried to fill in for her. She continued to choke and gasp for air. My gut somersaulted when I saw fresh blood dripping from her nose and pooling in her hand.

Was this how I would have met my end? How my death would have played out if it weren't for Ryker? Only an outlandish coincidence had kept me from dying here alongside Sera.

Fury twisted my insides, stirring my wrath against Rapava and even Dr. Holt. What gave them the right to play God with us? To not care about the consequences of their creations? How could they not consider we were *real* people with feelings, hopes, dreams, not merely cells from a petri dish?

As I watched Sera spit more blood into her hand, I knew I would do whatever it took to end Rapava. To destroy DMG for good.

Sprig nudged a box of Kleenex on the side of the table, still staying out of sight. I didn't know how she would respond to Sprig. Even if she hated DMG, it didn't mean her prejudices against the fae had changed. It was better if he stayed hidden.

I tugged the tissue out of the box and wiped the blood from Sera's face and hands. She grabbed for my wrist, her eyes wide, her breath growing choppy and irregular.

"I must. Tell. You." She panted, agitation tugging at her voice.

"Sera, you need to rest."

"No." Her grip on my arm tightened. "He's already..." She coughed even more violently, her withered frame convulsing.

"What?" I leaned in closer to understand her.

"Star-ted." Like someone poked a deep hole in a water balloon, blood trailed from her nose and the corners of her eyes. "Stop. Him."

"Oh god, Sera." I clutched the back of her head as she fell back.

"Zoey..." she muttered my name, her lips covered in blood.

"Shhhhh." I crawled on the bed, holding her. "It's okay, I'm here."
So you won't have to die alone.

"Save them." Her body jerked, and she moaned in pain. "Rescue her."

I couldn't stop the whimper from pushing past my lips, and I gripped her closer to me, trying to hold her frame in place. Red liquid soaked my shirt.

She smacked her lips, trying to talk again. "I'm. Sorry."

"Sorry for what? Rescue who?" I rocked her back and forth, not relenting on my firm hold.

"I knew..." With another fit of violent tremors, more blood poured from her nose and eyes. "Shhiisss—heeerrreee." Her words trailed off in a hiss. She jerked again, gave a terrible series of gasps, and then went still. Both ice and fire cascaded over me. I shook my head back and forth, trying to stifle a cry.

"Nooooo." I continued to sway her, but Sera's body remained still in my arms. "No. Sera…"

She was dead.

Sharp cuts of sadness slashed at my heart, coiling me forward over her body in pain, echoing out in a sob. Grief I had held back from losing Lexie and Daniel swamped my chest, unfolding with even more density. I pulled her body firmer against mine, shaking.

"*Bhean.* Are you okay?" Sprig jumped off the side table, his little voice unsure. But I could not answer him. Her death hit me harder than I thought it would. Maybe because with Lexie and Daniel I never had time to fully mourn their loss. Or because theirs had hurt so deeply I wouldn't let myself feel it. Sera had opened the barrier I put up, letting the utter agony of all the people I lost crash in. Hot tears slid down my face, choking my throat with cries.

An irritating sound came from the background, but I felt numb to sensations. The only thing I experienced was pain, loss, and being left alone.

"*Bhean?*" A tiny hand rubbed my leg. Through my blurry vision I saw Sprig beside me on the bed. "I hate to do this, but we got to go."

The here and now came back in an instant. The annoying noise in the background was Sera's heart monitor, letting everyone know she was no longer with us. Voices and movement coming from the hall pierced my ear.

The commotion moved toward the room.

Hell.

"Now, *Bhean!*" Sprig jumped off the bed.

It tore at my heart, but I moved away from her, letting her go. I knew Sera would not want me to get caught now. She wanted me to stop Rapava and have her death stand for something. I would not let her die being another unknown victim of DMG's.

Sera, Daniel, and Lexie were my crusade. My reason to get up in the morning and keep fighting.

"Bhean!" Sprig screeched, jumping up and down underneath the open panel where we came down. The commotion was moving closer. We only had seconds.

Giving Sera's hand one last squeeze, I dashed for the rolling table. It wasn't sturdy, but it would have to do. I rolled it to the opening and climbed on. Sprig bounded up my back and through the hole.

Footsteps pounded outside the doorway. Nerves cringed my stomach. I only had one shot. Adrenaline hammered through me and with a grunt I sprang into the gap, pushing the table back toward the bed with my feet. My ribs cracked against the metal partition as I landed. I scrambled to inch farther up. Sprig uselessly tugged at my shirt, trying to help. People bounded in the room, my legs still exposed, partially dangling from the ceiling vent.

Fuck.

I held my breath, waiting to be discovered.

It sounded like three women's voices as they moved around the bed. I stayed frozen for one more moment, confirming they hadn't noticed me.

The beeping of the monitor ceased. "Time of death. Twelve twenty-eight," one of the women spoke, and I recognized her voice. Delaney.

Their focus was on Sera. For now.

I slowly pulled my legs up, inching them so as to not draw anyone's attention.

"I'll go let Dr. Rapava know and confirm what he wants done with her," a deeper-voiced woman spoke. I knew her too. She was one who had come in a lot when I was locked in the room. She was the cruelest when injecting me. She loved to twist and dig her needle into my neck or arm.

Bitch.

The heavy tread of footsteps retreated from the room.

"Guess that leaves us with the paperwork." The last woman sighed. "Bitch."

Evidently I wasn't the only one who thought so.

"It's sad. Sera was one of us," Delaney said, compassion clear in her

45

tone.

"Please. *That* one was not one of us. Could you even call her human? She was a lab experiment."

My teeth crunched down, biting back my incense.

"Tina," Delaney exclaimed.

"What?" Tina paused. "Fine. She was human. But you can't deny she was also a bitch. A Collector, seer. She thought herself above everyone. Every time she came here, her nose was so far in the air, it could have been ploughing the ground level, six floors above."

Sera knew them? Had been down here? When I was a Collector, Rapava kept us far from this section. I knew there were scientists and testing going on, but I didn't know the scope of it. And I hadn't met any of them.

Peter, Liam, Marv, Hugo... all of them were here when I was trying to escape. They all seemed confident, as if they knew what was going on for a long time. Had they always been familiar with this area or only after I left? Were only Daniel and I not included?

Jeez! How blind was I?

Maybe I had wanted to stay in the dark. Deep down I sensed bad stuff was happening, but if I didn't see it, then I didn't have to acknowledge it and do something. With every turn, I realized I'd only scratched the surface of what was going on here, how deep it went.

"*Bhean*, come on. They're gone." Sprig yanked on my arm. I had been so lost in my thoughts I hadn't even heard them leave. I shifted around, glancing down to be sure they left, and shoved the panel back in its place.

"Damn! That was close," I mumbled. "Extremely happy you stayed awake. It would have been much more difficult to escape with you snoring." I glanced over my shoulder at Sprig. "And... I spoke too soon."

Sprig was passed out cold.

I snickered, embracing him with one arm. "I missed you." I nuzzled into his soft fur. I never wanted to be without my ADD, narcoleptic, honey-addicted monkey-sprite.

Ever.

He curled on my back when I placed him there, and I crept on my hands and knees back to my room through the section of vents.

On my way to Sera's room, I remembered some of the panels were fragile from age. Unfortunately, in the dark I couldn't remember where they were. I slid my knees across the thin board, the material groaning under my weight. Sweat dripped down my forehead as I moved carefully over each section. I huffed with relief when my foot crossed over the weak square. "Let's not do this again," I mumbled to myself. A droplet of liquid fell on my lashes, blurring my vision. My hand automatically wiped it away, tipping me off-kilter. My hand shot out to the next panel to stop myself from toppling over. I heard wood creaking and then felt nothing under my palm. I leaned so far forward my body followed as my stomach bottomed out.

Whoosh. Air skimmed my ears as I fell. A startled cry came from Sprig, his nails digging into my skin through my shirt. Impact came so fast I didn't even have time to scream. My face struck first, and instantly I knew I'd fallen on a person.

"Uuuffff." Air rushed out of the figure I landed on.

Fear and shock overrode my immediate reaction to flee.

"Wow... this is crazy. A girl landing face-first in my crotch was exactly what I wished for tonight," a man spoke.

The voice. I picked up my head. In the dark I could barely distinguish his outline.

"You even brought your own monkey... kinky. I like it."

No. It couldn't be. There's no way. Against my will, hope ballooned in my chest.

"Croygen?"

A click of a button announced a light before it came on. The room dimly sparked with a glow from a small flashlight. The soft ray of light in his hand shadowed and illuminated the sharp, distinct features of the dark-haired pirate.

His black eyes danced with humor. "Now, don't let me interrupt. You were about to make me believe in the power of wishes."

47

EIGHT

Croygen.

He was here.

Tears sprang to my eyes, different emotions moving through me. Before I even realized it, I leaped forward, burying my face into his neck.

"Oh, no. No. No. No," Sprig whined from where he had fallen on the floor. "You? Thought we got rid of you."

"I-I can't believe you are here," I whispered and lifted my head, reassuring myself he was really here and not a figment of my imagination.

I had seen *his* eyes the night Rapava drugged and locked me up. I thought it had been my mind trying to find comfort in all the fear and pain. I had forgotten about it till now.

"Yeah. Me neither." He let out a heavy sigh.

"You don't have to be." Sprig scuttled up the side of the bed next to us. "Can this be like the TV show where we vote you off?"

"And I was hoping, rodent, you weren't included in the package." Croygen laid his head back.

"Wh-what? I'm not a rodent." Sprig's chest puffed with indignation.

Croygen snorted, the vibration humming against my body. It was then I realized I was lying on top of him with his hands on my lower back.

"How are you here?" Shifting, I sat at the edge of the bed, heat prickling my cheeks. "Why are you here?"

"Why are you covered with blood?" He propped himself against the wall, his gaze moving down my face to my shirt. The room was rectangular and only big enough to fit a metal cot, a tiny sink, and toilet in the corner. It was a white-walled prison, but instead of bars, a thick plated window was next to the door so the captives could be observed.

At least my room came without a peek window.

"Not mine." I glanced at my stained shirt and hands. I shook my head, hoping the images would go away. I couldn't think about her right

48

now. "Did DMG catch you?" I asked, but I already knew the answer. "No, *you* don't get caught. What are you doing here, Croygen?"

He snickered, folding his arms over his chest. He was wearing the thin gray scrubs they issued to every prisoner. Nothing was left to chance, like personal clothes or items. Even if they told me I was not an inmate here, I knew different. They dressed me the same as the fae. Giving me my boots back was the doctor's way of trying to instill a sense of security. Something of mine. A gesture of goodwill. Or maybe a way to control me.

No personal items. "Wait! How did you get a flashlight?" I pointed to the four-inch torch.

Croygen scoffed. "Please. It was unbelievably easy to nick off the doctor. I'm a professional, remember?"

My lids narrowed. Everything about Croygen was a bit dodgy.

"Look at you, all full of suspicion. You think I'm on DMG's side?" Croygen arched one eyebrow.

"I. Don't. Know."

Sprig crawled up my leg. "Don't trust him, *Bhean*. Pirates are liars and thieves."

I nodded and both of us turned to Croygen, our arms crossed.

"And what are you?" Croygen challenged. "But a liar and thief also."

Sprig and I continued to stare at him.

"Seriously?" he exclaimed. "After all I did to get to you, you really think I'd go against my own to help the DMG? Humans?"

"For the right price," I replied.

"Wow." He shook his head. "I think Ryker has influenced you way too much." Suddenly his face was only an inch from mine. I sucked in air. Being this close to him unnerved me, but not for the reasons they used to. Croygen was quite attractive; there was no denying it. I used to see fae first and find myself repulsed. Now I only saw the beautiful man across from me. "I want to know what *your* instinct says. What do *you* feel, Zoey? Am I here to betray you?"

I watched him, his features growing sharper the longer I stared. My gut said he was friend not foe. It could be wrong. Croygen was good at deceiving.

"No. I don't think you are." My fingers wrapped around his collar and pulled him in. "It's why I really don't trust you. Now tell me why the fuck you're here."

A wicked grin engulfed his face. "Damn, I am really starting to get

49

what Ryker sees in you. That was hot."

"Croygen!" I tightened my grip on his shirt.

"All right." He brushed my hand off, leaning back. "You take the fun out of everything."

"Talk, thief." Sprig bristled.

"Tradesman."

"Croygen," I warned.

"Yeah. Okay." He huffed, standing up. "I'm here because I don't have a choice."

"What do you mean?"

"It means I am no longer obligated to Ryker." He walked to the small sink against the wall and leaned over it.

"What?"

"I don't know how it's possible. Nothing about you or how you got Ryker's powers is normal. All I can gather is when they finally claimed you, the oath binding me to him transferred to you."

"Say that again, buccaneer?" Sprig crawled off my leg, moving to the middle of the bed.

Croygen glanced over his shoulder, his black eyes going right to mine.

"It means I follow *you* now. If you are in trouble, I sense it. No matter where you are I will be able to find you." All humor dissipated from his features. "Where you go... I go."

My mouth parted. He was not pleased, but his words caused a strange intimacy between us. Something I never imagined having with Croygen. Ever.

"I'm gathering this is not something either one of us can change or stop."

He shook his head. "No."

The intensity of his gaze forced me to look at my lap. I thought back to when Ryker's powers became fully mine. It *was* around the time Croygen started to treat me differently. I remember being a little confused by his change of attitude toward me. Never in a million years did I think he was "attached" to me.

"So, what do we do?" I motioned between us. "How does this work?"

"We don't do anything." He grinned. "Well, unless you have something in mind." He winked.

I rolled my eyes. Here was the Croygen I knew.

"Zoey, it's not something you can do anything about. It is what it is. It cannot be broken until I fulfill my obligation." He rotated around and leaned against the sink.

"You mean, unless I am about to die and you save me, we will be... attached?"

"I like to think of it more as screwed or nailed together."

I rubbed my head.

"It is different from what I had with Ryker."

My head jutted up. "What does that mean?"

"Yeah, what do you mean, swine-buckler?" Sprig walked to the end of the bed. "Don't think your sword is mightier than the axe."

"Sprig." I grabbed him, pulling him back on my lap. "If you stay quiet for five minutes, I will try to steal you honey from the break room."

"Sweet love of the golden gods. Honey—"

"Sprig? What did I say?"

Sprig fumbled for his tail and shoved it into his mouth. "Vee, tis wops ee rom ralking," he garbled, pointing at his tail.

I grinned.

"Keep stuffing; we can still hear you." Croygen smirked.

Sprig threw both of his hands in the air and flipped him off. Croygen glanced at me, an eyebrow lifted.

I shrugged. "I didn't say he couldn't talk with his hands."

Croygen's tilted back his head and chuckled.

"Now, what do you mean it's different from Ryker's?"

Croygen frowned. "The link to you seems stronger, more out of my control. Which doesn't make sense. He was the one who saved my life, so why is it stronger with you?"

I couldn't answer that any more than he could. "How did you get here? I mean, you came all the way from Peru? For me?"

"It's not like I flew coach. I wouldn't do that for *anyone*," he stressed. "With our connection I can easily track you through the fae doors. It also wasn't hard to figure out where you were being taken once I saw them put you on the private plane in Cusco."

It felt strange to hear about what happened to me from someone else, when I couldn't remember it myself, like a weird video of my life. The movie flickered back to the last memory I had after Garrett, one of Vadik's men, chloroformed me.

"You were there that night," I stated. "I remember. I saw you in the alley."

Croygen nodded. "Yes. By then I already had the link to you, and I sensed you were following me out of town, trailing me. And when you suddenly pulled back, I got curious." He paused, glancing at his feet. "It was too late by the time I reached you. Garrett already had you. Unlike Ryker, who threw himself in the middle, I stayed back."

"Yeah, you're my hero," I quipped.

Sprig's middle fingers flew in the air again, wiggling around, muffled grunts coming from his mouth. I stroked the top of his head to calm him down.

"Look how well it worked out for you and Ryker," Cryogen retorted.

"Do you know where he is? Is he okay?"

"All I know is Vadik took him... and Amara." Her name came out strained. "I guess she went willingly." He shifted against the sink. "Ryker is no longer my concern. Finally."

"Please. You two are all bark. I sense the closeted bromance there."

Croygen's lids narrowed.

"Ryker was always suspicious of you, and the whole time it was Amara who Ryker should have been questioning."

Sprig tugged his tail from his mouth. "Purple-haired bitch! I never trusted her. I knew she was up to something, but did anyone listen to me? Nooooo." He jumped, throwing his arms up. Then he huffed and sat back down. "Are you hungry? I'm hungry."

"So close." I patted his head.

"What?" Wide-eyed he turned to look at me. "That had to be longer than five minutes. It was forever. I still get honey, right? Because I was silent for well over five minutes."

"It was barely two."

"Close enough."

"Sure." I rubbed behind his ear. His lids drooped quickly and in thirty seconds he fell face-first on the bed.

"Thank the gods." Croygen rubbed at his forehead, pushing himself off the sink. "That thing is too tiny to be so bloody annoying."

I ignored him and returned to our conversation. "You never knew Amara was deceiving us... you?"

"I should have, right?" A grin hinted at his mouth. "I mean, that's what she does, what she is. Probably somewhere I knew but clearly didn't give a shit."

I blinked, my mouth falling open. "Oh. My. God. You still love her. Even more now, don't you?"

"Yeah." The grin turned into a chuckle. "I do."

"You are a sick bastard."

"Don't I know it." He winked.

I groaned. I really shouldn't have been surprised the pirate was turned on by deception and duplicity.

"She's good. You have to give her that." My lips pinched together. All I felt was hatred for her. "Like you're an angel. Don't act like you don't deceive, lie, and cheat to survive."

He had me there. "Not to the people I care about."

"Really?"

Okay, that was false. All I did was lie to Daniel and Lexie, letting them believe the slivers of me that weren't the truth. Ryker was the first person I was completely honest with. "Let's move on."

Croygen eyes twinkled with smug triumph.

"Because of our connection, you followed me here and let yourself be taken by DMG. Why?"

"Being on the inside was the only way I could help you. This place is locked tighter than a virgin's knees. I knew if you were really in trouble and your life was on the line, I wouldn't be able to get to you from out there.

"It was easy to fool your buddies here into thinking they 'caught' me. Really, it was pathetic how simply they fell into my trap." He snorted. "Like I would ever allow myself to get caught on purpose."

And he wouldn't. Croygen was a chameleon. He could disappear in front of your eyes, blending into the objects around him. It was cool, kind of creepy, and annoying. But down here he wouldn't be able to use his powers. The injections of goblin metal and the layers of security they built up while I was gone made it impossible to get out of the building.

"I never asked before, but what would happen if you couldn't get to the person you owed to save them. Like me?" I motioned to myself.

"If something happened to you and my debt was still not paid..." He drifted off, his shoulders lifting up. "It's never happened. Ryker is the only life debt I owe. But I heard the debt grows heavier, while you grow weaker, then you die."

Holy shit.

Another oath. Another death. I bolted off the bed, walking for the door before twisting around and falling against it.

"So don't die before I can save you, all right?" Croygen commanded.

"Hell." I tipped my head back, staring at the hole in the ceiling I fell from. The panel I dropped through didn't break, only slipped from its holding, which was lucky. That would have been hard to cover up or fix. "This is all so fucked up."

"Yeah, meeting you has definitely been eventful and twisted, and especially hazardous to my health. And I've hung out with some of the most dangerous, scary-ass men in the Orient."

"And it's about to get more so."

"Why?"

"Because you have an oath to keep me alive, and Ryker has an oath to end it."

Croygen stared at me for a few moments. "You're kidding me, right? Please say you're fucking with me right now."

"I wish."

He rubbed a hand over his mouth, shifting around like he didn't know what to do with himself.

"When I thought I might be dying, I didn't know what was going to happen, and I reacted in the moment. All I knew was it would connect us no matter how far Ryker and I were separated. I wanted him to live."

Croygen held up his hand.

"Let me get this straight. The man I had dedicated my life to protect, for the last century, is the very man I will have to kill because he swore an oath to kill you?" He took a step toward me. "And if he fulfills his oath, I die. If I stop him, he dies."

"And I'm pretty much dead either way. Yeah."

Croygen regarded me, his face expressionless, except for the heated ire in his eyes. Then in a flash his countenance crumbled and a howl of laughter boomed from his chest.

It jarred me at first, the burst of mirth, but the twisted sick hilarity of our situation struck me too. A smile cracked my mouth, and I snorted briefly. It was like a trigger. Once one came out, the rest would not be contained. I bent over as more and more giggles erupted out of me. Tears leaked down my face. Croygen's laugh only spurred mine on. I gulped a few times, getting air as our merriment quieted down.

Sprig's body jerked, and he sprang up. "What? What? Breakfast? Yes, I agree." He glanced fuzzily between Croygen and me. "They have room service here, right?" Then he fell back over, snoring.

Croygen and I glanced at each other and burst out laughing again.

It felt like a giant boulder was temporarily lifted off me. So much bad lay ahead of us, more than I could probably handle, but it felt good to laugh, really laugh.

NINE

Leaving Croygen was difficult. He gave me comfort, a strange peace, knowing he was with me in this. Before, I would never have considered him a friend, someone I would let in. But being here, you got past the bullshit. His presence lightened me. I didn't feel so alone.

I departed, agreeing to try and come back the next night. To communicate during the day was extremely risky. I was never left alone.

It was strange for Croygen to be my anchor. Besides Sprig, he was my only link to Ryker, to the person I had become, to the life I wanted. Rapava's mind tricks and jabs at my former beliefs and actions were hard to keep brushing off. Having been forced to delve deeper into the character Rapava wanted me to be, it helped having Croygen and Sprig to never let me forget who I was now.

I would never again be a Collector or the girl I was before the storm. I had been through too much, seen too much, and my feelings for Ryker were far too powerful. Still, it didn't mean I was resilient to the relentless battle being inflicted on me daily by Rapava and my old Collector comrades.

At one time I believed fae were evil. While some were, Rapava showed me humans could be capable of far worse.

By the time I got back to my room and crawled onto my cot, I was exhausted. It had taken me awhile to scrub Sera's blood off me and my shirt, stealing the water in Sprig's cage they had for him to drink. I turned my top inside out, hoping no one would really notice till I could get a clean one. The memories of her violent death replayed in my head until finally sleep sucked me in, claiming me.

Fingers slipped along my backside, my naked skin tingling as his touch curved over my ass to my lower back. A smile arched my mouth before my eyes even opened. I turned my head to him.

Ryker was on his side, propped on one elbow, his jaw set, but his eyes glowed with need. We watched each other, his hand exploring my body.

"Why haven't you found me yet? Where are you?" I tucked my arms under the pillow.

"You know I'd be there if I could," he said.

"I'm scared for you."

"Don't be. Worry about yourself. You know, no matter what, I will find a way to you."

"Can it be now?"

The side of his mouth hooked in a half grin. He leaned over, his lips brushing over my shoulder.

"Croygen's here."

Ryker pulled back with a groan. "Wow. You know how to ruin a moment."

I snorted. "You know me."

"Yes." Ryker's eyes burned into mine. "I do know you. Don't you forget, Zoey."

"I'm trying not to." I bit my lip. "Actually, Croygen and Sprig help keep me grounded. I don't want to lose myself completely."

"You won't. You are way too strong. And stubborn." Ryker tucked a strand of hair behind my ear. His touch felt so real tears brimmed under my lids. "And I hate to admit this, but if I can't be there, I'm glad Croygen is."

"Now I know this is in my imagination," I chuckled.

"What? I don't feel real to you?" He trailed his hand down my side, peeling back the covers as he went.

"You do, that's the problem." Heat filled me as he continued. "I want to stay here. Escape from all the pain. Remain here with you forever."

Ryker stopped, his jaw grinding. "Then this has to be the last time we can be together like this."

I hated it, but I knew he was right. After losing Sera, I understood I needed to have nothing holding me back.

I drew in a long breath, the pain still cutting deep. "Rapava needs to be stopped. I get it. But being here compels me to want to stay in this bed forever. Be selfish. It would be so easy. But I know you are out there somewhere, and I want the real you."

"Even though I will be trying to kill you?"

"Especially because of that." I turned over on my side.

Our reunion would be problematic, but it still wouldn't stop me. If I were going to die, it would be at Ryker's hand, not Rapava's.

"You and I are survivors, and we'll do whatever it takes to live and be together. That is the love I want. Whatever the outcome." I sat up, looking over him. "You gave me strength at first. I needed to retreat to you. To feel comfort. I can't have it anymore. I need to turn off my feelings and become the person they want. Being here causes me to want you too much. I feel weak."

His hand cupped my cheek. His eyes softened as though he understood. He pulled me to him, his lips meeting mine. Desire zoomed over me, quickly deepening the kiss. I crawled onto him, straddling his bare hips. He rose hard beneath me. Hungry.

He grabbed my hips, lifting me up, then he tugged me slowly back down. Air gasped from my throat as he pushed inside me. His fist knotted behind my head, yanking my hair, his voice a harsh whisper. "Ride me. Wake me up, Zoey. Make me feel you so ardently in the real world, nothing will stop me from getting to you. So I can claim you again."

There was nothing but him and me. All my anger, fear, need, and sadness pushed out through my hips.

This was the last time, the last dream, and I knew it, and I let everything go.

Because tomorrow would come, and there would be no escape from reality.

The lights above my head fizzed, blinking on. I groaned, digging my head into my pillow, my eyes already burning.

Real life had arrived.

The memory of my dream flashed in my head and was quickly shoved out. *No more, Zoey. You need to focus on the here and now.*

It was up to me to get out of here. Play the game so believable they would eventually let down their guard, slip up. Until then, I needed to find out all I could of Rapava's plans. I needed to explore the bottom floor.

Sera had said Rapava had started something and asked me to save "them." I felt in my gut whatever she was talking about was on the lower floor. That was my new mission—find a way to that level.

The door to my room swung open. "Good morning, Zoey." Speak of the devil.

Dr. Rapava's abrupt footsteps advanced to the table where Sprig's cage sat. I curved my head to watch him lift the lid, his analytical gaze on the object inside.

"It's going to be a busy day for you. Today you will start training. You need to keep up your fighting skills. You will train in the morning and then do testing with me in the afternoon." Rapava lowered the top. "While you are training, I will be testing EP-One."

"EP-One?" I sat up.

"Experimental Primate One." Rapava shut the lid, glancing at me.

I quickly bit down on my tongue. *He has a name. A sprite name. Spriggan-Galchobhar.*

"I have high hopes for him. The faster I can discover why he worked, the sooner I can start reproducing more." Rapava strode to the end of my cot, everything from his voice to his body language was detached and factual. "We lost Sera last night, and right now my team is analyzing her body. I need to re-examine why your blood didn't work on her."

I forced my features into an unemotional blank slate. The impassive tone he used to talk about his "experiments" stretched the capacity of my acting abilities.

"I wanted Liam to train you, but today he is not quite up to his usual standards." *Yeah, he just lost his partner and, I'm pretty sure, the woman he loved.* "Peter will be taking over instead."

I groaned inwardly. Great. Peter was actually worse than Liam. His dislike of me over Daniel and my fae involvement had clearly turned to loathing. He would make me suffer.

Like I didn't already, every day. No matter what anyone said, I would always blame myself for Daniel's death.

"I need you dressed, fed, and ready to train in twenty minutes. Peter will be in the training room." Rapava turned and moved to the door.

My mouth dropped open in surprise. Was he letting me leave the room unsupervised? The idea made me uneasy. His trust was too easy, too soon.

The doctor opened the door. The nurse, Delaney, stood on the other side with a tray of bottles and needles.

59

"Delaney, after her injection, can you escort Zoey to this level's cafeteria? She will be eating breakfast in there, and afterwards take her to the training room?"

So... not alone. If it were only Delaney and not with another armed guard with her, it was like going from a tricycle to a two-wheeler with training wheels. He was slowly giving me more freedoms, showing trust, true to his character.

I didn't buy it for a moment. It was all an act. A test. But everyone I passed only helped me win the game.

He walked out as Delaney walked in.

She gave me a slight smile but quickly let it drop. I wondered if she realized her compassion toward me was a little out of place when she was about to shove a needle in my neck, treating me like another fae specimen.

She set the tray down, selecting a syringe. "How are you feeling today?"

Outstanding, fucking fantastic, joyous... this is like a tropical vacation.

"Fine."

She smiled in return. She had a kind aura. Even as she wiped my neck with an alcohol swab, I still couldn't totally hate her, even though I wanted to. She was part of team, and she knew what Rapava was really up to. But she was someone who, like I once did, thought fae were evil and what DMG was doing was beneficial. Hopefully she saw me as a Collector, a human, one of the "team," no matter how far I strayed.

"You know we lost Sera last night?" Her voice sounded timid and soft.

"Yes." I cringed as she drove the needle into my vein. "Rapava told me." Suddenly Sera's face, blood leaking from her eyes and mouth, fixed behind my eye. I had to shake my head to clear the image.

"I didn't know her well, but it's still sad... to lose someone in that way." Delaney sucked in her bottom lip. It looked like she was trying to push the memories of Sera's dead body from her head as well. "She was too young."

"She was a bitch," I responded, watching Delaney's eyebrows hitch up. "But no one should die like that. Violently and alone."

Her head tilted as she pulled the syringe from my neck, I could see the question forming on her lips.

Shit. "That's what I heard. Her death was brutal. I-I saw her earlier yesterday and she looked awful. She was still human, one of us, part of the team." Reflecting Delaney's words back to her from the night before was a manipulation. A trick to subconsciously bring someone in closer. My survival skills would always float on top when I needed the— whatever it took, whoever I had to con. The nurse injecting me with traces of goblin metal was not going to become a friend, merely someone to befriend and manipulate. I would do whatever it took to get the hell out of here.

Delaney smiled again, nodding in agreement. Her fingers touched my elbow, helping me stand. "Let's get you some breakfast."

I smiled. *Already working*. She had never touched me before.

"What happened?" She motioned to my top.

Hell.

I glanced at my top. Even with water I couldn't get the blood completely out. A light brown stain seeped through. "Coffee." I shrugged. "Knocked into someone yesterday."

She watched me then nodded. "Okay. I'll get you a new one on the way." She turned for the door.

"Will someone feed him?" I curved over to the table, peering into Sprig's cage. Curled in a ball, he slept soundly. "He gets irritable when he doesn't get food."

"Yes. Someone will bring him fruit for breakfast."

"What kind of fruit?"

"Usually bananas." Delaney opened the door, waiting for me.

Of course. Bananas. That would not go well.

Delaney found me a new top, and I buried my old bloody one at the bottom of the laundry, knowing no one would think twice about blood-stained fae-issued clothing there.

She then escorted me down the hallway and proceeded to a section of the building new to me. DMG was a labyrinth below ground and a full block long of seven-plus levels of corruption and secrets. Did the main branch of the government even know what was going on down here? Did they care? Rapava acted like he was free to do what he wanted with the DMG being his own private *X-Files*, ignored by the government.

When I worked here, I saw enough scientists eating on the main-level cafeteria, where the Collectors hung out, so I never questioned if there were other places to eat or how many mystery levels there were below my feet. I had been naïve, maybe out of willful ignorance more than actual naiveté. When I first arrived here, I finally had my life together and actually saw a future. I didn't want anything to take me off course. I should have known it was too good to be true.

We stepped into a room. It was smaller than the one upstairs, but it teemed with people—a sea of lab coats. Everyone wore them. Except me. In my gray scrubs I stood out like a beacon. Clearly Rapava wanted me to feel the condemnation of my "peers." A scarlet letter should have been stitched to my clothing. Disapproval, judgment, and humiliation were strong motivators.

A hush fell over the crowd as I walked through to the buffet line. My shoulders rolled back, my chin up. I would not cower or look embarrassed.

Delaney handed me a tray, and a strange sense of *déjà vu* enfolded me. Suddenly I was back at the warehouse, held prisoner, with a hundred other girls who were training to be pit fighters. *I think I'd rather be there.* I laughed to myself. At least there I understood the rules; I could handle myself. Here it wasn't a fight to the death with fists but with mind games and strategy.

Since I woke up from the forced slumber, my thoughts had wandered several times to the girls back at the warehouse, especially Annabeth. The sweet girl who, undoubtedly terrified, still patched me and held her own against the guard. I wondered if she were all right and if Duc, the leader of the Asian gang who took over Marcello's turf, had forced her into being an escort yet. She was not a fighter like most of the girls. Duc was turning the non-fighters into "companions" for his top clients. I cringed, shaking my head. The promise I made to get her out still sat heavy on my heart, but I could not dwell on things I couldn't change right now. When I got out of here, she would be the first person I'd try to save.

The cafeteria lady plopped a bowl of plain oatmeal on my tray, along with toast, then jerked her head for me to move along. The eyes glaring from behind me and in front of me tore at my dignity, stripping me of feeling human. When I sat at the table, everyone grabbed their items and exited the space in a hurry, clearing a wide berth around me.

I ignored them and poked at my oatmeal. Poor Delaney kept fidgeting and looking around, clearly wanting to be anywhere but sitting across from me. Eyes and whispers grew heavy on us, the cafeteria alive with murmurs.

"Okay, everyone," a woman's voice called out behind me. "Get back to work or mind your own business. She's *just* a girl trying to eat her breakfast."

I glanced over my shoulder. Kate's round, sweet face was lined with irritation as she scowled at everyone who defied her order. After a few minutes, everyone's eyes drifted back to their own tables, diminishing the spotlight on me.

"Delaney, I am sure you have other things you would like to be doing right now. I'll take it from here." Kate waved at her to move on.

Delaney glanced around nervously.

"Dr. Rapava will be fine with it," Kate encouraged. "I'll let him know."

Delaney released a relieved sigh. She sprang from the table and went out the door with efficient speed.

"Oh, and here I thought she enjoyed spending time with me," I quipped, shoving a spoonful of oatmeal in my mouth.

Kate lowered herself into the chair next to me, a cup of coffee and packets of sugar in her hand. She didn't speak, and her silence unnerved me. Kate was not the quiet type.

I set down my utensil.

"No. Keep eating," she whispered under her breath. "Look like we are having a normal conversation."

I retrieved the spoon, scooping up food. "Aren't we?"

"Depends on who is listening or watching." She ripped open a sugar packet and poured it into her coffee.

A jolt of adrenaline heated the back of my neck. When I was locked in the room, Kate's visit gave me hope and direction, but I had been slowly starting to think what I thought I heard in her words weren't true. The hope rushed back in like fresh air.

"Don't trust anyone," Kate mumbled. "You aren't safe."

"Two things I already know. And... are you... safe?" I replied between bites, trying to decipher what side she was really on.

"No." She stirred the black liquid, causing my mouth to water with the phantom taste. "I haven't been in a long time."

"What do you mean?"

"This is not the time for that conversation." She picked up the cup, blowing on it. "I'm sorry about Sera. Not being able to save her will always be my biggest failure."

Guilt pooled in my stomach, hardening into a clump.

"Rapava is getting more and more suspicious of me every day.

Watches me constantly," she whispered. "You must stop him. It's up to you to finish what Daniel started."

"Did you help Daniel?" Things were becoming clearer to me. Now that I'd seen the levels of security, I realized Daniel couldn't have gotten down here without help.

"Yes," Kate muttered. I couldn't stop the little twinge of betrayal I felt. They had both been aware of what was going on, working together but leaving me out of the knowledge of the actual experiment that was my life. "I caught him breaking into my office for a key. He was the hope I was waiting for. His determination would not relent until he discovered the truth." She glanced at the table, blinking the sadness from her eyes. "He confessed to me he loved you. Everything he did was for his family and you."

I gulped, swallowing back tears.

"Don't let his life or his love for you be in vain. I'm sorry it lands on your shoulders, but I can't help as I would like." Kate kept her face forward and emotionless, but her voice dripped with sorrow.

"Why?"

"Because…" She took a sip. "I have a daughter and three grandchilddren."

I understood. She had seen what happened to Dr. Holt's family. Rapava might have already threatened hers.

"Plus, I'm more useful if I stay on the inside." She stood up, slipping something under the coffee cup. "Have the rest of my coffee. I certainly don't need any more caffeine."

Kate's demeanor shifted, becoming less serious, like I had always known her. She made a face and giggled. "Now where are my glasses?" She patted her jacket pockets. I nodded at the spectacles on her head. "I'm always losing and misplacing stuff. My head some days..." She rolled her eyes with humor and turned to leave. "Better get yourself to the training room. Peter is not a patient man." She drifted out of the cafeteria.

I assessed the room through critical eyes. No one had seemed interested in our interaction that I could tell.

My breath locked behind my teeth as I inspected the object she slipped under the cup.

I stood slowly, not to cause any attention. I picked up the coffee cup, taking a sip, as I shoved the item into the waistband of my pants, catching it on the underwear band. The gray issued scrubs did not have pockets, naturally.

Without ceremony, I slipped out and headed directly for the training room.

The high-ranking, red-coded elevator security key card rubbed against my hip.

TEN

Kate was correct about Peter.

"You're late," he yelled. "You're wasting my time."

Before Daniel's death, he had been cordial enough to me, probably because of his buddy, Daniel. Peter had treated me like a kid, until I got in his face and challenged him to a fight. He was horrified to think about dueling a girl, one who only measured five foot five.

I remember Daniel leaning against the wall, grinning. "Don't underestimate her. She's a wicked fighter."

I was already in love with him then, but in that moment the magnitude of it bloomed in my chest. It was the first time I felt he no longer saw me as a child but as someone on his level, who could play with the big boys.

Peter ended up winning. I mean, the man was above six feet, had well over seventy pounds on me, and was trained by special ops. But I had held my own. I lasted far longer than he thought, and I got in some really good hits, knocking him on his ass. I was on a high until his foot met with my ribs. Daniel put an end to it then.

Peter's voice snapped me back to the present. "I do not want to be here. Every second you are late, the longer I have to be in this room." His glare of contempt made me miss Daniel so much it ached. I had thought Daniel was uptight and rigid, but Peter far outdid him. He was a soldier through and through. Unlike Daniel, Peter would never question orders or his government, even if it was wrong or he disagreed. He would do his duty, even training someone he despised because Rapava instructed him to.

"You hate me; I get it." I stepped to the large, built man. He shoved out his toned chest, glaring at me. Peter used to intimidate me, but I had grown so used to Ryker's build, he no longer frightened me. "But let's get one thing straight. I have never betrayed Daniel's memory. I loved him.

His death is something I have to live with every day. It eats at me I couldn't save him." I placed my hands on my hips, drawing in a gulp of air. "But I couldn't. No one could have. I battle with my own anger and guilt. I don't need yours on me, too. I'm sorry you lost a friend, but I lost my partner and the man I loved. So back off."

Peter's eyes widened in surprise.

Everything I said to this point was the truth. Daniel might have not warmed to fae like I had now, but he wouldn't think I was betraying him. He'd only want me happy. Peter might someday find out that Daniel kept a lot from him and was not as dedicated to the mission as Peter thought. But now was not the time, and I was not the person to tell him.

From here on, my tongue needed to twist with lies. It hurt my heart, but I felt Ryker behind me, whispering in my ear. *"Wrap your lies around their necks, pour them down their throats and into their ears. Cause them to believe so ardently they fall to their knees, needing more."*

"Do you know what I went through?" Air huffed through my nose. "I lost my partner, my sister, my place here, my friends…" I stressed. "That fae, the Wanderer, kidnapped me, tied me up, tortured me." I lifted my shirt to show him the deep scar from when the gas station blew up, and I was impaled on a magazine rack. Ryker had nothing to do with it, he actually saved my life, but I let Peter make his own conclusions.

Peter reached out his, fingers stopping just short of my skin. "He did that to you?" Indignation rose in his eyes.

"He tried to break me and weaken my mind through torment and control. And I can't say he didn't. It wasn't until I tried to run from here—when you guys caught me—the words I said—did I realize what had happened to me." I shuddered, shaking my head. "Then I realized something was really wrong with my mind. Seeing you all has now awakened the piece of me that was stronger than his manipulations.

"I also have no excuse for my behavior when you saw me in Bellevue, running from the bank. The day before had been a difficult one." I looked down, licking my lips. That was true. The day before we broke into the bank was awful because Marcello had forced me back into fighting. I also thought Ryker was dead. "But I played him, he bought my act, and thought I was on his side. In my heart I never forgot he was evil. I did what I needed to."

"Even fuck him?" Peter sneered.

I forced tears to gather under my lids. "You can judge me, but I did what I had to do. You have no idea what I went through each day. Daniel taught me how to survive. He told me the story about when you both were taken prisoner in North Korea. How you had to survive one day to the next. And no one, until they're in your shoes, can truly judge another on how to do that."

Peter stepped back, his face unemotional, but his shoulders appeared agitated and tense.

I would never diminish what happened to them, the true hell they had to endure, which bonded them. When you go through something like that, no one completely can understand unless they are sitting next to you.

But this was my war. Daniel made me read *The Art of War* at least a dozen times. *"Become relatable to you enemy. Find out anything you can on them, use it. It's how you become a person to them, Zoey. There's a connection. It can end up being the one thing that saves your life."* He would be the first to tell me to use this tactic.

Daniel's voice faded from my head. Peter paced around, rubbing at his head. Finally he let out a long sigh. "You're right, I'm in no place to judge you, especially when I've done the same exact thing." He stopped in front of me. "I've been so angry over Daniel's death, I pointed it at you. Blamed you. Let what happened after you ran discolor my thoughts of your actions. He would kick my ass for that." A brief fleck of humor lit his eyes before turning serious. "I can't say I agree with your choices, but if what you say is true, then I apologize. You're more of a survivor than I thought." He nodded. "Daniel would be proud of you."

I wanted to believe the Daniel I knew would be.

Ryker would find this hilarious.

"Can we start anew?" I held out my hand.

The initial response was quick, but I saw him look at my hand, his nose wrinkled, before his expression changed and he clasped it. He didn't want to touch me. Deep down, he still had a visceral reaction to fae. Tainted. Wrong.

I could work with it. We had made huge progress.

"Now. Let's get you back in shape." Peter pulled his hand away and proceeded to the mats. "If you thought Daniel was a tough teacher, just wait."

Exhaustion forced my eyes closed before I even hit the pillow. True to his word, Rapava forced me between training and tests for his study. By the evening I felt like nothing more than a pincushion between Peter's punches and Rapava's exams. Peter kicked my ass and took great pleasure in showing me what a tyrant drill sergeant he was. Then Rapava ran multiple tests and prodded me with every size needle there was. I had bruises and aches in places I didn't even know had nerve endings.

Even though I passed every mental and physical test they threw at me, I could tell Rapava and his Collectors were still skeptical. I stayed dedicated to the new leaf I turned over—to be re-established as a Collector.

"Is it safe to come out?" Sprig's voice drifted over to me from the cage.

"Probably not," I mumbled. Sprig and I had to maintain a respectful distance. I couldn't get caught crossing the line.

"You all right, *Bhean*?"

"Describe all right."

The metal of his cage clanged. I lifted my head to see him sitting on top of the box, watching me.

"Sprig…"

"Oh, sprite-munchers. Screw them, *Bhean*. You look like a black-and-blue piñata."

"I feel like one too."

"Don't they normally give you a cookie or something after you give blood?" Sprig hopped on the table. "You know, to keep your sugar levels up or something?"

I smiled and propped myself on my elbows. "They did. A whole box. I think they were honey lemon, but they were so fluffy and rich I could only eat one."

Sprig's eyes widened, his tongue licking at his bottom lip.

"Threw the rest out." I shrugged. "There was no way I could eat them all."

His jaw fell open. "Wha-wha-whaaaat?" he sputtered. "You threw them out? You didn't think about bringing them back to me?" He threw up his arms, undistinguishable words continued to come out of his mouth.

"Sprig," I commanded.

He quieted and looked at me glumly.

"They didn't give me any cookies. I was kidding."

He crossed his arms, sitting back on his legs. "You're mean."

"I know, but did you really think DMG folks were cookie-giving types?"

"No. But don't mess with me like that, *Bhean*." He wiggled a finger at me. "When it comes to food, you don't intercourse with me."

I burst out laughing. "Intercourse? You mean fuck with you."

"Yeah. Same thing."

"Not quite." I shook my head. "Slightly different context."

"You humans and your context." He crawled to the edge of the counter. "No wonder it took you and the Viking so long. He thought you tossed his cookies too."

I groaned and lay back on the pillow.

His comment allowed thoughts of Ryker to enter my brain. Thinking about Ryker was against my new rule, but the vivid sex dreams seeped through. Like I could still feel him inside.

No! Stop! I stuffed my face into my pillow, pushing back the barrier. *Dammit. I used to be better at shutting off. Becoming emotionless.* A Viking and a monkey completely undid all my years of building walls.

"Oh, *Bhean*." I felt Sprig land on my bed, climbing up my leg.

"Sprig," I hissed, lifting my head. "Go back. What if we're caught?"

"Screw those dingle-biscuits." He came between my arm and body and snuggled in. I didn't curl my arm around him, but it was enough for him to be there.

The lights clicked off signaling bedtime for the captives. Every night at ten o'clock on the dot we were plunged into the darkness.

"Sorry I brought him up," Sprig whispered, then sighed deeply. "Hate to admit it, but I miss him too. Even though he stole my churro. The delicious, warm, sweet, melt-in-your-mouth, large stick of heaven."

I snorted.

"I can see why you want him back. I saw it; it was not a stick but a seal clubber."

I rubbed at my face. "It's not only about the sex."

"Sure." His tiny hand patted my arm. "No cookies, but did you happen to spot anything else today? Perhaps honey? Like those bars you used to give me. Oh, what I wouldn't do for one of those right now. Oh, and what about those honey mango chips? To. Die. For. And one of those Inca colas. Or maybe—"

"Sprig?"

"Yes?"

"Zip it," I growled.

"Uh-oh, *Bhean* is grumpy, and there is no food or sex available here." He sucked in a breath and whispered, "I'm scared."

"You should be." I sighed. "Now go to sleep."

Tonight I wanted to sneak into the bottom level. Croygen's visit would have to wait. The plastic rectangle pressing against my hip called to me. My goal was to find everything I could on Rapava's plans. Knowledge was power, and I would destroy him with it. What would the higher-ups do if they knew the truth about this government faction and what it was really up to? Proof was the only way for them to believe. Whatever Rapava was doing down there had to be bad. I felt once I saw what was happening, the knowledge would only lead me deeper into Rapava's world, and to the truth.

I waited for Sprig to fall asleep. He would be upset, but I didn't want him to get caught with me. Of course, I was hoping it wouldn't get to that, but this venture was extremely risky.

He was restless, almost like he knew I was planning something. Exhaustion and his warm body next to mine were making it hard to keep my eyes open. I felt myself drifting...

Thunk! The sound of material hitting the tile floor sounded through the room.

"Ahhh!" Sprig vaulted up, tripping over my arm. "The gnomes found me. Hide the cake."

I grabbed him, covering his mouth.

It was pitch black, but my senses worked around the room, knocking against objects, trying to find the source of the noise.

Feet landed on the table. Boots. A grunt.

"Well, that was a pain in the ass."

Air catapulted out of my lungs. "C-Croygen?" I sputtered, letting my hand drop from Sprig, my eyes adjusting to the outline of a dark figure on the table.

"Like there is any other." He flicked on the tiny flashlight in his hand, pointing at his face.

"I wish there was *no* other," Sprig grumbled.

"What the hell are you doing?" I whispered, slipping off my cot and standing up. My gaze darted for the door, ready for a stream of hunters to come barreling through and seizing Croygen. The idea of him being taken away from me, now that I felt I had a thread of hope, generated a frantic, terrified feeling like a squirrel racing around in my stomach.

"You didn't show up." Croygen's form climbed down from the table.

"So you risked coming here? To see if I was all right?"

"Uh. Yeah." He sighed with exasperation. "That's why I'm here, Zoey. You think I like being in this hole in the ground, surrounded by human test subjects and forced to wearing this crap outfit?"

My lips bowed in a smile.

"I mean, come on, a pirat... *tradesman...* has a reputation to uphold. Sexy, smoldering, dangerous. This gray scratchy fabric is chafing my crotch and downgrading my threatening demeanor. Not sexy."

"Awww... is the delicate wee-li'l pirate's private parts inflamed and itchy? Might need to see someone for that. Besides your hand." Sprig leaped onto the end of the bed frame then to the table.

"But my hand is the only one who understands."

"Your hand is the only one who won't laugh at the size," Sprig snapped.

"Funny, most women—"

"All right," I said in a hushed whisper, moving between them. Their faces became more distinct through the shadows. "Think I've got enough visuals to keep me in therapy for a while. You two can bicker later. I was hoping to do this without involving you guys, but you're here and I can't put this off."

"Put what off?" Croygen tilted his head with apprehension.

"It seems we might have one person here on our side and willing to help us." I told them about my encounter with Kate earlier in the day.

"And you trust her?" Croygen's voice was full of doubt. "How do you know she's not playing you?"

"I have to agree with the butt-bandit, *Bhean.* She's one of them. She could be tricking you."

"Because I know," I replied, still eyeing the door. If they were or could be watching me, someone would be here by now. "I can't tell you how or why, but I do. I think Rapava is threatening her family. She has to do what he wants. Even coming to me today was a risk for her."

"It could all be a setup." Croygen crossed his arms.

"It could." I shrugged. "But I'm willing to take this chance. I need to go there. I need to see firsthand what he is doing with Dr. Holt's formula and my DNA. I can imagine, but I need proof. Documented proof."

"Wait." Croygen raised his hand. "You want to go down there? Are you nuts?"

"Ohhhh, nuuuutttsss…" Sprig exhaled dreamily. "Like the honey-dipped ones. Or even the cinnamon-sugar type. Choco-late! Diggle berries, I would even take the salty kind right now."

"I'll give you salty nu—"

"Stop right there." I pointed at Croygen, cutting him off. "Look, I'm going. That's final. You can stay or go; it's up to you. Though right now, I really want to leave both your asses behind."

"Zoey, do you get how dangerous this is? What if you're caught?"

"I will deal with it then. I'm not going to sit on my ass anymore and wait. I completely understand if you want to stay back. This is my undertaking, not yours."

Croygen groaned, rubbing his face. "Seriously, how did Ryker deal with you?"

"Salty nuts," Sprig responded.

It was my turn to groan. I turned, walking back over to the bed and sat, lacing my boots tighter. I never even took them off to sleep. I didn't know if it was because I wanted to be ready at a moment's notice or if it was more of a psychological connection to them. They had been with me since day one and were the only thing I had left which was really mine.

Standing, I wrapped my hair into a loose bun as I moved toward the table. Since my room was locked at night, I still had to use the vents to get to the elevators. I climbed on the table, and Sprig swung himself onto my shoulder. The key card Kate left me was still hooked in my underwear.

"You're not going without me, *Bhean*."

I heard Croygen exhale deeply. "Yeah, I'm going too. Who knows what trouble you'll get into without me?"

"Bhean, can we leave him down there?" Sprig whispered loud enough for Croygen to hear. "Please? Come on. It would make things much better here."

I glanced over my shoulder at Croygen's snarling face.

"We'll see."

ELEVEN

I landed on the tile, dropping from the air vent closest to the elevator. The lights were off in the hallway through this section. There was nothing but me, some unused labs, and fae-holding rooms. It was a perfect representation for me: not fae, but not safe enough to put among humans. I was in Siberia. Isolated and sequestered because I didn't fit anywhere.

The exits along the corridor illuminated our path. It was still a huge risk, especially because it was so quiet in the hall. At any moment we could be caught.

Croygen and I slipped down the hall to the elevator with Sprig snuggled close to my neck. I slid the card from its elastic hold and hit the elevator button. The ding echoed like a siren down the vacated passage.

My breath hiccuped in my lungs. I bit my lip, scanning for any movement. The doors clanked and slid open, a welcoming entry to our doom.

"Last chance," Croygen muttered.

I paused but quickly shook my head and stepped in. "No. Without this proof, we have no chance."

"Not dramatic or anything," Croygen grumbled.

We slunk inside and pressed our backs to the wall, hiding on one side. The card stuck to my sweaty fingers. I took a breath and then glided it into the slot and pushed the last button.

Every second felt like thirty. Fear ticked time slower.

Close. Now.

The elevator took another moment, taunting me, and then finally obliged my wishes. The reflective metal of the doors outlined two figures as both doors clicked into one. Then the box released its hold and plunged us farther into the building. The elevator came to a halt and I reached back, grabbing Croygen's hand. If the doors opened and someone stood on the other side, we were dead.

The bells dinged, and my fingers crunched down on his hand. I could feel him stand taller, his muscles tensing, readying himself for what may be on the other side.

It was strange, but in that moment, I had no doubt he would throw himself in front of any threat and protect me. It was an odd adjustment to realize Croygen had my back. Or my front. He would die for me. Not that he would be happy about it. He'd bitch the whole time, but he'd do it. It placed him into the group I would defend with *my* own life. Croygen... who would have thunk it?

The metal gates opened. My heart leaped into my throat.

We were greeted with empty darkness and only lit exit signs, computers, and equipment showed the entrance. I felt my heart crawl back down my throat, struggling over the patchy dry spot. I swallowed and stepped out of the elevator. The sounds of machines rumbled softly in the background.

"Okay, I can't say my pulse didn't just max out," Croygen whispered close to my ear as he stepped around me. "I feel naked without my sword."

My fists were usually the only weapon I needed, but this was a different kind of fight. I would have loved a blade or gun.

A short way down the path the hall came to an intersection, dividing the area into three more directions. "Right, left, or straight?" Croygen asked.

I needed to check out every way, but an animal chirp came from the right.

"This way." I followed the rustling noises. Sprig stayed uncharacteristically quiet on my shoulder—until we crept into the room making the noises.

"What the...?" Sprig pushed away strands of my hair that had fallen down.

My eyes scoured the room, taking in the inventory of animals locked behind cages. Mice, rats, hamsters, rabbits, birds, and a few cats and dogs lined every inch of free space in the room, covering walls with cages stacked on each other like a game of Jenga.

"Jesus." Croygen stepped farther in the room. "It's like I'm back in the oriental trade a hundred years ago."

"It's disgusting." Each cage was packed full, especially the rodents. The smell of the animals and their feces was so pungent I crammed my hand over my face and nose, the strong odor attaching to my tongue, building the taste in my mouth. "Ugh." I gagged. There had to be at least two hundred or more of mice, rats, and hamsters. At least fifty rabbits, ten cats and exotic parrot-type birds, and five small to medium-size dogs.

I wanted to vomit. As revolting as it was, I hadn't come here to rescue animals. Anger rose and I had to turn around, stomping out. Croygen followed close behind.

"You okay?"

"Far from it." I gripped my hands into fists. I never had a pet growing up and never thought much of it. Since Sprig had come into my life, not that he was a pet, he made me see what it might be like to love and protect something small and not human. He changed my views on a lot of things.

"Let's keep going, before I lose it and let them all loose." I marched down the way. When we came to the intersection, I took another right, heading for the first door. The handle pulled down, creaking the door open. I stepped in and stopped. Tingles of fear washed over my skin and covered me in goosebumps.

Jars of various sizes and widths lined the wall. Each held fleshy-looking items. I took a step closer, trying to decipher what I was looking at. My hand went to my mouth. Clumps of chopped body parts floated in translucent thick gel: eyeballs with strands of veins dangled after them like jellyfish; a small brain bobbed in another looking like a pink cauliflower; a lung; a liver; a clawed foot. The list of body parts filled the wall. By the shape and size, I could tell they weren't all from animals. A faint glow from some of the jars let me know many parts came from fae. My seer sight wasn't as strong since getting Ryker's powers, but it was still there.

"Holy... shit," Croygen uttered next to me. Sprig whimpered, clawing in deeper around my neck.

Croygen stepped past me, examining the labels on the containers. "Snake-shifter fangs, domestic rat's body, fae-raven's feet." He went down the row reading the objects in the jars. "What the hell is he doing?"

Through the horror, I knew I had suspected something like this, but seeing it in person felt different. To realize this wasn't some movie set, but a true Frankenstein lab, whirled bile in my stomach and up into my mouth. My body curled forward, responding physically to the scene. I turned away, needing distance from the carnage. Maybe if I saw this a few months ago, I would have chalked it up to what Rapava had to do to save cancer victims or disabled children. For me this notion had been thrown out a while back. I was also a different person. Even if I never received Ryker's powers and was still fully human, I would no longer be able to tolerate this kind of experimenting.

Rapava was not curing disease; he was destroying fae. I felt a sudden, visceral disgust at myself. If the night of the storm never transpired and Ryker was never forced into my life, I might still be all right with them experimenting on fae. Back then I thought of fae as the enemy and that their lives were nothing compared to the humans we were saving. At the time, I'd felt greater sympathy and anger for how the animals were treated than for any of the fae.

Now I wanted to punch the shit out of my old self.

How could I have been so narrow-minded and absolute in believing what I was told about another race? If Ryker and I could come together, hope existed for others. Even Croygen had warmed to me. Sprig and I were the poster children for human-fae relations.

"Hey." Croygen nudged my arm. "Let's keep moving." He glanced around nervously.

My feet moved as though of their own accord away from the display and into the next room.

A gasp fled my lungs at what I saw next.

Oh. My. God.

A horrendous wail came from Sprig, icing my veins. I couldn't breathe. Or move. All I could do was stare, my brain trying to catch up with what it was seeing.

Croygen ceased his tracks.

"I think we just went past creepy and entered sadistic."

Sprig hugged my neck, burying his head into my hair. I didn't blame him. This had to be too much for him. "Don't look, buddy. Okay? You stay right there." I tugged the band around my bun, letting my hair fall around him like a protective wall. I couldn't imagine what it was like for him to witness this sight, to experience this pain over again.

In the room stood eight five-foot cylinders lining the wall. In each floated a different type of monkey in a gel liquid. They were hooked to breathing tubes and monitors recorded their vitals. The primates in the tubes were made of different monkey parts. One had the head of an orangutan and hands, body, and feet of a gorilla. Others varied in size and type. The other side of the room was a mass of dissected monkey parts, like some twisted horror movie.

"This doctor of yours is a sick fuck."

"Don't you dare associate him with me," I growled, bile coating my mouth, my eyes still locked on the animals. Rapava had been "experimenting" on monkeys for a while. It was how he created Sprig, but my gut told me he had rededicated himself to the venture since my return. The conversation the day Rapava first showed me Sprig came back to me.

"I never thought of that before."

"Of what, sir?" I gulped.

"Both animal and sub fae seek a master. Someone to command them..." He drifted off, lost in his own thoughts. *"I will allow you to supervise him. It will be an interesting case study."*

This was part of Rapava's plan. Not only to create his tweaked human army, but to Frankenstein an animal horde alongside it. These monkeys were trials.

Sprig's little body quivered against my neck.

"It's okay." I nuzzled my face into his fur. "I won't ever let anyone hurt you again."

He only gripped me harder.

I wanted to go. To get him away from this, but I needed more proof. I needed to investigate the other rooms where the testing and experimenting of animals still occurred but was vastly ignored by the public. Again under the philosophy of "if I don't see it or acknowledge it, then I don't have to do anything about it."

I could no longer look the other way.

But this wasn't the thing to shut DMG down. Neither were the grotesquely severed parts of fae in the other room. I needed to get my hands on the files I'd lost, which showed they were producing and experimenting with human babies. This might get some notice. I would need as much data as possible. Right now I didn't even have what Daniel left me.

"Come on. I need to keep searching." I grabbed Croygen's arm and led him to the door so I could look out before we fled.

"What do you plan on doing when you find something?" Croygen whispered in my ear.

"You don't have a camera or anything, do you?"

"What do you think? I come loaded with technology?"

"And here you brag about being fully equipped."

Croygen snorted. "My gear is only used in the moment, not to capture a moment."

I smiled, but it felt forced. Too much heaviness sat on my heart. I used to be a lot tougher and could block out my emotions. I needed to become that girl again. There was more ahead; there was no doubt of that. And whatever I discovered I would have to face Rapava and act like everything was fine, and I was still going with the program. It was going to get extremely difficult, and I needed to be even tougher.

I peeked my head around the door. "Clear," I muttered.

Sprig jumped from my shoulder and clambered down the hall toward the elevator.

"Sprig?" I whispered hoarsely after him. He ignored me, slipping into the shadows. "Sprig."

"He'll be fine." Croygen came behind me. "He can hide anywhere."

"I know, but—"

"He might need a moment. How do you think he feels after seeing that?"

"Awful. It must have brought back the most horrendous memories."

"Come on." Croygen cut around me. I slipped into the hallway after him, pressing my back against the wall. Keeping low, we both slunk along the corridor. At the end of the hall was a thick metal door. A key card slot and thumbprint security tablet hung next to it.

"Hell."

"You think this Kate would give you a piece of her thumb?"

"Eww," I uttered over my shoulder.

"What?" He tapped at the pad of his thumb. "Just a little shave off the top."

I turned away from him.

"What's your great plan then?"

As I rolled ideas around in my head, I felt Sprig's nails in my pants as he climbed my leg. I grabbed him and settled him back on my shoulder, my hand reaching for him, petting his fur. He let out a sigh, his trembling subsided, and his body became more relaxed. Soon he would be asleep.

"Shit. I don't know." I was coming up with nothing. And I knew what I needed to stop or destroy Rapava was most likely behind the door. The truth was so close it was hard to walk away. But morning was coming, and we needed to devise a new plan.

My lips parted to tell Croygen, when a ding chimed down the corridor. The elevator hummed as it settled on the bottom floor, priming to open its doors. Panic shot down my spine into my feet.

The doors began to divide. I froze, watching in slow motion the moment of our discovery.

Out of the corner of my eye I saw movement. Croygen barreled into me, his arms wrapping around my waist as he picked me up. He dove into the monkey room, Sprig and me falling to the floor with bruising force.

A chirp erupted from Sprig, and I snatched him up, curling him to my chest to keep him quiet.

"What was that?" A man's voice trailed down the hallway.

"I don't know," another man spoke, his voice more nasal and cross sounding. "It's like we're working at a fucking zoo now."

"Someone's grumpy."

"Screw you," the nasal guy replied. "I'm getting the coffee started."

"Blacker the better. This is going to be a long day." A buzz came from above. Lights blazed in the hallway. Then, one by one, each fluorescent light flickered along the long corridor.

Croygen motioned me from behind the table. I crawled over, sliding next to him.

"We might be fucked." His dark eyes still sparked with amusement. "What I would give for either one of us to have our powers."

Yeah. That would be really helpful right now.

I peered at Sprig, his wide eyes were on me, but he tapped at his mouth, telling me he'd stay quiet.

"It's not only me, right? He's making us come in earlier and earlier, right?" the nasal man grumbled.

"Just get your coffee. And get some for me too. I'm gonna get started on EP-Five."

Experiment Primate Five.

Croygen stiffened next to me. "It's not 'might' anymore. We truly are screwed." He stared straight ahead. Following his gaze I saw the letters EP-FIVE on the tank in front of us.

"Of course."

Shoes squeaked across the tile, venturing closer to us.

I clamped my teeth together. This was not how it was supposed to end. And I knew there was no way to explain this. It was done. I was done. And I brought two other victims with me. Anger and fear filled my gut like lead.

A hand clasped mine. I looked at Croygen's hand on mine, then to his face. His black eyes were fixed on me. "I'm not letting anything happen to you. We will fight. If we have to battle our way out of here, we will."

I blinked, shocked by his sentiment.

"Don't get all sappy on me. I'm only saving your ass because it's really bad for my outcome if I don't. And there are still far too many bar wenches out there to bed."

I grinned, squeezing his hand back.

Steps pattered closer and closer. The presence of someone entering the room prickled at my senses.

Croygen gave me a pointed stare, his head bobbing slightly.

One.

Another bob.

Two.

I sucked in a breath.

A third nod.

Three.

My legs coiled, ready to jump up.

"WHAT. THE. FUCK?" The nasal man's voice shot down the hallway. "Jim, get in here."

The man we were about to attack, Jim, took off at a jog, racing the length of the hallway. "What, Jeff? What happened?"

"All the animals have escaped," Jeff hollered back. "I mean *all* of them."

"What do you mean escaped? Someone had to let them out."

Both Croygen and I looked at Sprig. A coy smile tugged at the edges of his mouth and he shrugged.

"Right now, monkey, I want to kiss you." Croygen grabbed my arm, pulling me to my feet.

"Don't cause me to have to get vaccinated again," Sprig replied.

Croygen and I darted for the hallway. We snuck down the passage, stopping at the intersecting hallway. The elevator stood only a few yards away.

Croygen craned his neck, trying to spot the location of the men.

"Let me get a broom." Croygen jerked back as Jim stepped back out into the hall. "Round them up first before Rapava gets here, then we can divide them. Jesus, this was not how I wanted to start the day."

Once again Jim was about to discover us. Adrenaline pumped in my ears as I glanced around wildly looking for any escape.

My eyes landed on a closet door and without a thought yanked Croygen toward it. I wrenched the door open, hauling both of us in it. It was small and stuffed with lab coats, mops, and cleaners.

"Zoey," Croygen hissed as I shut the door. I whirled around in the dark, cramped space. He stood there, a broom in his hand.

"Oh. Crap."

Croygen shoved the broom next to the door and plunged the two of us behind the mass of hanging lab coats. Sprig squirmed in my arms as Croygen drew me against his body.

The door creaked open, light spilling into the space. Between the white coats I could distinguish a man about my height, a little overweight, with dark brown hair, and a round baby face.

"Broom, where are you, broom?" He muttered to himself, his hand going for the chain to turn the light on in the closet.

Croygen stiffened, crunching me harder into his chest, trying to condense our forms as much as possible. I could feel his heart against my ear, thumping as violently as mine. Sprig's pulse felt like a hummingbird, pulsating so fast I wasn't surprised when I felt him go limp, passing out under the stress.

Please don't snore. I sent him psychic pleas.

Jim stepped farther into the space, missing the broom leaning on the same side as the door. His finger reached out about to divide the wall of fabric.

Fear slipped through my clenched teeth.

"Jim!" Jeff bellowed from the hall, causing Jim to jump. "What the hell are you doing? Get the fucking broom. They're getting out of the room."

"I'm getting it." Jim looked over his shoulder to yell back at his friend. "Ah. There you are." He reached out, clasping the handle in his hand. With a yank of the cord, the light went out as he retreated out of the room, swinging the door closed.

Croygen exhaled, his head tipping back against the wall.

"Little too close." My shoulders fell with relief.

Croygen's head popped up, his eyebrows curving up, his eyes centering on me with a no-shit expression.

A grin wiggled on my mouth. "Like you don't do this kind of thing simply for the hell of it."

He smirked, his eyes glinting in the dark. "Haven't needed to since meeting you."

It was in that moment I became aware of our aligned bodies, the proximity of our mouths, his arms wrapped around me, the dark intimate space we were in, and the intensity of the situation happening around us. I stepped back at the same time his arms dropped away from me. We turned away from each other.

"We still aren't out of here yet," I said, securing Sprig's sleeping form in my arms. He was tiny, and I would have felt better if I had my bag or even a pocket to put him in.

Croygen pushed out from behind the lab coats, sneaking to the exit and peering around the door. "Clear," he said back to me, all trace of his earlier playful mood vanished.

I took a step through the coats to trail him when something caught my eye on a bottom shelf. A cheap, red, shiny fabric. I leaned over and pulled it out. It was a cape.

"Zoey? This is not time for a wardrobe change, unless you really will turn into a superhero and get us out of here." Croygen waved me forward.

Superhero. Costume.

A nagging sensation rattled me. It looked a lot like the costume worn by the girl Duc had me fight in Seattle last time. The girl who begged for me to end it and who, like Annabeth, wanted nothing more than to leave that life far behind.

It was a coincidence. It had to be. Probably left over from an employee's Halloween costume. The chintzy polyester fabric hung from my fingers like an emblematic red flag, a reminder to not forget the girls forced to work for Duc.

"Zoey!" Croygen hissed.

I wanted to hold on to it, to keep the cape with me, but I shoved it back on the shelf, pushed away the tickling in my gut, and turned back to Croygen, letting it go as I focused on our getaway.

Once again my heart stuck in my throat as we crept out of the closet, heading for the elevator. The later it became, the greater the chance of other employees coming to work, or even worse, Rapava.

I followed Croygen out and across the intersection of hallways. I could hear the men yelling and clapping in the room where Sprig had freed the animals. Croygen punched the bell for the elevator, and the doors immediately opened. We slipped in, urging them to close, grateful the men were too distracted by the escapees to acknowledge the elevator.

"Tell me we are not going to do that again." Croygen placed his hands on his knees, leaning over.

I didn't respond.

"Zoey?

"I have to." No matter how far I had to dig or how unsafe it became,

I would uncover all of Rapava's secrets.

Croygen snorted, shaking his head. "You really are hard on a man's health, aren't you? Death to all who know you."

Truer words were never spoken.

With no more close calls or incidences, we returned to our rooms, Croygen mumbling a complaint as he crawled down the vent.

"For a pirate, you really are a pussy." I scooted across on my elbows, feeling the fur of a rat brushing against my arm.

"Please, I've crawled through sewers, outhouses, and garbage bins to escape."

"And you're bitching about this?"

"I didn't say I enjoyed those either."

Sprig stayed silent the entire way back, even though he was awake. I knew the sight of the monkeys really upset him.

"I'm figuring you want to do this tomorrow night as well?" Croygen asked when we got to my room.

I dangled my legs down the hole over the table. "What do you think?" I smiled before dropping down.

"Just once I'd like you to respond with, 'Why no, Croygen, let's do what you want.'"

"We are being sneaky, breaking and entering, and trying to steal priceless artifacts. I thought this was right up your alley," I whispered.

Croygen's head peered over me. "Yeah, that's a normal night for me. I was hoping to throw in some kinky sex in the middle of that. Spice it up." He winked. "See you tomorrow." The slab of ceiling slid over, blocking the opening.

"Keep your blade sheathed, pirate," Sprig grumbled, hopping out of my arms and onto the table. He crawled into his cage.

"Hey." I sat on the counter next to the crate. "You want to sleep with me tonight?"

Sprig huddled in the corner. "No."

The pain I felt for him sliced my heart. "Do you want to talk about it?"

"No."

I pinched my lips together, not knowing if I wanted to cry or scream. The physical and mental agony Rapava put him through created a fire in my chest, igniting even more hatred for the doctor. Sprig had never discussed what happened to him, not in detail. And tonight would be no different, but someday I hoped he'd be able to talk to me.

I reached down, my fingers twirling softly through his fur, stroking behind his ear and down his back. Eventually his body relaxed under my touch. He sighed, shifting to look over his shoulder at me.

"I miss Pam," he uttered quietly.

I rubbed at his head. "I know, buddy. I know."

All of our things were taken from us and were back in Peru, among them: Daniel's *The Art of War* book, the picture of us, the video recorder, and Pam, Sprig's stuffed goat/friend. Probably thrown out or hocked. The items I had on me the night of the abduction, my clothes and bag, had probably been burned by DMG. Getting my boots back defied my few expectations. But DMG had issued them to me in the first place. Returning them to me was probably their way of saving money.

I couldn't tell Sprig we'd get another Pam because I knew she wasn't merely a stuffed animal, something you could replace. She was his security, his comfort when he felt scared or lonely. There was only one Pam.

There was only one of him, also—not a monkey, but no longer a sprite.

I could relate to this as I was not exactly a fae, but not solely human either.

TWELVE

The lights assaulted my eyes not long after I closed them. It felt like grains of salt were stuck to them every time I tried to blink.

Right on schedule, the door opened and Delaney entered. Like when I was in the hole, each day an interchangeable nurse brought in shots to keep their patient's abilities subdued and controlled. Delaney stepped in the room, her gaze drifting over my face as I sat up. "You look tired. Didn't you get enough sleep last night?" Paranoia swarmed over. *Was she making a jab about my activities last night? Did they know what I did?*

"No," I said warily, rubbing my face.

"Why is that?" She cocked her head, appearing concerned. She wasn't acting like they knew I broke into the top-secret floor. Rapava was too arrogant to think I could get away with anything locked in my room. This was his flaw. His overconfidence in thinking he was the smartest one here would be his downfall. My gain.

I dropped my hands in my lap. "Maybe because I'm still treated like a criminal."

"You know how to fix that; simply continue to do what Rapava wants. He will eventually give you additional freedoms the more you prove yourself." Delaney regarded me through her lashes. She set the tray down and picked up the syringe. "Until then, I can give you a sleeping pill to help you relax at night."

"A pill?" I inhaled sharply as the needle dug into my neck vein, liquid burning icily into my bloodstream. "Because I don't want more of this."

"Yeah." She took the out the syringe. "I can leave a couple of pills for you."

"Thank you," I replied gratefully. I had no intention of ever taking them.

The door opened again, and Rapava stepped through. I forcefully swallowed the bile which rose at the sight of him, last night's images

86

roaring through my mind.

"Good morning, Zoey." He nodded at me, his blue eyes taking me in. "It looks like you did not sleep well."

"No."

He stared into my eyes. It felt he was looking into my conscience. "Night filled with activity?"

My muscles locked up, dread coating me like pancake batter. "W-What?" *Hell. He knows.*

"Your dreams." He stepped to the bed, reaching for his pocket light. "The training must be overstimulating your mind and keeping you up. I presume you still have the active dreams like you used to?"

I always had violent dreams, but when I first started at DMG they got so bad Rapava ran some tests on me. It was a couple of months before I slept a full night. The headaches and nosebleeds began right after. Now I could see they were probably connected.

"Yes." Air rushed down my trachea. "Yes. I keep waking myself fighting with my sheets."

Delaney smiled, but Rapava watched me blankly before clicking on the mini flashlight, which looked similar to the one Croygen stole from him. "Look up." He tugged at my bottom eyelid, peering into my pupils.

I tried to keep my breath even as he examined me. His detached manner always left me feeling as if I were in quicksand. I never knew what he was thinking, which was probably how he liked me to be.

He frowned, clicking off the light.

"What?"

Rapava picked up a clipboard. "Delaney, will you go prepare the examining room? I need to run more tests."

"Yes, Doctor." She nodded, her gaze meeting mine with soft, concerned eyes. She touched my shoulder before heading out of the room. She was sympathetic to me. I needed to act on and use that more. She might be a beneficial acquaintance to have, even if she was unaware of my true motive.

Rapava waited for her to exit before he addressed my question. "I really hoped for you to do more training today, but the tests I ran on your blood came back almost all negative for fae blood."

"What does that mean?" I knew exactly what it meant. I didn't have Ryker's blood. But I played dumb.

"I am not certain. Most likely the blood was contaminated in the lab somehow." He scribbled a few notes on the clipboard and set it down. "I don't think it's anything we need to be concerned about, but I want to run a few more tests today."

I swallowed over the disgust caught in my throat. "Of course, anything you need, sir."

His expression grew smug, a glimmer in his eyes. "I am happy you feel this way, Zoey. Your contribution is already making a huge difference."

Severed primate parts floated behind my eyes and I nearly gagged.

"Glad to help." The words slid off my tongue. "I was actually hoping I could do more."

Rapava tilted hid head, his curious eyes never leaving me.

"I do not doubt there will be," he replied. I waited for more, but he turned away. "Get dressed and have a quick breakfast. I will meet you in the examining room in twenty minutes." He shut the door behind him.

I sat there a little stunned and surprised. *Delaney isn't walking me today?*

I quickly dressed and checked on Sprig. He was still fast asleep or pretending to be. I patted him gently before heading out. He was my tiny anchor, keeping me grounded to what really mattered.

Though I rarely saw anyone when I went to the bathroom or walked to the cafeteria, my senses told me I wasn't alone. Liam was somewhere in the shadows, watching and keeping tabs on me.

I didn't defer my walk to the cafeteria; the secret eyes kept my path straight. It was hard when I passed Croygen's hallway not to want to sneak a glance, but I forced my head straight. The key card rubbing against my lower back was a silent reminder I would see him tonight. The thought of leaving the card behind to be discovered overrode my fear of getting caught with it. It was a gift I didn't want to part with.

Kate was nowhere to be seen in the cafeteria, which disappointed me. Even if she were there, she probably wouldn't risk talking to me again. But she was the olive branch I needed. The only other turncoat in this war.

Eyes watched me as I ate my oatmeal alone. No one dared to even sit at a table near me. *Wow! I actually haven't left high school.* I snorted, shoving another spoonful into my mouth. Except in high school people sought me out, usually for protection. All the way through school, my round, sweet face made me have to prove over and over why they should fear me. I always did. Soon, even the biggest and toughest were trying to associate with me. I ran with a rough crowd during the week and an even wilder one on the weekends.

"Rapava told me we have to cancel our session today," a voice spoke above me. I looked up to a tall blond. Peter's stern gaze met mine. His arms were crossed.

"Yeah. More tests."

"Too bad," he replied. "Your roundhouse kick is shit, and your arm strength is pathetic."

"Not my decision."

Peter frowned. "It simply means I go harder on you tomorrow. Be prepared to get your ass handed to you again. And maybe you should cut back on the sugar." He pointed to the pile of honey packets on my tray, then whipped around and sauntered away.

A grin tickled my lips. That was the closest to approval and acceptance Peter would ever show me. This was how he treated me before the "incident." A surge of confidence and optimism pushed me off my seat. I threw away my dish and headed out, snatching the extra honey packages and stuffing them in my sports bra.

My plan to re-establish myself, become one of them again, was slowly working. Peter was one of my toughest opponents. If I got him, the rest would follow.

Even Rapava.

When I walked from the cafeteria, my confidence fell away the nearer I got to the lab. Every hour, every minute of being stabbed, cut, examined, drugged, and prodded wore me down. Whatever Rapava was trying to figure out, he was being obsessively thorough.

Every tube or syringe he brought near me and shoved in my vein or down my throat, I bit back my tears and repeated: "Whatever I need to do to help." My will was slipping; I could feel it. Every day the injections tore my powers from me, while the testing challenged my resolve. The only thing keeping me going was my determination to ruin the man doing this.

When underground, I only knew time by the lights turning off or on. A couple of times Rapava's wristwatch faced me, so I caught the gap in hours passing. When I last looked it was well past four in the afternoon.

"It's good to see you being yourself again." Dr. Rapava stared at me over his clipboard, gauging my reaction. His eyes were always scrutinizing and critical, staring at me as an experiment rather than a person.

Blood dripped down my arms from the abundance of needle jabs. Exhaustion and pain lowered my defenses, and I didn't trust myself to speak. A big *fuck you* lay on my tongue, seeking release.

"I know you are working hard to return to your former station here, to earn the respect back from your peers. Me." Rapava set down the chart. "I feel the more progress you attain here, the less those dreams might keep you awake at night."

Quicksand. It was under my feet again.

"You were always more intelligent than Daniel. I could see you would soon outgrow him. You were a quick study, understanding dangers Daniel never could." Rapava's voice and face were expressionless, never clearly revealing if the threat I sensed was real. "You remind me of me when I was young. You came from nothing, but you bucked the system, climbed out of the gutter and became something. You are a fighter and survivor, Zoey, no matter the odds against you. I am enormously proud."

I chomped down on my tongue, keeping myself from rejecting our comparison with abhorrence.

He clasped his hands together, a pinched grin on his face. "Because you have been good, I want to give you more incentive to keep on your path." Rapava strolled to the internal phone and spoke quietly into it. *What was he up to?* My eyes tracked him as he came back, untying the straps around my arms. The blood from my wounds was clotting. I missed the fae powers; with them I would be able to heal a lot faster.

"I understand your need to keep the fae contained and under control, but don't you need their powers? Their powers and willingness to fight against their own kind?" I shifted to the edge of the seat, too weak to stand yet.

"Yes to both," Rapava replied, leaning back against the counter. "I am working on one so the other can follow. It is going slower than I hoped. Until I can fully control their minds, I will have to keep their powers from being used against me."

"Control their minds?"

"It's another formula I am working on. You will be meeting one of my test subjects soon."

This man's god complex multiplied every day.

"You might be able to help me."

I forced myself to breath in and out evenly. "How could I possibly help?"

"I've heard rumors that you and your fae companion were in possession of a certain stone. A stone which holds great power, enough to control every fae."

Don't react, Zoey.

Quickly my mind tried to gauge Rapava. He wouldn't mention it unless he knew for sure of its existence and my proximity to it.

"Yes. Like the others searching for it, I tried to discover its whereabouts. I thought the fae's and my connection would shed some light on the location." I twisted the fib out of my mouth. "I was never able to learn anything except it's hidden somewhere between China and Magnolia."

"And you believed it?"

"It was something I overheard the Wanderer say when he thought I was asleep. I have no reason not to believe it."

Rapava stared at me. A trickle of sweat wound around my spine.

"Come, Zoey. I think we both know you are smarter than that." The intensity of his gaze was causing me to want to wiggle, but I stayed put. "It is a lot closer than that."

It was like fire shot from my feet to my head with a zap. *Keep calm. Keep calm.*

"You're probably right, but I'm no longer in the situation to ask," I countered.

"If you were, do you think you would have the talent and capability to retrieve this information?"

"I would like to think so," I replied stoically.

"Would you do anything to obtain what I need?"

I gulped. "I would do anything in my power, sir."

A knock shook the door, and a strange gleam sparked in Rapava's eyes as he straightened and moved toward the door. "I will keep it in mind."

Hell. I felt I had walked into a trap—one he had set for me.

Rapava opened the door to Liam and a figure standing next to him.

My attention was so focused on the knots in my stomach and trying to stay composed, I didn't really take notice.

"Come in, my dear." Rapava motioned for the person to enter, dragging my attention to the door.

Everything ceased.

Air drained from my lungs and I slowly rose, my head shaking back and forth in immediate denial of my senses. My entire universe swayed under me, and I grabbed on to the lab table to steady me.

A lanky, petite frame with crutches outlined the outer door. She stood stiff and guarded.

No. I'm hallucinating...

Rapava signaled again for her to enter. "Come in and say hello to your sister, Lexie."

THIRTEEN

Lexie alive?

I couldn't move or breathe, too afraid I would shatter the illusion if I made a sound. My sister was alive. My brain struggled with what my eyes took in, and what had really happened.

"But... I-I saw... you... the fire," my voice choked.

"You saw her chair," Rapava said.

I turned back to the girl. Lexie still stood in the doorway, staring at me with a cool aloofness I had never seen directed toward me. *And she's standing.* My brain understood this change, but it was not my focus. Nothing mattered except her.

I didn't even remember moving until my arms were wrapped around her. Standing, she was an inch taller than me, her skinny frame engulfed by my arms.

"Lexie." Tears spilled down my face as I pulled her closer to me. Her beautiful wavy black hair tickled my nose, creating more tears. The happiness of seeing her and holding her again was so overwhelming it took me awhile before I realized she was not hugging me back. I pulled back, my hands not letting go of her. "Are you okay?" I touched her face as my eyes scoured her frame.

"Yes." Her voice was like a hand came in and squeezed my lungs together. I pulled her back into me, letting the tears fall freely now.

"I thought you were dead." I rocked us back and forth.

She stayed board-stiff in my arms.

"What happened? How did you get out?" I brushed the tears away, leaning back to see her face.

"Lexie contacted us before the fire." Rapava's voice was like acid in my wounds.

Keeping her clutched to me, I swung around to him. "How could you keep her from me all this time? Why did you let me believe she was

93

dead?"

"She asked for us not to tell you at first," Rapava replied.

"What? I don't understand."

"Lexie came to us about a month before the fire. She figured out you had been lying to her and followed you one night. She's a smart little girl and when she asked to see me, I obliged. She knew she was dying, Zoey, a painful, cruel, slow death. She offered herself as a test subject for a chance at life, to walk again. How could I refuse? It was the least I could do for her." His words dug into my chest and twisted around. "When she couldn't get a hold of you the night of the fire, she called us. Hugo and Marv barely got her out in time. Too late for your caregiver." The way he said it made me believe they could have saved her and chose not to. "Lexie was barely alive the brief moment you came back here last time. After hearing about Daniel, I didn't want to give you hope and take it away again. By the time she was out of the woods, you were gone."

What a fucking liar.

"With or without you, I saw no reason to let this special girl die. As you see, Lexie has been given legs. The transplants are not adapting liked I hoped, but she can stand with help now, which is progress. I hope to keep advancing in my treatment for her."

My gaze shot to Lexie's legs. They were covered by baggy pants and bent under her weight, crutches under her arms. But she was standing.

"Lexie." My fingers cupped her face, the need to touch her and make sure she was real overwhelmed me. She watched me. Finally her silent aloofness caught up to my mind. "What's wrong? Why aren't you talking?" More silence. "Why isn't she talking?" I shot over my shoulder at the doctor.

"I think it is time to take Lexie back to her room." Rapava nodded his head at Liam.

"No!" I reached for Lexie's wrist.

"I think this is enough for the day." Rapava stepped between us. "If you continue to behave, you can spend more time with her tomorrow."

"Lexie!" I shoved my way through the doctor and Liam.

"Good night, Zoey." Lexie looked at me, her head tilted, her eyes watchful.

"What did you do to her?" I shouted at Rapava.

Liam pulled Lexie back out of the room as I leaped for her. Rage balled my fists, ready to strike anyone keeping me away from my sister.

"Zoey, stop!" Rapava commanded. "I know you are emotional right now, but don't let all your hard work go to waste. Don't force me to keep Lexie away from you permanently."

My struggle fizzled at his threat.

I whispered her name as Liam took her away. She glanced over her shoulder at me, and a brief emotion I couldn't decipher filtered over her face before she turned. Her crutches clicked down the hallway, disappearing from sight.

I swung around, no longer able to hide my feelings. Fury burned my throat. "What did you do to my sister?"

"She is the first human to receive my new mind stimulus. I needed to try it on humans, especially ones receiving fae blood, to see how it works."

"You're mind-controlling my sister?" My lips hitched in a snarl.

"I am not doing anything she didn't agree to do." Rapava crossed his arms defensively.

"She's twelve."

Strain whitened his lips. "I am not the bad person here. She wanted me to test on her. To help her walk again. This will aid others like her. She's a special girl. I have only her well-being and best interests in mind."

Another lie. Even if he believed it. I'd experienced him explain what he was doing in the labs, the way he could make it sound heroic and noble. It was not hard to see anyone, especially a dire and desperate preteen, falling for his spiel.

"It is not harming her in any way. It's a simple formula. I can assess her mood and responses. But it's only for short bursts of time, and it has yet to work on the fae mind."

This must be why he kept our visit short. Soon she would break away from his control. Hopefully she could develop an immunity to it like the fae. This was the true reason for his interest in the stone. My anger was shaking loose the monster inside me who thrived on pounding an opponent till they were unconscious and who craved the doctor's blood on her lips.

"She's a *little* girl. Dying and desperate for hope. How could you take advantage of her like that?" Vehement rage rattled my body.

Rapava cocked his head. "You want to assume responsibility for your sister's care?"

"Yes." I didn't hesitate in my response.

"Fine. Your sister's care is completely in your hands." He dropped his arms, an edge creeping around his vocals. "You want me to find a permanent cure for her to walk again? Have her stop being my test subject? Then do what I ask, and I will do everything in my power to keep her protected and healthy."

Rapava's words hit me harder than if he attacked me. His veiled threat meant he could just as easily end her. His past had ripped any empathy and compassion from his soul. I had seen it happen before on the street. When pain and loss had consumed someone so much, they no longer could feel. And everything bad they did was rationalized in their heads to be okay. Walking the line of madness.

And my sister's life was now riding on a whim of a madman and my behavior.

The lock clicked behind me, and I beelined to my bed, sitting with my head in my hands.

"*Bhean*." Sprig crawled out of his cage. "Wow, you look like crap again."

I didn't move.

"*Bhean,* are you okay?"

"No." I bit down on my lip. Tears choked my throat. "I'm not."

My sister was alive. She was a being mind-controlled. Another victim of Rapava's Frankenstein army. But she was alive. It was only fact that truly mattered. The rest I could deal with later.

Lack of blood, food, and being saturated by extreme emotions caused me to crumble weakly back on the bed, curling onto my side.

Sprig hopped over to the bed, coming over to me. Seeing his sweet little face, I reached out, pulling him into me, crushing him into my chest. At the moment I didn't feel like talking or telling him about my sister. I would, but first I needed to absorb it was true. To wrap my mind around seeing her again. Rapava's threat. Everything was jumbled and surreal.

Usually Sprig would say something silly, but he seemed to understand my mood. I needed him near, giving me comfort. We stayed like this for a while before I felt him wiggle against my hold.

"I am sorry, *Bhean*, but your boobs are poking me." He pointed between my breasts. "They keep crinkling. That's not normal, right? You aren't stuffing your bra to impress people, are you? Is this a fetish I don't want to know about?"

Crinkling. Stuffed bra.

"Oh, I forgot." I slid my hands in my sports bra.

"Seriously? With me here?" Sprig covered his eyes.

I tugged out several packets from my bra. "I got these for you at breakfast."

He peered between his fingers, his eyeballs moving over the items in my hands. "Is... is that…?"

"Honey?" I smiled. "Just for you."

Sprig's mouth and arms dropped. "For me?"

I tore one open, the smell of the sweet syrup filling my nose.

Sprig's hand shook as he reached out for it. "It's a mirage, isn't it? You are not really real." His finger poked into the plastic. Then he snatched it out of my hands. The honey was in his mouth before I could even blink, and he licked every inch of the packet dry.

"More. More. More." Like a junkie, his hands opened and closed with need. He downed the last two the same as the first.

"Ahh!" He bounced around on the bed. "*Bhean*, you're the best. That was so awesome. Can I have more? Oh, did they have those granola bars? What about churros? Oh, my pixie sticks. I want Izel's pancakes." He zipped around the room, jumping and swinging from every item he could. "Can you hide those in your bra too? Oh-oh-oh, I'm calling you Honey Tits from now on."

"Please don't."

"Why? Your boobs delivered the nectar of the gods."

"Now you're making it worse."

"Your bra is the stuff of legends."

"Don't make me regret my choice."

"I will take over the world." He leaped for the bed, missing, and face-planted on the floor. Snores quickly followed.

I leaned over, scooping him up. He curled onto my pillow, mumbling in his sleep. I curved around him.

Even when I felt myself losing grip on reality, crumbling under the force of the outside world, he brought me back.

With so much to think about, my brain gave in to Sprig's rhythmic breathing, caving under my exhaustion, and I let myself join him in slumber.

FOURTEEN

"What the hell?" Croygen's whisper floated over to my bed, waking me up. Sprig stirred next to me. "I thought you'd be waiting in the vent, screaming at me for being late." His feet softly landed on the counter.

"We're not going, Pirate." Sprig climbed my arm.

"What? Why?" Croygen snuck over to the bed. I laid on my side staring into the darkness. "What happened?"

"Because, ass-bandit, *Bhean* isn't feeling well."

"Excuse me? This coming from someone who licks his own ass."

"You're just jealous."

"Yeah. Kind of."

"I can't go." I finally spoke. "I'm done with all of it."

"What? Why?" Croygen hissed. When I didn't respond, he crouched closer. "What changed, Zoey? Does Rapava know? Did he threaten you?"

"No." I sighed, sitting up, placing Sprig on the bed. "Not exactly about that. His threat was more about keeping me in line."

"A vague threat is keeping you from discovering more? What happened to the Zoey who said she'd do whatever it takes? Are you really giving up that easy?" Croygen sat next to me. "I didn't swipe the nurse's cell phone camera for nothing. Come on, we can't stop now."

"The threat isn't vague," I barked, more anger rolling from my words than I expected.

"Then what was it about?"

I jumped to my feet, emotion shooting up through my legs. "He has my sister."

"What?" both Sprig and Croygen exclaimed.

"My sister is alive. She's been here the whole time."

"Holy honey-stuffed cannoli! You didn't say anything earlier." Sprig put his hands on his hips.

"Sorry. I was still processing."

I told Croygen and Sprig a rushed version of everything about my sister and what transpired in the room, catching them up.

"Shit! He has her here, experimenting and mind-controlling her, and now using her as leverage to keep you in place?" Croygen massaged his forehead.

"Pretty much."

"He's making you look like a shiny turd, Pirate." Sprig hopped on the table, crawling up my arm to my shoulder. "Though a turd just the same."

"Again coming from someone who flings his own."

"I might look like a monkey, but you know I'm a sprite, right?" Sprig sat back on his legs. "We only fling our poo on the summer solstice."

Croygen ignored Sprig, leaning against the wall and rubbed a hand over his mouth in thought.

"I can't go down there."

His lids narrowed. "You're giving up?"

"I have to."

"Why?" He threw up his arms. "I thought you wanted to end DMG. To stop the torture and experimenting."

"I do, but…"

"But what, Zoey? Is one life worth all the others here?"

"Yes!" My reaction was instant. "You don't understand. She is my sister."

"You think she'll be better off if you stop?" Croygen pushed off the wall, leaning over me, getting in my face. "She's simply going to end up another freak, like your monkey here."

"Hey!" Sprig retorted.

"Or *dead*." Croygen snapped, then turned way, proceeding to the table. "But it does save me from having to protect your ass tonight." Croygen jumped up. "I guess I can leave since I'm not needed here anymore… Oh right, I can't really get out of here. Another trapped rat to be dissected and tested on." The way his boots hit the counter, I could sense his anger.

I wanted to stop him, to explain, but I couldn't. He was right. Still, I could not put Lexie's life in peril. He slipped the panel back on and withdrew into the darkness.

I circled the room like a captive lion. *Lexie.* I still couldn't believe she was alive. The longer I went without seeing her, the more I doubted what I'd seen. My heart wanted to explode with happiness, but at the same time fear swelled through me that she wasn't real. Not the girl I raised anyway.

I spent time rehashing our encounter and her withdrawn, vague attitude, which was far from the girl I knew. The little sister I raised was vibrant, funny, and blunt. The change was thanks to Rapava's mind-control injections. Like acid, rage burned holes in my esophagus at the thought. I wanted to kill him, to douse him with a mind-controlling substance and shove needles into him as I dissected him. I wanted to do everything to him he did to us.

Sleep stayed away and during the dark hours of the night, I realized a very unsettling truth: *Croygen was right.*

Playing by Rapava's rules would not help her. Or anyone here. Her existence would not be better if I stopped uncovering the truth. If anything, her life would be harsher. None of us deserved this. This was no life. And like Kate and Daniel both said, it was up to me. I would need to be even more careful, but I would not stop. Not till he was dead and this place was gone. We would get out of here—escape the walls imbedded deep underground.

My thoughts also went to Lexie. I recalled all the times she may have hinted at knowing more about my involvement with the secret government division. I could see it now, in the tiny things she'd say, the random comments. Why didn't she ever tell me she knew? Why did she keep it from me?

All those things could only be answered by her. And I had no idea when or if I would ever get the chance to ask.

The next day, Dr. Rapava told me that after I trained, I could have a short visit with Lexie. Peter pounded my ass, yelling I was not concentrating.

Yeah. No shit.

Finally he let me go, walking me to the room where I waited, impatiently, for Lexie.

The door opened, Rapava stepped through first. Lexie shuffled in behind him, crutches under her arms, a blank look in her eyes.

Rapava's mindless drone.

"I'll give you a few minutes to catch up." Rapava scanned both of us, like he was doing me the biggest favor. He stepped out and closed the door.

My arms wrapped around Lexie's slender body and squeezed her tight. I never wanted to let her go. "I've missed you so much." I stroked the back of her head. "I am so sorry. If I'd known you were alive... here... I would never have left you. Ever." I pulled back. "You understand this, right?"

She nodded, but it seemed to be more of a reflex.

"Lexie, do you know who I am?"

"My sister," she responded formally. "We were in foster care together. You raised me." Her words were remote, monotone, as if she were merely stating facts back to me but did not actually remember them.

My hand went to her face, searching her eyes for a hint of life. "Do you remember what I got you for your last birthday?" I needed a connection to see how deep this mind-control drug went. Did she still have her memories?

Her eyebrows crinkled, then smoothed out. "You got me an automated dog." She pressed her mouth together, looking at the floor. Her voice became softer. "Because I really wanted one. And Joanna wouldn't let us have a real dog."

"What did you get me for mine?" Hope caught in my lungs and I sucked in. I dropped my hand from her cheek, clutching her arms.

Her gaze went distant. "Red nail polish."

"Why?" I whispered.

"Because I told you Daniel would see your red nails and think about sex," she replied. Her voice never fluctuated. Robotic.

Disappointment weighted my shoulders and my arms dropped away. She had all her memories but relayed them back like she was looking through a plate of glass. No emotion. No connection.

"When did you find out I was lying to you? When did you first come here to meet the doctor?" I asked.

Lexie looked up, but her eyes never really focused on me.

"Lexie?"

"I don't remember."

Lexie had a memory of a steel trap. She could recall things I wished she'd forget. This felt odd.

"What happened the night of the fire? When did they get you out?" I

101

heard Rapava's side, I wanted to know hers.

"I don't remember."

"What about your legs? When did you get them operated on?"

Her lips turned white. "I don't remember."

He was messing with her brain. Big time.

"Do you remember anything about the night of the fire?"

"Marv and Hugo got me out. Just in time."

My heart squeezed with physical pain as she regurgitated exactly what Rapava told me. Tears slid under my lids. I pulled Lexie to me, wrapping my arms around her. I didn't care if she wanted to hug me back or if she felt anything. I needed to hug her, to have her safe in my arms for a moment. She was alive. That's what was important.

Similar to the day before, she was stiff as a board against my snug embrace. I continued to hold her when I sensed something happening. It was slight, but I felt the muscles along her back and shoulders give way under my touch. She lifted her arms, hugging me back.

I gulped, swallowing my emotion, not daring to react, too afraid to move and break whatever moment we were having.

One by one I felt her fingers grip the back of my top, her shoulders relaxing. I reacted, not able to stop myself. My head darted back to look at her. She blinked, really taking me in.

"Lexie?" I whispered.

She held her breath, then slowly nodded. "Zoey…" Her arms came back around me, pulling me to her. "Oh my god, Zoey."

A dam burst in my chest, a sob echoing up. "Lexie." I repeated her name, feeling for the first time like I had my sister back—at least a glimpse of the feisty twelve-year-old I knew.

"Zo-ey." She struggled to get out my name. "It's not what you think."

"What's not?"

The handle of the door clinked and began to open.

Lexie glanced over her shoulder, her face showing signs of fear. Then she gripped me tighter, her lips close to my ear. "They started the fire. Lightning never struck the neighborhood," she rushed. "They killed Joanna."

"What?" Her words sent a pool of sewage into my gut. *Started the fire? Killed Joanna?*

"Time is up, Lexie." Rapava entered and grabbed Lexie's shoulder, pulling her away from me. His face was etched with angry lines. "If your sister keeps progressing and doing what I ask, you will be able to see her tomorrow."

Lexie kept her eyes on the floor, swaying on her crutches.

"You would like that, wouldn't you, Lexie? To be allowed to see Zoey again?"

"Yes, sir," she replied. Even I could hear the fear in her voice. Rapava frowned, and his fingers clasped around Lexie.

"Let's go."

"No." My mouth opened, leaping forward along with my body.

Rapava's eyes darted to me, full of warning.

"It is your decision, Zoey. How much do you want to see her on a regular basis?"

"You can't keep her from me. She's my sister." I could feel my will rising up, big enough to escape the room.

"Actually, she's not. She is not your blood relation, nor did you ever adopt her. She belongs to the government. You have no claim on her." He tugged on her arm, and she hobbled after him, out of the room. "Liam will escort you back to your room."

He stepped out, walking alongside Lexie, a threatening grip on the back of her neck.

Liam stepped up, holding the door with his shoulder. "Come on. I have better things to do than babysit you." He motioned with his head for me to leave.

Drawing in a deep breath, I followed him. Until we disappeared around the corner, I kept looking over my shoulder, trying to get a last glimpse of Lexie.

"They started the fire. Lightning never struck the neighborhood. They killed Joanna." Lexie's claim swirled round and round in my head. DMG purposely set our house on fire, killing Joanna. Why? To get to Lexie?

I never loved Joanna, but she had been in my life since I was eleven. There was a level of caring somewhere there. I dreamed about moving out and never seeing her face again, but I certainly never wanted her dead. Rapava killed the only parent figure I had even really known, burned the home where Lexie and I grew up together. Rapava took this away and more. The fire he started at our house jumped to the neighbors, burning the whole neighborhood down.

He probably ordered it to be done without even a thought to the lives he could take.

Sacrifice a few to save the masses.

My fear of Rapava only deepened. There really wasn't anything he wouldn't do.

We were in greater danger than I thought.

FIFTEEN

After Liam returned me to my room, I paced and plotted. Sprig was absent. I had no doubt he was probably being tested upon. I needed to act now, to get into the protected room. Whatever was behind those doors was my prize. Either I got the information I needed soon, or we needed to escape.

On both counts, Kate was my only hope.

Hours went by and still Sprig did not return. It didn't help my nerves, but soon I fell back on the bed with exhaustion.

The endless roundabout thoughts in my head drew my lids closed. I needed a break. Just for a moment…

"Zoey!" A man's voice bellowed my name so full of fear and agony it sent a chill down my spine.

Bolting up, my lids popped open, my lungs gasping for air.

The sound of the doorknob twisting jerked my head quickly to the door. Someone was coming in. I fell back down, slamming my eyes shut, pretending to be asleep. My heart pounded from the strange dream, mostly lost to me now, except for the way my name rang in my head. I turned over, keeping my head facing the opposite wall, hoping whoever entered would think I was sleeping and leave me in peace. It was a struggle every moment to keep up my façade—to pretend Rapava wasn't the devil and my sister's life didn't hang from a thin thread. I felt close to breaking.

"Hey! Did you hear me? Get up," Liam's deep voice commanded. "Rapava wants you."

I didn't move.

"It wasn't a question. Get up now." Irritation rolled off his tongue, whipping me in the back.

Silence.

"The thought of touching you disgusts me, but I will pick you up and carry you there."

I grunted in response. Today I wasn't in the mood to play the good little soldier. The chance to cause Liam distress would probably be my only perk of the day. But I also couldn't afford to hurt my progress and lose my visits with Lexie.

I dragged myself up, retying my boots. I swear some days they were the only thing propelling my feet forward. I snuck a glimpse into Sprig's cage. He was curled in the corner, fast asleep. Blood and wounds dotted along his arms and sides. As I watched his tiny body roll up defensively, I felt like kicking down the doors of this foul place in my rage.

Liam escorted me down the hall and into the elevator. He slid a card into a slot and pushed the last button. I subtly glanced at the card in Liam's hand before he shoved it into his pocket. It was a red-coded card. We were going to the bottom floor.

The elevator descended, levels below the surface. I gulped, my nerves coming alive and waking me up.

Why would he need me here?

The horrors on this level were enough to haunt me forever. Rapava requesting I come down here? Not good.

We rode the elevator in silence. Liam stayed as far away from me as he could, but still close enough for him to grab me if necessary. After losing Sera, his reactions toward me were more negative, as though "fae" was a disease he could catch.

The doors beeped and opened.

"Move." Liam kicked at the heels of my boots. I bit my lip so as not to snarl at him. Liam turned us along a familiar long corridor, and we moved to the secure doors at the end of the hall. My breath caught in my throat. *Was I going in there?* Was I finally going to see the terrors behind the door? Was I ready?

"Here." Liam's finger pushed me to a door right before the divide. One I hadn't noticed the night I was down here. This door also had a key code safeguarding it. Liam tapped a code into a panel at the door. He was fast, but I caught the two last numbers: four and nine.

When the door lock released, he opened it and nodded for me to enter. The room was dimly lit. Dr. Rapava stood waiting for me on the far side of the room. The room reminded me a lot of others I had been in. A room within a room. The outer room was arranged like chemistry class: beakers and test tubes covered the shelves and tables. The inner room's windows were covered with automatic blinds, keeping me from seeing what was on the inside.

"Thank you, Liam." Rapava nodded at him, taking a few steps toward me. "You may wait outside. I don't think this will take long."

Fear bristled my skin, but I kept my expression blank. Foreboding and anxiety locked my limbs, as though I could never be ready for what was coming.

The door clicked behind me, locking as Liam shut it, leaving me alone with the doctor.

"Don't worry, Zoey." Rapava waved me over to him. Neither his voice nor face held any sort of softness, making his words hard to believe. "I merely need your assistance."

I swallowed back the fear, schooling my face. "How may I help you, sir?"

"Remember when you said you would help in any way you could?"

The thin hold I had on the façade I maintained was about to be challenged by my own words. I kept my mouth closed, waiting for him to continue.

"I need you to assist me with interrogating a fae. Your seer sight and knowledge of their world will be extraordinarily helpful in this matter." He kept his eyes locked on me. "You *do* want to help your sister, don't you? Want the best for her?" I could feel the layers of meaning rolling out of his words.

"Yes, of course." The question was an ultimatum. Of course I wanted to help her, the best for her, but we both knew this was not the real matter here.

"If you help me with this fae, I will not only make your sister's case my priority, but she will no longer be used in my new drug testing. You can be with her anytime you want."

My chin jerked up.

"You miss your sister, and I am sure she misses you. If you do everything I ask, prove yourself to me, show yourself as genuine to our cause as you once were, I will be sure Lexie gets the best treatment and is discontinued from any more mind testing." He let voice trail off. The unsaid "if you do not" threat hung in the room.

The thought of my sister being free filled my eyes with emotion. To be allowed to be with Lexie all the time, to have her back fully, mind and soul, felt like a gift. But DMG's gifts were not without teeth and claws.

My knuckles curled toward my palms. I wondered if this was how he was raised, by intimidating, bullying, and threatening. It was now the only way he understood to deal with people. To control them by fear.

"Will you aid me?" Rapava slanted his head, his crisp gaze fixed on me.

Why did I feel I was about to be handed the ultimate test? My feelings for fae, no matter how much they had altered and softened, would never compete against my sister. She was everything to me. I would do whatever I needed to protect and save her.

Really, Zoey? Could you kill and torture Sprig? My mind shot at me. My stomach sank at the thought. There was no way I could hurt him. But what would I do if he were on the other side of the curtain? Or Croygen? *Please, don't make it either one of them and I will be okay.*

"Yes, sir." My stomach rolled as the words came out of my mouth.

"Good." A strange smile stretched Rapava's mouth and I had a sinking sensation in my stomach. I struggled to swallow, keeping my gaze firmly on him. We stood assessing each other before he gave a quick nod.

"I'll be turning off the lights. You can go to the window. It will not be able to see you."

I turned to the glass and moved close. Rapava went to a switch on the wall and flicked it down, plunging the room in darkness. The light bled through the blinds of the inner room and cast shadows all around.

A buzz hummed in my ear, the curtains slowly rose, displaying the figure behind the curtain.

My world dissolved under my feet, tearing breath from my lungs. My heart curled up and shattered into pieces.

Of course.

Ryker.

RYKER

SIXTEEN

"Promise me."

"No." My muscles trembled under my skin, desiring action. I knew what she wanted of me. But I couldn't. Didn't she see that? She wanted me promise to kill her before she died of the weakness in her.

"Promise me."

It was like her voice was charmed, twisting my certainty and determination to dust. Her vivid green eyes held a power over me no one had ever before. Without realizing, I nodded. "I promise."

As I uttered the words, blood pooled out of her mouth, sliding over her chin. Red liquid dripped from her eyes. Her body went rigid as her black pupils bore into me. A fire surged up behind her, burning shades of scarlet and auburn.

Her lips parted, and streams of black liquid coated her mouth. "Loving you only brings death and devastation." She sneered and her eyes reflected the flames, appearing cold and inhuman. "Your lover, family, unborn child... me. When will you pay for the suffering you bring to us, Ryker, the Wanderer?"

I jerked awake, my chest pumping frantically up and down. The dream evaporated into a sour lump in my stomach.

Blinking, I glanced around the dank cell keeping me prisoner. It was a room built out of thick stone, deep underground. The single metal door had a small opening at the bottom for food and a slit cut out at the top for viewing their hostage.

I had no idea how much time passed between consciousness and

109

unconsciousness. The first couple of times I woke, the separation between dream and reality was hard to decipher. The goblin poison inflicted from the blades caused a fever so ravaging I had no sense of truth or logic. Over time, the discomfort of frozen stone seeping through my sliced clothes, penetrating deep into the slashes carved in my skin, told me this was real. I trembled, sweat coating my forehead. Metal cuffs dug deep into my wrists. The throbbing could have been eased if I sat up, but I didn't move, punishing myself. The pain of the knife cuts sliced across my arms, neck, and stomach were nothing compared to the anger and torture billowing inside.

She was gone.

And I did nothing.

My fists clasped into tight balls. The chains rattled, and my muscles convulsed with violent tremors. The goblin poison kept me weak, slowly killing me. I might have welcomed it. I was dying anyway... but something kept me from letting myself give in to the reaper.

A girl and a promise.

Zoey.

The image of her being dragged away circled my mind like a whirlpool. Around and around, faster and faster till it made me sick. The fever growing in my brain churned the voices and faces into a blurry portrait.

Sprig's cries flashed in my head—his screams for Zoey, before he was silenced.

"Bhean!" Loud, high-pitched chirps and wails bounced off the buildings of the small village, shredding my eardrums.

"Shut up!" Maxen, one of Vadik's minions, violently shook Sprig's small body.

"No!" Sprig cried, his arms stretching out as Zoey's body went limp. "Bhean!"

I shoved off my knees, barreled forward, my instinct moving me straight to her. Knives slashed across my skin, the toxins working deep into my bloodstream. A roar tore from my throat.

Crimson death.

It was the best way to describe the boiling anger crashing around inside—my desire for the blood I wanted to spill on the cobblestones underneath my feet. The rage tinted my vision as if it couldn't be held in my gut and chest alone, bubbling into my eyes. It was the sign the monster within wanted out to destroy anything and everything in its path—the part of a Wanderer most didn't know about. Or didn't want to.

Many had heard the rumors but not seen a true Wanderer firsthand. I was feared for good reason. I didn't shift into anything, except a larger, angrier version of myself when provoked. It was enough. My adoptive father spent years teaching me how to calm and control the fury within by doing meditation and Kalaripayattu, an ancient martial art from India. Mind over instincts.

And in one evening it all crumbled to dust.

One girl.

One human girl.

My world, and everything I struggled to tame, were gone.

"Silence him," Vadik demanded.

Maxen tightened his fingers on Sprig's throat, crushing his windpipe. A cry strangled from Sprig before his body fell limp.

A thunder of rage pushed me past my own pain, where I felt nothing. I don't know when the little pain in the ass got under my skin, but my need to protect him, to keep him safe, clawed my throat and pushed me onward.

Another sharp sting stabbed my side, and my gaze darted to the nuisances. The hilt of a goblin blade stuck out from my stomach.

My eyes flashed back to my attacker then over to Cadoc. His arms curled under Zoey's lifeless body, picking her up.

"Take her away. They are waiting for her," Vadik ordered, his voice sounding farther away than where he stood. Shaking my head, I try to clear my senses. Cadoc nodded and turned.

"Who's waiting for her? Where are you taking her?" I tried to demand, but the words came out mangled and garbled.

Vadik motioned to Maxen, glaring at the monkey hanging from his fingers. "Take that thing with her. They wanted it as well."

No! It was like my feet grew roots in the earth; picking them up was like tugging at knotted rope. I stumbled forward. I felt nothing, but my body was no longer listening to me. I grunted, taking another step toward Zoey and Sprig before my knees crashed to the cobble. The world spun around me; thick bile coated my throat. I reached out, trying to keep myself from completely losing my center of gravity.

Vadik sauntered up, a smug smile twisted on his mouth. "Your mistake was thinking you were smarter than me, that you could outplay me. I know you have the stone on you." He squatted in front of me, his hand cupping the back of my neck, keeping my head upright. "You will pay for your disobedience." He withdrew his hand and I fell, landing on my side. My body twitched and jerked uncontrollably as more poison seeped into my blood.

Helpless, I watched Cadoc carry Zoey off, slipping into the shadows. I still felt her. The promise I made would tie me to her till my death. Or hers. My lids lowered, following the images into darkness.

A hand stroked my face, stirring me awake. *Zoey.* My eyes stayed shut, taking in the pleasure of her touch, the moment of peace before Sprig would be yammering relentlessly to get breakfast. Her fingers traced the side of my face, her nails lightly tracking back into my tight braids. A soft exhale tumbled from my lungs. Her hair tickled my face, provoking me to open my eyes, but they were determined to stay down like heavy curtains.

"I'm here," she whispered in my ear, her breath hot on my neck. Only one part of my body reacted to her words, the rest of it stayed fixed in place, ignoring my commands to move. Her hand skated down my chest, sliding over my pants, till they found me. Her hand massaged at the fabric, my dick responding. "Is this what you want?"

A moan broke out in reply. Her response was to rub harder. I couldn't seem to shake the sleepiness keeping me from moving, to touch her. I wanted nothing more. From the day she walked into my life she caused violent emotions to stir in me. From hatred to wanting to fuck her so fiercely we both would drown in my lust. It was a thin line, and I fell over it. She crawled in and was all I craved now, all I wanted. I hated a human had this much control over me.

Soft lips kissed my neck, working up to my chin. Teeth scraped at my bottom lip, and I felt my cock grow harder. Her hand worked beneath my pants, grabbing my shaft.

Everything except my dick was numb, which magnified the sensation. *Why can't I wake up?* As good as it felt, I wanted to touch her back, to see her green eyes watching me.

I felt her climb on me, her legs constricting around my hips, but still my lids refused to open. *What did we drink last night?* No memory of the previous evening flooded back. All there was fuzziness and flashes of images I couldn't pinpoint.

"I know you want this," she purred in my ear, rubbing herself into me. "You want me."

Yes. It frightened me how much I wanted her. And *nothing* usually scared me.

"Tell me, Ryker." She kissed me, her fingers gripping my shaft again. "Show me. Fuck me."

I paused. Zoey could be aggressive and unrelenting, but the words struck me as odd. It wasn't like her to command or say it. She would simply act.

Lips crushed into mine, demanding me to react.

"Zoey," I mumbled between breaths. Wanting to forget my doubts and continue to enjoy the moment. But I couldn't deny something was off, the way her figure fit on mine, the way her lips felt, the taste of her kiss.

"Yes, Ryker. I'm here," she spoke against my mouth. "Tell me where the stone is. I want to keep it protected."

Another flicker went off in my head. *You know where it is,* I thought.

"Tell me again. You know how easily I forget things."

I hadn't realized I spoke out loud. Dream and reality fought for dominance in my head.

Another warning went off in my gut. Zoey would never forget where the stone was. She was the furthest thing from forgetful.

My forehead creased in confusion. Deep inside a restless energy was building, contradicting my weak body and mind.

Legs squeezed tighter around my hips, moving up and down, creating friction as she rubbed herself against me, and purging me of any thoughts. A force tugged at the buttons of my pants, popping them open.

"Fuck me. Hard. Like we used to."

As good as it felt, things seemed wrong. I groaned, trying to pry my lids open. When they finally flickered up, I blinked rapidly, trying to make sense of the blurry outline on top of me. With every blink it morphed more into a solid figure—one with long, deep plum hair and dark eyes. Reality came flooding back.

Dread surged energy in my limbs, and I pushed at the hands tugging me free of my briefs. "Stop." The word sounded more like a grunt.

Amara's gaze flashed to mine, her face contorted with hunger and determination. "Don't deny it. You want this as well. You know how good I feel." She unzipped her pants, pushing them over her hips. Her hand continuing to stroke me.

My denial caught in my throat. I couldn't refute the carnal response. The bliss of the way she kneaded and rubbed me. It was strange for this to feel so right and so wrong. I had been with her for a long time. Most of it seemed natural... normal. Then her horrendous betrayal came back, flooding me with rage. But in this exact moment I probably would have ignored it, letting the primal instinct take what it wanted before pushing her away. But the shame and hatred at myself for letting it happen was nothing compared to the harsh reality of realizing it wasn't Zoey. That was the proverbial ice bucket.

It was Zoey's head I wanted to fall back in gratification as she rode me. It was her face I imagined. The thought of the hurt across her expression at seeing me with Amara halted me. The pain and sadness she felt would be quickly shoveled behind a barricade of indifference and defensiveness. It would be in the tiny movements she made, the way her eyes darted to the side, the way her mouth flattened into a line, or how her chest pushed out like armor. The pain I would see deep behind her wall of anger and rage.

So many had hurt her before. I didn't want to be another one who proved to be the same. The woman on top of me now only brought out hatred and violence at both her and myself.

Amara gripped me firmly, pushing her underwear down.

"No!" I seethed, grabbing for her hands. With the building rage, I shoved her off onto the ground. My limp muscles struggled to move, scrambling back to the wall away from her. My spine crashed against the stone, the chains keeping me contained to only a few feet of space.

Righting herself, her lids narrowed into slits. "You are turning me down? For what? A *human*?"

"And because you're a conniving, deceitful bitch."

"You don't know what I had to do to survive."

"Vadik's whore. Fuck me because you are commanded to," I sneered. "Your lover tells you to go screw another man for information, and you do it. Very obedient of you, Amara. Do you sit and stay too?"

Her hand jetted out, and a sharp sting sliced across my cheek.

"Don't you dare judge me!" Amara rose to her feet, leering over me. "I do what I need to do."

"Clearly."

Red dots freckled her cheeks, anger hunching her shoulders.

"The great Vadik still not enough for you. You still need to ride me? Did he order you? Hoping I was delirious enough to talk?"

"Fuck you." She clenched her hands. "I loved you."

I laughed. "You don't love anyone but yourself."

She leaned over, clutched my chained wrists, and pushed them back into the wall. Her face an inch from mine. "And you don't either. It's what made us perfect together."

"Perfect?" I tilted my head up, staring into her eyes. "It was all a lie."

"Really? The night in Turkey or the weekend in Greece weren't real to you?" A coy smile curled her lips. "You couldn't stop wanting to be inside me. We broke the bed twice."

It was true. But I never thought I was letting myself be deceived. I knew what she was. Most of the time I liked that about her. We did make a good team. She would target our next victim, get closer, learn about them, before I would jump to where their fortune or treasure was hidden, robbing them blind. I should have known it then—seen she was doing the same to me.

"What do you want from me, Amara?" I inched my face closer till our noses almost touched. "You want me to tell you I enjoyed fucking you? I won't lie. I did. But you and I both know it was nothing more."

"And your human was?" She sucked in her breath at my proximity, licking her bottom lip. "Please, I think we both know it was only the novelty of screwing a *human*. Fragile, sweet, ordinary Zoey."

Those were three things Zoey was not.

My arm moved before I even realized it, my hand gripping her chin, my fingers pushing in till she flinched. My voice grew low and steady. "Don't ever speak her name again."

Amara watched me, deciphering my true mood.

She yanked from my grip, standing straight, buttoning her pants. "Whipped by human pussy. Never thought I'd see the day."

My teeth ground together. Anger restored my energy.

"Enough, Amara," a voice came from the door. "Stop playing with your food."

The door squeaked open, and Garrett's slight form outlined the doorway.

Amara's eyes fluttered with annoyance, an expression I knew well, before glancing over her shoulder. "Following me?"

Garrett smirked. "I came to see you fail once again. Haven't you learned? He doesn't want you anymore... if he ever did."

"Screw you."

A glimmer of humor blazed through Garrett's green eyes. A knowing smile hitched the side of his mouth. "Did Vadik tell you to come here?" Garrett stepped deeper in the room; his gaze drifted salaciously over her figure.

"No." Amara crossed her arms, shifting her head to stare at the floor.

"So, you came to get rejected by a man who can barely stand or form a sentence?" Garrett clicked his tongue. "Shameful, Amara, and incredibly sad."

"Shut up," she growled.

"Funny. I don't remember hearing that from you before. Thought you liked it vocal."

Amara rolled her shoulders back, stiffening her posture, her nose flaring. If looks could kill, Garrett would be dead on the ground.

Her response only formed a bigger smirk on his face as he turned to me.

"What a sight." Garrett strolled over, gratification at seeing me at his feet sparked haughtiness in his stance. "The once great Wanderer is no more than a toothless, sad bastard." Smugness galloped over his face, his lip hooking up in a laugh. "Look at you." He motioned to me. "Beaten, bloody, weaponless, shoeless, and feeble as a baby."

I finally noticed I was still dressed in the same stained, ripped clothes. And I was barefoot. The absence of my boots stirred me to sit higher.

Did they take them? Look? Did they know?

"As fun as it is to come here and view you like this, Vadik wants to see you." Garrett yanked me onto my feet. My legs buckled under my weight, the room spinning. One of his minions, a massive fae with dark hair and eyes, entered behind him. Cadoc was Garrett's muscle. The fae was huge, a boulder of a man. He was a few inches shorter than me, but he was almost as wide as he was tall. The bulges protruding from each arm were like mounds of densely packed earth, rippling with every move. At one time I could have fought him. Today I was not at my best. Not even close.

Weak and magic-less. But my pride still did not relent. I puffed out my chest, glaring at Cadoc as he stepped to me, releasing me from the cuffs chained to the wall. The itch deep in my gut stirred again as I recalled he was the person who last touched her. A memory of him carrying Zoey off rushed into my head.

"Where is she?" The words snapped from my mouth before I could stop them, barely loud enough for Cadoc to hear me. It was pointless. He was an underling and did what he was told, no more.

He said nothing as he retied my wrists and tugged me forward. I stumbled and gritted my teeth, fighting against the weight bearing down on my frail body. The fever still ravaged me.

Cadoc pushed me forward, my mind spinning with every movement. Sweat trickled down the side of my face. I was determined to stay upright if it was the only thing I managed. Garrett and Cadoc walked me out of the room with Amara following behind. Garrett glanced over his shoulder, a frown creasing his forehead.

"He shouldn't be moved. He's still ill," Amara declared.

Garrett's eyebrow cocked up. "Don't tell me you of all people care about his well-being? You who's been lying, cheating, and deceiving him for years?" A huge smile spread on the Irishman's face. "You sure didn't seem to care about him the other night."

At one time I might have cared what Amara did... or who. No more.

She ignored his insinuation. Garrett shook his head and faced forward again. Two more of Garrett's men joined the group, walking behind to box me in. I wasn't stupid enough to try to escape. I had no axe, no magic, and barely any strength to stand. The fever continued to rage through my veins, pumping out drops of sweat down my face and back. The more steps I took, the more my legs shook, and my stomach cramped into knots. As much goblin poison as I took in, I was surprised to be alive at all. But a conflicting ache in the pit of my soul made me restless, desiring to move, to keep walking.

The connection to Zoey was distant enough to ignore, turning it into white noise. I redirected my focus on the surroundings, tailing along through a maze of corridors, up a flight of stairs, and down a hallway. There was little doubt I was in Vadik's compound, which was rumored to be somewhere in Seattle. *How long was I unconscious?* It was hard to know. The trip from Peru to Washington wasn't as long for fae as for humans. Fae doors sprinkled all over the world would shorten our trip to minutes or hours, depending on the moods of the doors that day.

My feet pushed between the hand-sewn oriental rugs and dark wood floors. The house was the type you would imagine if someone said they lived in a modern Italian-inspired villa. Intricate iron railings, antique furniture, curved arched doorways, and large paintings hung on the walls, depicting landscapes, oceans, and dead, rich ancestors. Wealth from "old money" oozed from the pores of the large house. In my haze I couldn't lock on anything particular, all portraits blurring into a haze of undistinguishable faces and streaks of color, although something struck me about some of the paintings, like I had seen them before. I knew I hadn't, but the sensation of *déjà vu* coiled around my mind.

Garrett finally stopped in front of double curved oak doors and knocked.

"Enter," a deep voice called from the other side. Vadik.

My muscles constricted in defense as Garrett opened the door and motioned for Cadoc to bring me through.

Vadik sat at a desk with his fingers steepled together, leaning back in his leather office chair. His white-blond hair was slicked back, emphasizing his dark navy-blue eyes, which sparkled with arrogance and ruthlessness.

A huge bay window framed him, sun sparkling off the deep blue lake. We sat high enough to look down at the dozens of white yachts and sailboats floating and darting across the water like bleach spots on a blue canvas. A private yacht berthed below bobbed in the house's boat dock, eager to go play in the sun. The green, dense forest beyond only emphasized the stark white of the boat's sails and contrasted sharply with the few boats whose owners were rebellious enough to pick another color to flaunt on their sails.

I knew this area—Bellevue, Washington, along Lake Sammamish. I had stolen from a few properties over in the prestigious West Lake Sammamish area. Maybe it was why some things in this house looked familiar. *Had I stolen from here?* I didn't remember ever being in this house, but my mind wasn't functioning properly.

Cadoc pushed me close to the desk. He held up a lot of my weight, and I pushed my shoulders back, trying to stand straighter. Besides not wanting to show how weak I felt, Vadik inflicted a hatred so deep, I had to swallow back the urge to leap over the desk and rip his head off his body.

"I have to admit, I am surprised you survived. You were out for almost four weeks. There were a few times we didn't think you would wake," Vadik said evenly. "You are stronger than I thought." He dropped his arms and sat forward. "But then again I probably shouldn't be too astonished. You are the fierce Wanderer, are you not? You were conceived to fight, to survive, to escape. Possibly even death."

I pinched my lips together. I had many questions, but none were about me. With men like Vadik, you let them talk. They loved to hear their own voices too much to stay quiet.

"Silent and stoic." Vadik kept his eyes locked on me. "Living up to your name... oh right... except for actually not being a Wanderer anymore."

My feet shifted underneath me as if burrs were stuck to the bottom of my feet.

"How does it feel to no longer have your magic?" Vadik's eyes flashed, a slight grin curling his mouth. "Now a human has your powers—a Collector, a seer who wants to destroy us, dissect us like lab rats?" He piled each word on top of the other, building them up to taunt me. "Now you are dying a slow painful death. You will grow feeble... useless. Dying like a pathetic human if you even last that long since many enemies will come for you. And none of them will give you the quick death you will beg for."

If he wanted to piss me off, it was working.

Vadik pressed his lips together, his jaw straining before he let out a breath. "Your stunt is causing me a lot of headaches. I am not sure if you are extremely foolish or exceptionally ingenious."

My brows furrowed, confused at what he was talking about.

"You don't remember, do you?" Vadik scoffed, shaking his head. My silence was enough of an answer for him to continue. "We were returning through the fae doors, and you decided to chuck both of your boots through an opening, which simply *happened* to be a multidimensional door." One eyebrow cocked as if to say *you knew exactly what you were doing.* "They could be anywhere, and most likely not together."

We stared at each other. Something in his gaze unnerved me, almost like pride.

"I knew you would keep it close." Vadik's head shook slightly, mumbling to himself. "I should have seen it. The most obvious and careless place to hide one of the most powerful objects in the world. In. A. Boot." He cleared his throat, returning his focus to me. "Now it is out there, lost. And no one will ever realize a legendary treasure is in the discarded shoe they just walked by. Some homeless man will probably be walking around with the *Stone of Destiny* in his heel." He let his irritation swallow his sentence and hang in the air.

I no longer had the stone, which meant I was no longer beneficial to him.

"What do you want?"

A gratified smile rose on Vadik's face. "At first I considered your life, but I've had time to rethink your usefulness to me. Anger made me rash." He sat back in his chair. "But disobedience will never go unpunished. You will pay for defying me."

"If you don't want me dead, then you must want me for something."

"I do." Vadik's demeanor was calm like a huge lake, but what was below in the depths and darkness is what you worried about. "Death would be the easy way. This isn't a one-time deal. Your existence is mine to own. As it always should have been. You will do everything I say."

"No. One. Owns. Me."

A knowing smile played on his mouth. "There you are wrong."

"I don't have my powers; I am worthless to you."

"Maybe. Maybe not." His navy eyes glinted. "You could get them back."

Vadik's words cleared through the murkiness in my head, recalling why we wanted to challenge him in the first place. He was right. A man was being held here who possibly could restore my magic.

"Regnus," I responded. Regnus was an extremely powerful shaman, the head of the shaman leaders. He raised Amara after she lost her parents. I met him once through her. He was a known recluse and stayed hidden from people, and he only allowed her to get close.

Amara told me Vadik kidnapped Regnus. He was the reason we were coming here. But that's when I also believed Amara had been abducted the day of the fae storm. I pushed away the dread seeping down my throat. I swallowed. "Regnus... you think he will be able to extract them from Zoey? Can he do it? Without her here?"

Vadik leaned back in his chair, watching me for a while, his brow creased. I didn't understand his sudden silence. A trickle of sweat ran down the back of my neck. Vadik tilted his head, his gaze finding someone behind me. "Another thing you forgot to tell me about, Amara?"

I felt and heard her shift behind me. Instinct rolled my gut into a knot.

"I see." Vadik shook his head, humor danced in his eyes.

The sickening feeling in my stomach expanded. "Where is Regnus?"

Vadik stood, straightening his suit jacket. "Ask her."

I looked over my shoulder at Amara. She glanced away, crossing her arms.

"Amara." Vadik's voice was full of adoration. "My little deceiver. Such an incredible talent for it. The best I've ever known. Her tongue is truly talented. She can't help it; she whispers in your ear like a snake charmer, weaving truth and lies together so well you can't tell the difference."

"What is he talking about?" Deep down I already knew the truth but needed to hear her say it out loud.

She sighed, turning her face to mine. "Vadik never had Regnus. I made it up."

"What?" I growled.

"I needed you to act." She shrugged her shoulders. "You needed a reason to move. To go after the stone, and I gave you one."

"Was there ever a moment you spoke truth to me?"

Her dark chocolate eyes locked with mine. "Yes." I could feel the underlying meaning in her gaze, but it fell numbly on my heart.

"So where is he?"

She glanced away

"Amara. Where. Is. He?"

She faced me; her chin set high.

"Dead."

"What?" Rage burned like fire in my lungs. The years this woman put things over on me. I felt stupid, blind, and gullible. I understood being a "storyteller" was part of her nature, the type of fae she was. But I had foolishly let myself believe I was one she wouldn't deceive. We worked together because we were both liars, thieves, and survivors. This was our truth.

I was simply another naïve asshole who fell for her charms, beauty, and wicked tongue. It was disturbing to think there probably wasn't one person in here she hadn't used it on.

"He's been dead for a while."

The entire time she let me believe there was hope. It never was an option. Disappointment crept into my lungs when the truth hit me. No Regnus. The shred of hope I was holding on to broke. There was nothing to save Zoey or me. It had to be death for one of us.

And it was going to be me.

A deep rumble came from my chest. Cadoc grabbed me and held me back from attacking Amara. My body pushed forward, leaning toward Amara as she backed against the wall.

"If you knew he was dead, you never would have come here. With

Regnus in play it got you either to go for the stone or to come here. Whichever way…" Amara trailed off.

"You got what you wanted. A job well done," I replied, turning away from her. I could no longer look at her face. I was more disgusted with myself. She worked it so I would have to tell her the location of the stone, give her the actual stone, or willingly go to Vadik's, walking into a trap.

She was good; I'd give her that.

I turned back to Vadik. "I will not let Zoey die."

"No? This works for me too." Vadik slipped his hands in the pockets of his pants, walking around the desk. He was almost as tall and as wide as me, though he commanded more attention. Cruelty danced in his aura, what you expected from a demon. Back when the fae and human worlds worked together, superstition ran high. Demons were feared and honored as much as the gods. However, I always had a healthy disgust for them. I stayed clear of them as much as humans.

"Your little human and her pet have made me richer. DMG wanted her badly and paid obscenely for her return."

"What are you talking about?" I blamed my fevered brain for not connecting dots fast enough.

"DMG has been a profitable acquaintance."

Anger hitched along my spine. "You work for DMG?"

"I do not *work* for them." Vadik's eyes flashed black before returning navy. All demons in their "pure" form had black eyes, but the exact level of a demon revealed itself in their natural color. You knew what level of demon you were dealing with whether they were dressed in business attire or jeans. Yellow or yellow-green was the most dangerous of demons. His navy eyes told me he was not the highest, but he certainly wasn't at the bottom. Far from it. If yellow was the top, like the general, then navy was the major. Powerful enough to be feared.

"They *kill* fae."

Vadik took a breath and leaned back on his desk. "I am a businessman. I provided a service. Merely because we are fae doesn't cause me to feel kinship to all fae. Like humans, there are those who are not worth saving. I provide leads to their whereabouts. It has made me a hefty income."

"So, you sell out your own kind for money?" Disgust coated my words.

"Power runs the world, ours and theirs, whether it comes in money or objects." He inhaled, peering at me as if I were a silly child. "They were going to get the information from someone. Why not me?" Vadik's nonchalant attitude caused me to grip my confined hands together. I always sensed he was ruthless and power hungry. It was why I kept the stone away from him, but I didn't realize how evil he was. "I get what I want... until it no longer works for me. DMG has gone past their usefulness. There is something there I want more, something I want back."

My shoulders tensed.

"Your human."

"She is *not* my human."

"Oh, I think we both know that is a lie. Your weakness for humans will always be your downfall." He grinned. "Or in this case, hers."

I gritted my teeth.

"I've come to understand if you kill her, your powers will be restored. If you do not, she will be the useful one."

"Stay away from her."

"You and I both know that will never happen." Vadik stood, walking to me. "I am being kind giving you a choice. She is actually the better choice. She can bring in money as my thief and my fighter."

My nostrils flared. He wanted me to ask. I hated he would get exactly what he wanted. "What do you mean?"

"At first I thought she was insignificant, a human who could easily be replaced or gotten rid of." Vadik set his stance, challenging me. "However, she is anything but. I should thank you. Such an incredible find, especially now that she has your powers. Finding her a part of the underground fight club opened my eyes to a whole new revenue."

Again, I felt my stomach drop in anticipation, seeming to know where this roller coaster was going.

"It was easy to get rid of the human man and his pathetic excuse for a gang running the underground fighting ring and take over the business. Humans pay to see and bet on fights, drink, and indulge in all their favorite sins with my girls. At the same time, fae pay for the service to freely take from a concentrated pool of humans. All are drunk, emotional, and greedy. Everyone is happy. And I do very little." Pride emanated off his skin. "Zoey will be my lead fighter but will also be stealing more out of their pockets and homes."

My tongue seemed to swell in my mouth, I could no longer breathe.

"You can see why I would prefer to have her. But I will let you decide. I know you declared a promise to her." Vadik lifted his chin, his gaze directly into mine. "You won't be able to help yourself. You will go after her. And I will follow."

The monster in me, the one I worked hard to control, broke down the door, thundering to the surface. It did not think. Only reacted. My shoulders expanded, enlarging and coiling. I could no longer see anything but red. I did not feel my pain or the fever raging in my body.

My hands still in cuffs, I swung my paired arms like a bat against Vadik's skull. The cartilage in his nose crunched against the metal cuffs, and the force threw him across the desk. Objects went flying, hitting the floor and walls.

Cadoc's fingers wrapped tighter around my arm, but I twisted out of his grip, rushing forward and slamming Vadik into the desk.

Shouts reverberated off me and hands grabbed for me, but all I saw and heard was my anger.

Crimson.

The control I fought to contain gave way. The rage inside became my voice. And it kept repeating her name over and over.

Zoey. Zoey. Zoey.

My fist smashed down onto Vadik's face, and my elbow cracked into Cadoc's. Out of the corner of my eye I saw a floor lamp swing down, striking the back of my head. My body dipped when it hit, but I didn't feel any pain, my focus lasered on the man underneath me.

"No. One. Will. Touch. Her." A roar came from me. Blood from my head wound trickled into my eyes. "No. One. Hurts. Her. But. Me." The moment the words were out of my mouth and soaked into my mind I halted. An image of choking her to death fired through my veins, stirring a deep drive. A carnal but robotic notion. Was that all this was? I didn't want anyone to take my kill from me?

Fuck.

Scarlet drained from my sight, clearing my vision. Several hands yanked me off Vadik and hauled me back across the room. A gun was thrust to my head.

"If you move, I will gladly pull the trigger," Garrett snarled in my ear. "Just give me a reason. Please."

Vadik sat up, taking a handkerchief from his pocket and wiping the blood from his nose. "I think I know what the promise entails now."

I growled.

Vadik patted his nose again; the blood already stopped. He stood, straightening his wrinkled suit with cool, detached motions.

The icy aloofness provoked a deep fear in me. I knew fury lay under his reserve, a rage which would put my monster to shame.

Fuck with a demon and you were going to get more than the horns.

A tight smile stretched his mouth, and he took measured steps to me. "You will take me to her."

"No."

His eyes flashed. He crouched down in my face, his voice vibrating with wrath. "Let's see how you feel later. You will be begging for your death... or hers."

The last thing I saw was Garrett's arm coming for me before he slammed the butt of the gun into my head.

SEVENTEEN

The tops of my feet dragged across the floor, hitting the stone stairs as they hauled me to the basement. My head lolled and bobbed, not able to pick itself up yet. As the monster I didn't feel pain, but now it was back with a vengeance.

Long ago, I'd almost burned to death. It took me months to come out of my coma, my fae powers keeping me asleep as I healed. I no longer had this luxury. I was still fae, so it eased the pain, but I was more human in healing. Every hit hurt worse than it ever had before. I was changing, my body slowing down. The fever sapped my energy, which pissed me off. I did not handle being fragile very well.

Several other men joined Cadoc in towing me back to the cell I'd been calling home. I recognized some of the men from my encounters with Garrett. One blue-haired guy ran ahead, pulling the extra chain off the floor until it hung from the ceiling at eyeline.

I'd been around too long not to know what was ahead of me. Torture had not advanced much with fae. They liked the old-school ways. I grunted and struggled. Cadoc and another fae grabbed my arms and wrapped the metal cuffs around my wrists, clicking them into place. The blue-haired fae yanked the pulley. My arms shot over my head. The bones and muscles along my shoulders and sides popped as my weight tugged back on them. The clanging chain echoed off the walls. My joints wrenched from their sockets. The tips of my bare toes skimmed the floor.

Shoes clicked across the stone floor.

"You're still the same. Disobedient and impertinent," Vadik hissed, I heard the whip snap as he opened it up.

My fingers rolled into fists, preparing for the pain. But no matter how much you do, you can never prepare for this kind of torture. The sound of the leather cracked in the room only an instant before the switch lashed across my back. My mouth slammed together; a groan caught in my chest.

The whip struck my back again.

Then again.

"Is a human really worth this?" Vadik growled.

I didn't respond. She was worth more.

Agony sliced down my back as he snapped the whip. My skin split. The leather strap slashed across the open wounds. My knees dipped and dizziness overcame me, building and exploding with nausea.

"You are a fool. I hoped better from you." Wrath coated every word he spoke. His resentment for me seemed deeper than what I'd expect from a bad business deal. But this was why people feared him—he was a demon who relished torture. You'd think he'd let others do this, not get his hands dirty. Not with me.

A bellow rushed out of him, his arm coming down, snapping the leather harshly.

My body jerked forward, curving with anguish. Against my will a moan escaped my throat. I slammed my jaw together, keeping Vadik from getting any more satisfaction from my pain. Sweat streamed down my face and blood flowed in trails along my back, dripping onto the floor.

"You need to learn I am in charge. You do not disrespect me," Vadik yelled, the violence giving more fire to his rage. Each hit only gave him more fuel, more drive, causing him to strike harder.

Hurt so unreal choked the air in my throat. Screams could no longer reach the surface, barricaded beneath the agony. I huffed. Saliva oozed out of the corners of my mouth. Snot bubbled out my nose.

Crack.

Crack.

Snaps of the whip echoed off the stone.

My vision blurred. Bile filled my mouth as the room spun. I drifted further from myself. My muscles let go, and I hung freely from the chains in the ceiling, ripping me a part.

"Vadik. That's enough," I heard a woman's voice cry, then the sound of a hand hitting flesh. A form fell to the ground.

"Do not tell me when it's enough," Vadik growled. "You want to be next? You are already walking a thin line with me, Amara. You can easily be replaced. No one will miss you. *No one.*"

Time and reality were getting hazier as I receded deeper into my mind.

"Now turn him around," a voice ordered.

I felt hands on me, pairs of feet scuffling over the floor. The chain above my head creaked as they twisted me around.

"Wake him up."

A sharp, foul smell spiked up my nose and caused my eyes and mouth to water violently. I lifted my head, blinking back sweat and blood.

Vadik watched me, his eyes completely black. Sweat and spots of my blood sprinkled his sullen white face. His cheek bones stuck out sharply, which only enhanced the terrifying monster he really was. A twisted smile grew on his lips when he saw I was awake. "That's better. I want you looking at me when I talk to you."

His words sparked something in my head, a deep instinctual fear buried far below. But my brain couldn't latch onto any reason or understanding. He flicked the whip with his wrist.

I knew what was coming. My punishment was far from over.

"Once again I will ask. Is this human's life worth this? The more you fight me, the more I will be sure Zoey gets *all* m y attention. You want to die, knowing you left that life for her? My concubine, my slave, my fighter?" Vadik said. "You can live or she can. But you will find her for me."

It took everything I had to unclench my jaw. "Fuck. You." Saliva and foam sprayed from my mouth.

"Bad decision." He lifted his arm.

As the switch made contact with my stomach, my threshold for unbearable pain hit its max. A howl ripped out from the depths of my guts. He quickly responded with another one.

Darkness reached up, covering my eyes and mouth, and pulled me back into the depths of oblivion.

I went willingly.

My lids blinked open to a small comfortable room with its peeling paint and white billowing curtains. Instantly I felt the warmth of her body pressed against my leg. I rolled over, the old comfortable bed creaking. I propped my head on my hand and watched her sleep. Her brown tresses only held a dim violet color now as they tumbled around her shoulders and down her back. This was the first peace I felt in a long time. No pain. No torment. Only relief and contentment at seeing her.

She was beautiful, but it was more than that. The girl was a force. No one I ever met, fae or human, compared to her. Even with all the horrible things she had gone through, she still fought with hope, love, and violent determination.

I hadn't let myself feel deeply for anyone in a long, long time. I hadn't wanted to. Until now. But she barreled down my walls with ferocity.

My gaze rolled over her sleeping form, taking in every inch, especially the way the sheet curved over her body. She wore one of my thin white T-shirts and a slip of fabric for underwear. The top was hitched up, displaying a strip of her bare back. I reached out my hand for her, catching the edge of the shirt, and dragged the fabric to the top of her shoulder blades. My fingers trailed over her spine, curving over her ass. She stirred under my touch. Her head turned over on the pillow till she faced me.

"Thought that might wake you up." I smiled.

"Ryker," she whispered.

"Miss me?"

"Yes."

The bluntness and honesty of her declaration stunned me.

"Wow. You said that without the least bit of sarcasm."

Liquid glistened in her eyes. A deep sadness and desperation echoed in them I had never seen before.

"Hey." My hand went to her face, cupping her cheek. "Are you all right?"

She leaned into my hand and bit down on her lower lip. She looked lost. Unsure. Seeing her like this caused panic to prickle in every pore.

"Zoey, you're freakin' me out."

She licked her lips, closing her lids briefly. "I know you're not real, but I need you... to get me through this."

The need to protect her, to shield her from pain, fear, or harm drove me to her. I pulled her to me, my lips brushing softly over her forehead. "You are strong; you can get through this. You don't need me, but I'll be here whenever you want."

"I wish you could tell me you were all right. That you got away from Vadik."

I could have told her, but the despondency in her demeanor made me lock the truth away.

"If I were free or capable, I would have already found you."

129

Stacey Marie Brown

She watched me. A fire flickered in her eyes, her gaze dropping to my mouth. It was like the fire in her eyes jumped to me, igniting a combustion through me. I grabbed her hips and pulled her onto my lap. She inhaled sharply, enhancing my need for her. To be inside her.

I knew this was a dream, and she wasn't real. But she felt hot, wet and her legs clenched my hips with desire. A moan emerged from my throat. I knew one thing. Even If I had never made an oath to her, nothing in this world would stop me from getting to her.

"Even without the oath, I would find you."

"I wish the vow worked both ways. I want to be able to feel you and know you are still alive," she whispered, grinding into my lap.

Fuck.

"You want to feel me, huh?" I grabbed her waist, flipping her back onto the bed. I nudged her legs apart and crawled between them. My gaze never left hers. I lifted her shirt up, my lips sweeping over her stomach, my mouth moving down.

"Feel this?"

I tilted her hips up, slipping her underwear down her legs. The sight of her almost made me lose control. My hands roughly traveled over every inch of her skin.

She let a small groan escape. Her arms twitched, looking like she wanted to touch me. Her face strained, and her eyes grew hazy. Faraway.

I felt myself drifting, reality breaking through. Dull slashes of pain ran over my torso, dragging me away from her back to the dungeon.

No.

I did not want this dream to end. She said she needed me, but I needed her just as much.

"Stop. Stay with me." I straddled her on all fours, stopping her struggle to touch me. "Just a little longer." I leaned over, my lips finding hers.

Tasting her felt like I finally found my place. I wanted to be so deep inside her neither one of us could find our way out again.

Even if this was a dream, for one moment I wanted to pretend it was true.

"I've done some interesting things, but this might be hitting a new level," I mumbled against her mouth.

"Why? You're not even real. This is all in my head."

No, it was in my head.

"Zoey, I will make you another promise. I am going to bury myself

into you so deeply and fiercely we are both going to feel it in reality."

I grabbed her ass, angling her to me. I sank into her, then plunged deeper, feeling like I had come home.

EIGHTEEN

Voices came and went, speaking words I could not understand and had no energy to try. Time had no meaning. Pain was the only way I could decipher reality, with sleep taking me away when it became too much. The fever was back, blistering my skin with heat.

Each morning and evening Vadik's servants came to feed me, clean my wounds, or bathe me. Two guards stood at the door. They fed me fae food, which helped ease my physical suffering and would help to heal me.

They stayed silent and left as soon as they were done. Keeping me alive and helping me heal was simply so he could torment me again.

Vadik was not forgiving.

Every moment was torture. The deep gashes across my stomach and back drove buckling pain through me. Exposed tissue and torn skin gaped like tiny, pink mouths with ragged teeth, open and screaming.

I measured time by the visits. Days if not weeks passed this way.

Eventually, they no longer chained me to the wall and allowed me to roam the small cell, if I got up. I barely did. The only thing in the cell was a bucket to piss in. Most of the time I slept curled on my side, to keep pressure off the deep wounds slashed across my back and stomach. The icy stone floor prevented my muscles from unlocking or relaxing.

The thud of the door snapped my lids open, then they slowly drooped again. Footsteps moved toward me.

"Roll him onto his back," Vadik's voice boomed through the cell.

Hands came down on me, pitching me over. I squeezed my lids tight, pain in my back throbbing and spiking every nerve.

"Are you done being stubborn?" Vadik's voice came from above me.

I wanted to spit at him, to tell him to fuck off, but my tongue and mouth wouldn't cooperate.

"Look at me and answer," he demanded with a growl.

His words caused a flash of fear to press down on my lungs, stirring a deep-rooted terror. It was a strange reaction. I took a deep breath, and the movement shoved my back against the floor. Pain brought my thoughts back to the horrendous aching I tried to ignore.

"Are you ready to locate your girlfriend?"

My lids lifted, blinking a few times. "Kiss my ass."

Vadik stood over me, his hair slicked back, his navy eyes narrowed on mine. He wore one of his incredibly expensive suits. The pressed immaculate outfit and clean manicured nails fostered the idea he never got his hands dirty.

It was all a façade.

"Do not disrespect me." The tips of his shoes dug into my ribs.

I ground my teeth together. "Why don't you get her?" I said through a gritted mouth. "Go get her from your buddy Rapava yourself."

A nerve in Vadik's neck twitched.

"Most humans are stupid. He is one of the rare ones who actually understands and fears our power. The domination we could regain, but he is quite good at keeping his location secret." Vadik slipped his hands into his trousers, his feet still clipping my side. "Our deals bring me money and supplies him victims to use as experiments."

"Your own people," I snarled.

A creepy smile flashed on his face. "Not all. He needs humans as well."

"What do you mean?"

He smirked but didn't respond.

Whatever his secret, I was sure it was dangerous. I actually didn't want to know. I had too much on my plate to worry about.

"Do you feel the oath nipping at you? Growing stronger every day?" Vadik leaned over me. "The longer you ignore it, the worse it gets. I could be patient and wait for the day you can no longer stand it, but I'm in a hurry." He stood straight again. "Anyway, by then you will tear her apart in a state of bloodlust. I would like her alive until I decide which one of you to keep."

Like a pet. That's all we were to him. Pets, minions, and slaves.

Vadik took his hands from his pockets, his polished cufflinks glinting in the dim light. Something about them caught my eye. I directed my gaze at the symbols of two dragons, their necks linking around each other. A family crest. The dragons sat atop a shield with a crown and boat on it. I couldn't make out the writing below the crown. The fine details of the crest were lost in the shadows. A flicker of familiarity crossed my mind. I had traveled to so many places, I could have easily seen the crest before. Maybe there was a reason Vadik hated me so much. Besides double-crossing him this time, I might have done it before, although he didn't seem the kind to keep our past dealings a secret.

"I will take your silence as a no." He clicked his tongue. At that, Cadoc and the blue-haired guy moved to his side. He nodded.

A whimper coiled around my throat, but I kept my mouth shut as the two men pulled me to my feet, latching the cuffs around my wrists.

I was strung up. My feet lifted completely off the ground. Once again my weight and gravity ripped at my body. The stretch of my agonized muscles and ligaments screamed in torture. My barely healing cuts tore open again as my skin stretched. Dots blinded my vision.

"Leave him like this for a while. Let him think about his options and which one will soon outweigh the other." Vadik whipped around, exiting the cell. The other two trailed on his heels, leaving me swinging from the ceiling.

Vomit hung around my throat. The pain finally forced me to exit the present and shift away to the only place that gave me comfort.

I woke with her next to me again. The feel of her skin sent heat up the side of my body. I rolled over, propping on my side. This was my happy place where I didn't feel the excruciating pain of my dungeon. Just her and me.

She lay in the exact same position as before: on her stomach, one arm curled around the pillow, head turned the other way. Her T-shirt hitched up, a slit of skin showing.

Like last time, I could not resist touching her. The feel of her skin beneath my fingertips ignited me. She turned her head to me, smiling. We watched each other, my hand exploring her body.

Her eyes grew sad. Almost defeated. "Why haven't you found me yet? Where are you?"

"You know I would be there if I could." I couldn't bear to add more sadness to those eyes.

134

"I'm scared for you."

"Don't be. Worry about yourself. You know, no matter what, I will find a way to you."

"Can it be now?"

With a smile, I leaned over, brushing my lips over my shoulder. Even the Zoey in my head was getting impatient with me.

"Croygen's here."

I jerked back. "Wow, you know how to ruin a moment."

"You know me." She grinned.

I would never admit this to Croygen, but it was the very thing I wanted. Someone to be there for her when I couldn't.

My past with Croygen was complicated. In one way, I didn't trust him, but I did with Zoey. He was loyal in his way. He'd been there in the background for decades now. As dysfunctional as we were, he was the closest I had to a friend. It gave me a little comfort to pretend he was protecting her.

"Yes." I stared into her green eyes. "I do know you. Don't you forget, Zoey."

"I'm trying not to." She nibbled on her bottom lip. "Actually, Croygen and Sprig help keep me grounded. I don't want to lose myself completely."

Even if it were all in my head, my subconscious did not want her to be alone and scared. It helped, even if it weren't true. I knew Dr. Rapava had Sprig, too, but in reality there was little chance they would get to be together, even if the little furball kept trying.

I reached out, tucking her hair behind her ear. "You won't. You are way too strong. And stubborn." Liquid filled her eyes. She felt so real; it was hard to remember she wasn't. "And I hate to admit this, but if I can't be there, I'm glad Croygen is."

"Now I know this is in my imagination." A smile exploded over her face.

"What? I don't feel real to you?" I teased my imaginary Zoey, my fingers roaming over her, pushing the blankets off.

"You do, that's the problem." Desire in her eyes mirrored my own. Damn this was a mindfuck. I could stay here, locked in this dream. "I want to stay here. Escape from all the pain. Remain here with you forever."

It was the problem. I wanted to quit and stop fighting, letting the dream take over my reality. But I couldn't. The girl I wanted was out

135

there, hurting. I had to stop this. Without this comfort, I would fight more to get free.

"This has to be the last time." *I pinched my mouth together in resolve.*

She drew in a long breath. "Rapava needs to be stopped. I get it. But being here compels me to want to stay in this bed forever. Be selfish. It would be so easy. But I know you are out there somewhere, and I want the real you."

"Even though I will be trying to kill you?"

"Especially because of that." *She turned over on her side.* "You and I are survivors, and we will do whatever it takes to live and be together. That is the love I want. Whatever the outcome." *She sat up, the sheet pooling in her lap.* "My dreams of you gave me strength at first. I needed to retreat into you. To feel comfort. I can't have it anymore. I need to turn off my feelings. Become the person they want. Being here makes me want you too much. I feel weak."

Even though she said it, I knew they were my words. My subconscious telling me to let this go and fight.

It was time.

I somehow knew this would be the last dream I would have of her. She needed me out in the real world. Not hiding away in my head.

I slipped my hand over her cheek, cupping it, and pulled her to me. Her mouth greeted mine. Instantly a deep craving took over me. I tugged the back of her neck, wanting her closer. She moved forward, the power of her mouth pressing me back. She draped her legs on either side of me. I slipped her underwear down her ass, pulling them lower on her thighs. She tugged her shirt over her head.

I grabbed her hips, lifting her up. She sank down on me, a gasp of air releasing from her throat. The utter pleasure on her face was enough for me to lose it. I grabbed the back of her head, my fingers tangling in the loose strands and yanked her to me. My voice was coarse and thick. "Ride me. Wake me up, Zoey. Make me feel you so ardently in the real world nothing will stop me from getting to you. So I can claim you again."

Whatever she was holding back, she let go. It felt like she was slamming her anger, fear, need, and sadness into me through her hips.

I responded with the same intensity, emotion, and passion.

It was a goodbye to the fantasy.

NINETEEN

"Ryker." A hand stirred my shoulder, arousing me from a deep sleep. "Wake up."

It was a woman.

Amara.

The sound of her voice instinctually sent a growl vibrating in my throat.

"Stop that. Anger at me can wait. We don't have much time." She tapped insistently at my shoulder. "Come on. Get up."

I groaned, trying to lift my lids, to look into her face. I was on the ground. The stone unyielding under my curled form. *When did they release me? How long did I hang? How long was I out?* All these questions rolled around my head but never made it out of my mouth.

"Ryker, sit up." Amara pulled at my arm, her eyes wide and full of anxiety. "We have to go. Now."

"What?" I blinked. I only wanted to continue sleeping. Being unconscious was the only time pain didn't consume me.

"Come on." She yanked at my bicep, causing me to groan as a sharp pain shot up my arm, curving around to my shoulders.

"I'm not going anywhere with you," I snapped, tugging away from her grip.

"I'm sorry I lied about Regnus. You can be mad at me later." She looked anxiously back at the door.

"Mad is too nice of word. What I feel about you goes *way* past that," I snarled.

"Detest me later then. Right now we need to go," she shot back, desperation laced in her tone.

Ignoring the agony I reached around, clutching her chin between my fingers, jerking her to me. She inhaled sharply.

"I. Want. To. Kill. You," I seethed.

Her breath was uneven, but her eyes never left mine. The stronger

137

she held my gaze, the more my anger evaporated. Her strength and determination was the one thing I actually respected about her. Like Zoey, she would never back down. She would do what she had to do to live. If a man did what she did, we wouldn't think twice. It was her nature to deceive and steal. How could I really blame her for being what she is?

I dropped my hand and turned back over. "Go where?"

"I'm getting you out of here," Amara replied.

"What?" My head whipped back to her. "Why?"

Amara ignored my question. Clasping my back, she prodded me to sit.

"We have to go before those idiots come back. Please, Ryker, just do what I ask."

"Why should I believe you are helping me? This could be a trap." I cringed at her rough contact.

Her forehead lined, the corners of her mouth drawing down. "I know trusting me is the last thing you want to do, but please, right now, trust me. Both our lives are at stake."

Once again, I could be a fool, but I did believe her. I saw how Vadik treated her. He would kill her without a thought. And the one thing Amara did well was save her own ass. If getting me out was helping her with that, then so be it. Both of us had the same goal—escape.

I dipped my head in a yes. She exhaled with relief and put her hands around my waist, helping me to my feet. I jerked, swallowing the wave of nausea.

"Sorry." She loosened her hold.

I swayed and stumbled to the side.

"Here." She got her body under my shoulder, holding some of my weight.

My overstretched muscles balked at the movement. Everything hurt. Everywhere she touched prickled with pain. I leaned against her and stepped when she did. I merely reacted to her pleas, my brain beyond muddled with pain to grasp what was happening.

"I want my axe." In the condition I was in, I *needed* it. And in all honesty, the weapon was such a part of me, more than my own arm, I couldn't fathom leaving her behind. Weapons in the fae world were alive. Had personalities. They grew attached to their owners as much as the owners relied on them. She was strong and fierce. We had been together for a long, long time. I would not leave her.

Amara scanned the horizon as we stepped from the cell. "They locked it up down the hall."

The guards who had been at my door day and night were gone from their posts. "Where?" I nodded at the empty positions.

"Men are easy." Amara spoke evenly but her eyes darted around with high alertness. "They each think they're getting a blow job in the laundry room."

I smirked. Simple but effective.

She directed us down the corridor to another bolted door. "It took three of Vadik's musclemen to carry it even this far." She smirked.

"Key?"

She lifted her eyebrows, pulling a keyring from her pocket and holding it up. "You doubt?"

"No." I knew her too well to have reservations. Amara always obtained what she needed.

She went through the string of metal keys, trying each one on the door, while I stood watch. It would have been nice to jump in and out of here. I missed my magic. A gap in my chest and soul waited longingly for the power to return.

"Hurry," I demanded, coercing her to glare over her shoulder at me. It took several keys, but finally the lock clanked over, reverberating off the walls.

I sucked in a breath, the door hinges screeching. She slipped in, and I followed.

My chest swelled. There she was, locked in a cage. My battle-axe. It was as if she were calling me; my feet moved obediently to her.

Amara had the lock open before I even reached the box. I reached over, my fingers wrapping around the handle. My lids closed as I felt her greet me, her power and excitement were like electric shocks into my skin.

"I missed you too." I picked the axe up, the harness still attached to her. As I slipped it on, reinstating her on my back, a loud noise banged from down the hallway, like a door slamming.

In sync, both Amara and I swung for the door. We had been in too many close calls together for the need to talk.

I hobbled after her to the stairs. There was only one way in and out of the dungeon. I lifted my foot to step on the first stair and clapped my jaw together. Every nerve throbbed, followed by a pulse of nausea. Bile clogged my throat. I wanted to puke and then pass out. Or the other way around.

"Hurry," Amara hissed in my ear.

"I'm trying," I responded through gritted teeth.

Another door slammed somewhere upstairs, and Amara halted, listening.

"Go. Go. Go." She hurried us up the stairs, her fear bleeding into me. I pushed through the sharp agony and commanded my feet to move faster. We reached the top of the stairs, and she poked her head out into the dark corridor.

"Okay." She waved me forward. We both stepped out into the hallway. Suddenly it was no longer pretend. I was only steps away from freedom. I had no idea what was outside the front door. I knew Vadik would have it heavily guarded, but the possibility of freedom spiced my tongue and cleared my head.

Amara grabbed my hand, lowered herself into the shadows, and pulled me down the hallway. Her attention was forward, mine behind us. The silence made anxiety thrum through me like the banging of war drums.

She took me along another corridor, my legs still trying to find a rhythm. She stopped and pressed her back into the wall. "All the exits have alarms and guards," she whispered.

"You had a plan for this, right?" My shoulder bumped into hers. The pressure against my wounds slammed my jaw together.

She shot me a look over her shoulder. "Yes. But you're not going to like it."

"Do I usually like your plans?"

She rolled her eyes. "You're going to have to trust me."

"Trust you?" I snorted.

"Right now I'm all you got."

"That only makes me more nervous. What are you up to, Amara?"

"Wow, I can't actually want to get you out of here because I care about you?"

I tilted my head.

"Fuck you, Ryker." She shook her head and turned away from me, taking apprehensive steps down the hall. I followed behind.

We entered a large formal living room, and I stopped dead in my tracks. Sofas and chairs faced the giant fireplace and another set stood by French doors topped with arched Palladian windows, which overlooked a backyard. In the middle of the lawn was a lit fountain, giving the outdoors an eerie glow. The lake beyond was lost in the sea of night.

What stopped me wasn't the ostentatious gardens and fountains in the backyard, the expensive furniture, or the garish displays of collected artifacts, sculptures, and relics. It was the singular painting. The only one in the room.

The painting depicted a woman.

I stared at the gorgeous woman portrayed in oils hanging above the fireplace. My heart fluttered in my chest with a feeling I couldn't decipher. A recognition. A distant memory.

The woman in the portrait was beautiful. Golden hair was braided and twisted in intricate designs hanging over her shoulder to her hips. She wore a long tunic dress, the same color as her hair, tied at her waist with decorative interwoven ropes of deep gold, red, and blues. The details along the trim and sleeves were lined with white. It looked to be from the eleventh or twelfth century. She wore a small jeweled headband. Her slight smile glinted her eyes with happiness and mischief, as if she held a fun secret you wanted to learn.

I was drawn to her eyes. I sucked in a sharp breath. Her eyes were so pale blue they almost looked white.

My throat constricted, and I struggled to swallow. Memories flashed through my head, more feelings than images, but those eyes smiling down on me rang strong in my soul. Then like a boulder, recollection barreled into my mind, hunching my shoulders. Seeing her flicked a switch in my brain I had kept off for so long—a long and forgotten memory buried deep in my soul.

I wake up lying in the middle of a huge four-poster bed, knowing the rich dark wood it is crafted from was hauled out of the nearby forest. Every day I escape to the security of their branches to either hide or play.

Elaborate tapestries hang over the cold stone walls, keeping in the heat. It's early in the year, but the air smells of spring. Buskerud flowers bloom around the window, their sweet scent hanging in the air. The dawn lets in a soft glow of the breaking sun.

This is my home. My room.

A beautiful woman walks to the bed, peering at me.

My mother.

"Good morning, my love," she coos softly. "You are three years old today, my sweet boy." Her long golden tresses reflect the light and halo the jeweled band around her head. The ends of her hair tickle my face as

141

she bends over me. "I love you so much." Her white-blue eyes water. She brushes away the tear hinting at the bottom of her lashes and shakes her head. "Can't let him see emotion," she mumbles to herself. Her fingers touch my chest. "Whatever happens, my love, know you are loved. No matter what, you will be free of him. I promise you. This is my gift to you. Both of us soon will be free." Her voice grows barely audible.

I don't know what she's talking about, but her melancholy creates a deep sadness in me. Reaching up, I touch her face. "No cry, Mamma."

Her fingers grasp my little ones, and she brings them to her lips, kissing them softly. "For you I will do anything."

Her words should have made me feel better, but they didn't.

"You're going to be strong for me today, right? You are my little man now. You must be strong for Mamma."

I nod, wanting to please her and bring back her smile.

She kisses my hand again and lets it go, standing straight. "Don't forget how much I love you. What I am doing is for you. I hope someday you will understand and forgive me."

The image of her fades, but it pushes another one to the forefront. A memory from later the same day.

Ancient fear from this part of my life now washes over me in waves, like I stepped right back in time.

A man is standing over me.

My father.

Terror keeps me from looking up, my eyes are locked on my birthday cake.

"But I want cake," I sniffle.

"I told you, you will eat your dinner first," he yells, and I feel tears pricking under my lashes.

"It's his birthday," my mother's kind voice comes from behind the man. "Let him have some cake."

Even then I knew what was coming. The sound of his hand slapping her across the face echoes in the large dining room. The room, like every other space in the castle, is cold and forbidding. My mother is the only warmth in this place.

"I am his father. He will obey me."

"But I want cake." I can feel tears pooling under my lids. Maybe if I had stayed quiet, kept my mouth shut, everything would have been fine.

"You. Want. Cake? Fine." The man grabs my uneaten dinner and flips the plate over. Peas, carrots, bits of meat sauce, and mush fall on top

of the birthday cake. A hand comes down and smashes the beautiful cake.

"Valefor!" My mother yells out my father's name.

A cry escapes my mouth as I watch the beautiful cake being destroyed.

"Now eat your cake!"

I stare at it, tears sliding down my face.

"Eat. It!"

I still don't move.

"You want your damn cake. Now eat it," my father's voice growls in my ear. I can hear my mother arguing with him to leave me alone, but we know he won't. His anger at my noncompliance causes him to howl.

"DO. AS. I. SAY!" My head is shoved into the sweet bread. Frosting and sauce sting my eyes.

"Valefor, stop!" My mother's voice is frantic and high pitched in the background.

"He must learn to obey me."

I struggle to breathe, but he holds my head down till I start eating.

Even now I can feel the bile coming up my throat. The various flavors coating my tongue like rotting ghosts. To this day I can't handle my food mixing. I never knew why.

I eat till I throw up, and then he forces me to continue till everything is gone.

"Now, will you obey me when I ask you to do something?" Father's question is more a demand.

I nod.

"Look at me and answer."

Anger suddenly burns inside me, and I lift my head, my eyes locking on his. "Yes. Father." I struggle with the word, not able to say it clearly, but he demands I call him that.

The man's face was suddenly clear in my memory. The rage shaping his features, his voice, crystalizing in my head. Air froze in my chest. My lungs no longer want to produce oxygen.

"No." I shook my head back and forth. The man's face hadn't changed much. Age had only distinguished him, but there was no denying...

Valefor.

Vadik.

The world under my feet disappeared, my stomach falling through the floor.

Valefor was a name of an ancient demon: The Duke of Thieves.

No. This can't be. This man. This demon cannot be my father. Though I can feel the truth of it in my blood. Literally. Wanderer didn't have to mean thief, simply a fae who jumped like I could. Yet thievery was an essential part of me—it was in my DNA to steal. To be the best. Valefor passed down the power of speed and dexterity, the skill of sharper hands, eyes, and mind.

If my father was a demon, what was my mother? How did I become a Wanderer?

Her white eyes in the painting stared at me, almost provoking me to remember. Then like the last, another recollection careened down on me, physically curling me over.

I sit on my mother's hip as she rushes down the hallway, wiping my face clean of frosting, vomit, and other food. Her mouth is twisted in anger, but her eyes are soft as she searches me over.

"I am so sorry," she whispers quietly. "He will never touch you again. I swear."

She doesn't head to my room or even hers but takes me to the east side of the castle, an area we rarely went.

Her mood keeps me silent. It isn't the anger or even sadness that frightens me, but her resolve. She holds her head high with defiance and strength.

Weaving us through a maze of hallways, upstairs, down, we finally exit the castle into the dark forest.

"Mamma?" I snuggle closer to her.

"Remember when I asked you to be strong and brave?"

I nod against her shoulder. "But I'm scared, Mamma."

"You don't need to be. Never again. But I need you to trust me, my love. Can you do that?"

"Yes," I say proudly. "I be brave, Mamma."

"That's my boy."

We walk for a while more, the night solid around us, and sounds of wild animals resonate in the depths of the forest. I wiggle in tighter to her.

A light in the distance perks up my head. A torch. Mamma's steps scurry faster.

We get close enough to the person holding the torch that I can see a woman. A cape and hood obscure her face in the shadows, but I see long white hair trailing over her chest to her waist. She is small but sturdy. Confident. The air around her is dense and chalky, almost like I can taste the grittiness on my tongue. I feel her energy bumping against my skin. She holds a lot of power, scaring me.

"You sure you are ready to do this, Ingrid?" The woman's voice is deep and rough.

"Yes, Margo." Mother stops in front of her.

The woman, Margo, pushes back her hood, revealing a young, pretty face, which goes against her gravelly voice. Her face says she is young and vibrant, while her voice and eyes convey she is old, full of life experiences. Her hazel eyes dig into my mother's before she nods. "Yes, I can see you are."

"I can't take any more. For him or me." Mamma adjusts me higher on her hip, kissing me on the forehead.

"I told you. The fae did not name me a high-ranking Druid for nothing. I warned you he was not what he seemed."

My mother blows out an irritated breath. "Not what he seems is not the same as telling me I was fooled into marrying a demon."

The white-haired woman swishes her hand. "It's not an exact science."

"Let us begin." Mamma looks over her shoulder nervously.

"Ingrid, I need you to understand what you are doing. This boy's magic is not supposed to come to him until much later. He's part demon, fae, and human. It's unnatural. His body and mind might reject it if you force it forward now."

"I am aware." My mother's voice tightens. "But you said you could see the power of the Wanderer in him. He will be able to jump." She takes in a shaky breath.

"I said he carries the possibility of having the power," Margo replies.

"Nothing is worse than the life he will have growing up with that monster. I will not let my son be tortured daily by that man. This is for the best."

"Do you know what you are giving up? You will never see him

145

again. He will never know his mother. He will probably lose all memory of you."

"Yes. I do. I will give up the world to keep him safe. And I willingly surrender my life for his freedom."

Margo presses her lips together, her lovely face showing sadness. She reaches up and touches my mother's face, stroking it softly. "I will miss you, sweet girl. I wish I could have helped you more than I have."

"You have been a dear friend to me. I appreciate all you have done." The woman drops her hand, her eyes clouding. She turns away, heading for a large stone slab.

My mother sets me on my feet and drops to her knees next to me. Tears swell in her eyes. "I know you will forget me, but remember. Here." She taps at my chest. "Mamma loves you. So much."

A single tear slides down her face. My chubby fingers reach up and wipe it away. It seems to only cause them to come faster.

"We must act now. The exact placement of the moon is crucial."

Mamma nods, keeping her eyes on me as she rises.

The woman places candles, a stone bowl, curved blade, a dead mongoose, and other items I cannot see on the rock slab.

"Okay, my boy. Be brave, be strong. No matter what darkness you feel inside, remember you have light too. Hold on to that." She takes my hand and leads me over to the stone. She picks me up and sets me on top. "Don't be scared, my love."

Margo starts chanting behind me, drawing out a knife, and handing it to my mother. I try to be brave, but when Mamma draws the blade across her wrists, letting the blood fall freely from her arms into the bowl, I start to tremble. She pricks my finger, mixing our blood, drawing a line across my forehead and down my cheeks in blood. The chants behind me grow louder and more passionate.

I felt something ignite inside me and I shriek. My mother crumples to her knees. I want to go to her, but the fire burning inside me keeps me in place.

Margo is screaming out the chants as pressure crushes me from all sides. It builds and builds till I wither in pain. Then something snaps inside and I scream. I see my mother drop back on the ground. Her eyes open, staring vacantly at the sky.

Then everything goes black.

146

TWENTY

"Ryker!" Amara's head poked out from around the corner, pulling me from my memories. "Come on. This is not the time to take in the art."

"Her name was Ingrid."

Amara glanced around nervously. "That's nice for her, but we've got to go."

"She was my mother."

"What?"

"And Vadik... he's my father." I stared into Amara's eyes, waiting for a reaction. Deep down I hoped the memories were false, but one glance at Amara, and I knew it was true.

Her eyes widened before she licked her lips.

"And you knew?"

"This is not the time."

"Not. The. Time?" I gritted my teeth, stepping to her.

"Let's get out of here first." She bounced on her toes, anxious to move.

"Why. Are. You. Helping. Me?"

"Because, even if you don't believe me, I do care about you."

"Care?" I snorted. "Yeah, that's hard to believe."

"Ryker..."

"How could you not tell me?" I seethed. "You enjoy fucking father and son?"

Her dark eyes darted to mine, flashing with anger. "He is not the type who asks; he takes. And I did not have the luxury of saying no. I survived the best way I could."

From what I recalled, it was the same way with my mother. I rubbed at my forehead.

"We can discuss how horrible I am later. First, let's get out of here."

I put my hands on my hips, shaking my head. "You are a piece of work, Amara."

"So are you." She whipped around and proceeded down the hall.

I took one step when a voice shouted from below, followed by an alarm, which blasted my eardrums with a sharp wail.

"Dammit," Amara hissed. "Guess who finally realized I tricked them?"

"Tricked, and no blow job... they're going to be pissed." I followed her. "So, what is your great plan?"

"We break out and steal his boat." She dangled keys in my face.

My feet faltered. "This is your great plan?"

"Do you have a better one?"

Sadly, I didn't. I wasn't going to be caught by this bastard again. Technically he was my father, but he would never be one to me. Dhir was my father. He raised me, loved me, taught and mentored me.

Amara raced along the hall, the voices growing louder around the house.

Every exit was equipped with an alarm, but they already knew we were escaping. "Why aren't we breaking down a door?" I demanded.

"They are not only armed, but some are triggered to spray acid on you." She darted down another corridor.

"What?" I peered behind me, feeling and hearing people moving toward us.

"He wanted the intruder to be slowed down."

"Fuck." It was helpful Amara knew things about the house.

"There are a few safer exits," she whispered over her shoulder.

The house sat on a slope, so on the backside you had to drop to the ground level. She slipped into a huge pantry with a slender rectangular window on the far wall. It looked wide enough for me... if I went sideways.

Amara ran for it. "I wish I could tell you it won't hurt." She reached the window. "But it will."

My body reeled from the thought of more pain.

Pounding feet echoed off the kitchen tile. "I heard them this way," a man yelled.

It's funny what adrenaline and desperation can do. I grabbed my axe and swung at the window, shattering the windowpane before I went sailing into the glass shoulder first.

A mosaic of glass shattered, slicing my thin shirt and burrowing into my skin as I fell through. My stomach dropped at the weightlessness, while my mass dragged me to the ground with bone-crunching impact. Air pushed from my lungs when I landed, knocking me immobile for a moment. I heard Amara fall next to me, her frame hitting the grass with a sharp grunt. Glass sprinkled down on us and crunched under our bodies as we sat.

Alarms from our escape throbbed in my temple, but no acid. At least Amara did her homework. Fae wouldn't die, but it would cripple us and send us in hibernation till we healed.

We both stood. Men's voice shouted from the opening above. There was a low popping sound. The manicured lawn, with its shapely topiary and gracefully designed patio, didn't give us much disguise. The yacht stood only a hundred yards away. If that escape didn't pan out, we would swim and get lost in the sea of darkness.

A bullet zipped past my ear. "Shit." I ducked and reached for Amara, pulling her close as we ran across the lawn. Vadik's guards came from everywhere, shooting at us with silenced guns. I pushed my legs to move faster. Then pain exploded in my shoulder and I fell.

"Ryker!" Amara reached for me, but her gaze was fixed on the dozens of men advancing toward us. "Ryker, come on."

She whirled around, footsteps moving in around us. Panic struck her face, and her body moved more wildly. Then she took off, running for the boat.

She was going to leave me. Her life was at greater risk than mine. Vadik still needed me. She would be killed instantly, and she knew it. More to the point, Amara always picked herself first.

With a roar, I dragged myself up. The ground pounded underneath me with the vibrations of approaching feet. I could see her on the private boat dock, vaulting onto the beautiful yacht. A rope tying the boat flung onto the berth, freeing it from its warden.

Prior to the breakout, Amara must have cut all lines connecting the boat to the dock, minus the one which kept it from drifting away from its mooring.

My bare feet dug into the dirt, pushing me forward. Blood seeped down the side of my body. My toes had barely crossed onto the dock when the motor of the boat rumbled to life, purring in the water.

A force knocked into me, stumbling me to the side. A man rolled past me, bounding up quickly.

Cadoc.

He withdrew the knife from his belt and sprang for me. I twisted, getting out of the way by a hair. My muscles along my side strained as I reached for my axe, pulling it out of its halter.

He wasn't a talker, which was the only thing I liked about him. Garrett would be jabbering my ear off till I wanted to drive my own blade into my chest. Cadoc didn't waste his breath. He did his job. That was it. He came after me again, the metal of the blade whooshing by me as we danced around each other, both taking swipes.

Then I heard the sound of the boat motor changing, digging deeper as it backed away from the pier. *Fuck!* My only escape was leaving me. The boat moved away from the quay. Panic tapped at the monster inside me. Growling like a beast, I hunched down, running for Cadoc like he was a ramming cage. I hit him with as much force as I could, causing him to land on his back and slide down the pier.

I leaped for the boat, barely making it. Hope flared in my chest as the boat moved farther and farther out.

Then I felt something enter my side. I glanced down to see the end of a knife sticking out between my ribs. I glimpsed over my shoulder. Cadoc still laid on the deck, half curled up, his arm over his head as if he just threw something. My eye went back to the hilt sticking out of my body. I didn't feel any pain but sensed myself falling forward.

My eyes closed before I crashed face-first onto the deck of the yacht.

Icy water along my forehead roused me. My eyes still didn't want to open. I heard low indistinguishable voices mumbling around me.

"I gave him fae food and my own personal healing remedy," a familiar woman's voice spoke close to my ear. "The fever is still not down. He should be healing faster."

The only thing I felt was the desperate need to move. To go find a girl.

Killkillkill. The desire hissed in my head.

"He was beaten, almost whipped to death, hung by his wrists, and then gutted with a dagger. You think a bunch of weeds and spices are really going to help him?" another woman's voice replied, sounding annoyed and farther away.

Find her. Kill her. I gritted my teeth. I focused on the voices around me, taking my mind away from the urge.

The woman near me sighed, dampening my forehead again. "I need to go create more. A bit stronger this time. He needs to wake up. It's been too long."

A chair creaked, footsteps crossed the floor, then feet padded up the wooden stairs. The smell of herbs and medicinal plants filtered into my nose. The odor was familiar. Comforting. The scent instantly told me where I was. How I got here was the question.

I forced my lids to pry open. "Elthia?" My voice cracked over my dry throat.

I heard someone move and a face peered over mine.

"Amara?"

"You're *finally* awake." She sat in the chair next to the bed. My mind flickered to when Zoey had been in this bed, and I was the one sitting in the chair. It felt a long time ago now. We were both such different people then.

Now I was a son to a demon.

The sudden need for Zoey to be next to me, help me deal with this discovery, twisted in my chest, startling me. I wasn't used to the intense emotions she brought out in me. When I shut the door on someone, I also shut out my feelings. I never let myself miss anyone. Even at the beginning, the girl inflicted anger and disgust deeper than any other before her. Now thoughts of her elicited the exact opposite.

Zoey was in every molecule of my skin. I wanted to blame it on the oath, that the promise caused me to feel this intensity. But it wouldn't be the full truth. I had felt this way before I made the pledge.

I lifted my head and looked around the room. No doubt we were at Elthia's. This place had at one time been my residence, if I could even call it that. After losing my human family, I never had a place to call home. I embraced my name and my title with fervor. I lived up to my reputation. The fewer strings, the better. The Wanderer never stayed anywhere long enough to call a place home. Elthia's dwelling was the closest I had come, which was still a far cry from home. I had been with Amara the longest, but she had the same philosophy on staying in one place as I did. Liars and thieves had to keep moving before they got caught.

"What are we doing here? How?" I tried to sit up.

"Take it easy." Amara helped me sit up. "You've been unconscious for a long time."

"How long?"

"Nine days." Aggravation flavored her words.

"Nine days?"

"Almost ten. But who's counting." She crossed her legs and leaned back in the chair. "I guess with them hunting us it's for the best, but it sure is great to be stuck with another one of your ex-lovers. Fun."

"How did we get here?"

"She brought you." A voice came from the other side of the tiny room. Elthia stood at the base of the stairs. I hadn't heard her come down. Her blonde dreads were woven in a loose side braid, laced with a colorful head scarf. She wore cream-colored baggy hemp pants and a flowery loose tank, which showed off the ink lines vining and flowering up one of her hands to her shoulder. Fabric braided bracelets decorated the other wrist.

Elthia held a bowl in one hand and a cloth in the other. Her bare feet padded noiselessly over to the foot of the bed. "You were conscious enough to get to my front door but no farther. I will not tell you how we got you downstairs. How's your head?" She dipped the cloth into the bowl, wetting it.

"Hurts less than the rest of me." I pushed myself higher against the wall. The single bed was far too small for my frame.

"This is the second time you've appeared at my door, close to death." Elthia shook her head. "You were in a lot less trouble when you were with me."

"And probably bored as fuck," Amara mumbled, but clear enough we all heard her.

Elthia took in a deep breath. She lowered her lashes, holding the air in her lungs for a few beats before letting it go. Her lids opened and she rolled back her shoulders. I could tell she was trying to control her anger. She liked serenity and tranquility in her life, meditating and working with herbs for new healing potions. She was exactly what I needed at that time in my life, but Amara was not far from the truth. It wasn't long before I became restless and needed to move on. Elthia's roots were embedded here, and she was happy with that. I never would have been. One of the many reasons we didn't work.

"We were on a boat... how did...?" I trailed off, remembering the last moments of the night before I blacked out. I had been shot and stabbed. I glanced at my bare torso. Gauze was tapped across my shoulder and stomach. The skin was red, bruised, and torn, but the pain was manageable. Probably because of whatever painkillers Elthia was giving me.

"I knew we didn't have much time before Vadik would be sending out a search squad of helicopters and other boats. We took his boat to the other side of the lake and dumped it, stealing a car."

Pays to be a thief sometimes.

"How did you move me?"

"You stayed conscious enough to get from the boat to the car. I drove here. Got you in and dumped the car in Salmon Bay."

I didn't recall any of this. "How did you know to bring me here?" I asked, knowing I'd never mentioned Elthia to her. We never talked about our pasts.

She scoffed. "Like I didn't know everything about your past. Before I actually met you, I did all my research, from learning how you like your coffee, to what type of bourbon you like, to everyone you ever slept with. Elthia stood out because she was the only one in centuries you spent more than a few weeks with." She leaned forward in the chair.

I expected every revelation of Amara's true character to irritate me, but she really couldn't help her nature. Did it make me trust or believe her? No. But I was past anger with her. And she did get me away from Vadik.

My father.

I shook my head, pushing the thought far from my mind. Someday I would have to confront him about my mother. She took her own life because of him, for me.

"If I know about her," Amara nodded at Elthia, "Vadik probably does too. We've been lucky, but we need to get going."

"Amara...?" I wanted to ask her what she knew about Vadik, how long she had known I was his son, but nothing came out.

"We'll talk later." She glared over her shoulder at Elthia. "When we're *alone*."

I sighed and nodded. It wasn't information I wanted anyone else to know.

"You said I've been out for nine days? If he knew where we were, he would have come by now."

Amara wrinkled her nose. "She put some rancid-smelling herb around the house the first night. Says it blocks people from entering."

"It only keeps them out," Elthia stated. "The last time I had to go out to get something, I noticed my house was being watched. You are no longer safe. They are only waiting for my protection spells to wane."

Once again I was putting Elthia in danger being here.

"Amara, can you give me and Elthia a moment?"

Amara pressed her lips together unhappily before she slid out of the chair. "I need to take a shower anyway. The herbs here seep into your pores. I smell like a spice rack." She glided up the stairs. A few moments later the bathroom door slammed shut.

"She's lovely." Elthia faked a sweet smile.

"Yeah," I chuckled.

"Ryker, what are you doing?" Elthia slipped into the vacated seat, setting the bowl on the table beside me.

"Trying to survive."

"No, with her." Elthia pulled one leg on the chair with her. "Her aura is dark. She only knows lies."

"She's a con artist. It's who she is."

"You deserve better than her."

"Don't make me out as some great guy. You always did that. I'm a swindler too, no better."

"You don't fool me. I can see you. You want more." Her head tilted to the side. "You have changed since I've last seen you. You've lost something but are no longer searching." Elthia always had this way of seeing past your façade, sometimes in a creepy, unsettling way. "Where is the human, Ryker? The girl, Zoey?"

Hearing her name was like a dagger to my gut. *Killkillkill.* I turned my gaze to the unlit fireplace.

"Ryker." She shifted, creaking the chair.

"I know." I shifted my gaze on her. "We'll go."

Her caramel-colored eyes drifted to her foot propped on the chair. "I am sorry, but I can't keep—"

"El," I stopped her. "I. Know." It was not fair of me to keep using her. We were no longer together, and I would never feel toward her what she wanted.

Her mouth pinched together and she bobbed her head in an abrupt nod. "All right." She shot out of the chair and grabbed the bowl on the table. "Let me go mix you a healing remedy to take with you. You are not healing like I hoped." She whipped around and moved toward the stairs. She paused. "I loved you, you know. Still do. But I need to move on."

"You deserve way better than me."

She snorted. "I know I do." She took a step up the stairs. "Find Zoey, Ryker. She is the reason you are no longer searching and may be your only chance to find the peace you long for." I thought how wrong she was, but before I could respond, she ran up the stairs, leaving me alone with the truth of her words.

TWENTY-ONE

An hour later, after a shower, a huge dose of medication, and more of the awful healing crap Elthia forced down my throat, I was feeling stronger. Good enough to move to my next location. The urge to locate Zoey, to know she was all right, was temporarily overpowering my need to kill her. I had to keep my mind clear and not give in to the craving.

Elthia had clothes I'd left behind when I lived with her, as if she hoped any day I would return to her. It pained me when she pulled out the pair of boots she bought me when we were still together. I never really liked or wore them.

"I should have cleansed you from my life a long time ago." She stood from the far recess of the closet that held my leftovers and walked to the door. She leaned against the doorjamb, watching me pull on the boots. "I guess I always hoped one day you would want to settle down, and I would be the one chosen."

I kept my focus on lacing my boots.

"But I see the truth now. I actually saw it the moment you brought her here." She folded her arms with an exhale. I knew she meant Zoey. "Even then, the future was with her."

I sat up, putting my attention on the woman in front of me. Elthia was beautiful, amazing in every way. She just wasn't the one for me.

I never thought I would find someone I wanted to be with. Amara was the closest I'd gotten to a mutual understanding, but I never was in love with her.

Now everything had changed.

"I'm sorry, El."

She pinched her lips together and nodded. "It's okay. You can't pick who you love, right?"

Isn't that the truth? I stood and collected her in my arms, hugging her tight. I sensed once I walked out the door, things would be different. For her sake, I hoped so.

"Ryker, come on," Amara yelled from the kitchen, breaking the moment.

Elthia pulled back. "I will not miss *her*."

I snorted.

"Seriously, Ryker. Watch her. She's not to be trusted."

Don't I know it. I nodded and kissed her gently on her forehead, then turned and walked out of the room.

"You are taking forever." Amara had pulled her hair into a high ponytail. She wore dark skinny jeans and a black top with brand-new boots. A dark, sleek leather messenger bag was slung over her shoulder. I didn't even have to guess that all the stuff was stolen. And from an overpriced store. Amara's taste was exorbitant. Even a simple outfit had to be designer. She always tried to get me to dress in nicer stuff, but no matter how many expensive jeans she stole for me, it never worked. Wasn't me.

We both looked like cat burglars. Black head to toe.

I had scarcely slung my axe on my back, trying to avoid my freshly bandaged shoulder, when a blaze of light blasted through the kitchen window. The force of the explosion tore me off my feet, throwing me against the wall. Glass sprayed down like water from a broken hydrant.

My ears rang with a high-pitched buzzing, but I quickly scanned the room. Amara lay not far from me, her hand grasping her head, blood oozing through her fingers.

"Amara!" I scrambled up, crawling over to her, dodging the debris. Fire caught the drying herbs hanging above the table, wolfing them in a gulp and spitting out a spray of flames.

"Ryker!" Elthia screamed from the hallway as she ran toward us.

Another blast hit the side of the house, causing the foundation to shake and Elthia to stumble into the stove.

"Amara?"

"I'm fine." She drew her hand away from her head; it was stained with red.

She would heal, and right now I had to get us out of here.

"I thought this place was protected?" I hollered at Elthia, the blaze catching the beams of the roof, crackling as it ate its way across the ceiling.

"Herbs and spells aren't foolproof." Elthia crouched, crawling over to me. "But I was careful about keeping it active and potent. I am sorry. They must have found a hole."

It was my fault. I brought this danger to her door.

Boom! Another fireball hurled through the broken window. I grabbed Elthia and Amara, covering them with my body as much as I could. Fire roared, nibbling at the furniture, old books, and spices.

"Back window." I tugged on both of them. Elthia's place was a little cottage. The only escape routes were the front door and the back window. Or so I thought.

"No." Elthia shook her head. "This way."

She spun toward the stairs leading down to her secret room.

"What are you doing?" I yelled, the flames growing a louder voice.

"Follow me," she said over her shoulder and continued down.

I looked back at Amara. Her face held the same doubt. But what was our choice? The front door was on fire, and we couldn't crawl out the back window. They'd have this place surrounded.

Sweat trickled into my eyes and smoke clogged my lungs.

"Fuck," I roared before following Elthia below. Amara stayed close behind me as we crawled on our hands and knees, keeping low to avoid the smoke and flames. I motioned for Amara to go down the stairs before me.

A blast from the back window hurled her down the flight of stairs, and she crashed to the ground. Flames ignited along the hall, billowing with rage toward me. I grabbed the trap door, flinging it on top of me, closing us off from the upstairs, making me glad we didn't try the back window.

I climbed down the steps. The room had no windows or doors except the trap door. I felt like I was following Elthia into a death trap.

Amara stood, brushing herself off. "Great. We're stuck here like rats. Now we're going to burn to death. Fae can die from fire, you know?"

Elthia ignored her and ran for a closet in the corner.

"I built this after you left." She pulled things off the shelves, then slid them out. "I knew you hated this place and its lack of escapes." She threw the last shelf to the side. The heat and sound of the fire pushed down on us. "I was going to surprise you when you came back. You never did."

A strange pattering sound tapped above us, like rain pelting a metal roof.

"What the...?" Amara wiped at her face, then looked up. Drops of water leaked from the gaping floorboards over us.

"Shit." A heavy drop splatted on my shoulder. Vadik's men were stifling the fire so they could enter. They burned the spell away, now they could cross the threshold.

A rush of water pounded against the ceiling and created a downpour that squeezed through the floor and pelted us. Voices hollered soon after. They were coming in for us.

I hurried across the small space, water rolling down my face. Elthia pushed on the back wall of the closet. With two heaves the false back popped open, revealing a tunnel.

"Holy shit." Amara stood next to me, her ponytail already dripping down her shirt. "I change my mind. I like her."

"Don't be offended, but I still don't like you," Elthia retaliated.

"None taken."

Footsteps pounded on the floor above our heads as more liquid rained down on us.

"Find them," a man shouted. "Remember, bring him back alive. Kill her... and whoever else has been helping them."

It was all the incentive I needed. I pushed Amara forward, rushing us to the opening.

I heard the trap door rattle, squeaking open. "Down here."

My adrenaline pumped in my ears. Boot treads rumbled down the stairs. I grabbed the closet door and shut it to give us an extra moment before they determined why there were shelves on the floor. My eyes didn't adjust to the blackness like they normally did, but I could distinguish enough. I swung the false opening closed.

"Run," I shouted when I turned around. And they did.

We all understood we didn't have the luxury of time.

Elthia led us out of a manhole a distance from her home. When I pushed the cover off, the moonlight shone in the clear night. We were silent as we reached the surface wet, singed, and in shock. I glanced at the smoke billowing in the distance.

Elthia stood next to me, her shoulders slumped as she watched her house literally go up in smoke. No matter what, she could never go back. Because of me she had lost her home, all her notes, potions, books, and memories.

"I am sorry," I muttered. The words sounded hollow and pathetic on my tongue, but I didn't know what else to say.

She nodded and looked away. "When I said I wanted to cleanse you from my life, I didn't think to this extreme." No humor sounded in her voice.

"Guys, we are still being followed." Amara bounced impatiently behind us. Her sensitivity to Elthia's loss was zilch. Amara never had anything that meant anything, besides herself.

Sadly, I related. Except now, there was a girl and a monkey-sprite calling me home.

"Go," Elthia ordered me.

"El, I'm not going to leave you here."

"Yes, you are. It's you two they want." She heaved out air, placing her hands on her hips. "I'm gonna disappear for a while."

"El—"

"Move." A burst of anger coiled from her, her gaze flashing to me. "Run before they find you."

I felt a nerve in my jaw twitch.

Her face softened. "Seriously, Ryker, go. I'm going to be all right. You know I will."

It took me another moment. I could see Amara dancing around in my periphery, ready to go.

Finally, I nodded.

Elthia bit her bottom lip, but a strength encompassed her expression. She turned and walked away.

I knew this was goodbye, I could see her letting me go with every step she took away from me. I was happy for her. She deserved happiness.

Amara and I ran into the darkness of the city. The streetlights were off, but as we jogged, I could see by the lights coming from some houses a few places had electricity. We crossed the bridge from Fremont back into Queen Anne. We weaved our way through the neighborhoods, hoping to lose ourselves and cause our tracks to be hard to pick up.

Wanting to stay out of the main downtown and Belltown, where the fae storm had caused the most damage, I steered us to Magnolia, hoping to find a vacated house there. It wasn't hard. We found a studio apartment close to the rail tracks. It wasn't big and only had one bed, but neither of us cared. It was only for one night. The painkillers Elthia gave me were wearing off. Pain, exhaustion, and hunger caused my muscles to shake.

"Sit down." Amara pointed to a chair. "I'll start a fire and see what there is in the cupboard to eat."

I turned to do what she said, catching myself in the mirror. My face was streaked with black soot and the top of my head was singed, blackening my blond hair. I had lost weight, sharpening my cheekbones. There was no longer a glint to my eyes. My fae magic was gone, creating a hollowed-out man.

Human.

"Are canned carrots, soup, and an extremely out-of-date box of crackers okay?" Amara's voice broke through my reverie.

I looked away from the mirror. "Yeah."

"Oh, and there is some honey in here too," she said. "It never goes bad, right?"

Honey.

Sprig.

Memories came flooding back to me of every laugh, smile, and moment I had with Zoey and Sprig... the little bubble we had lived inside in Peru, even when we were on the run.

My gaze went back to my reflection, staring at the man in the mirror.

I was in love with her. I didn't simply care for her, or want to be with, but completely *in love*. This idea was not easy for me to process. I had cut ties to people the day my adopted family, baby, and lover were killed.

Zoey, and even the little furball, dragged emotions from the far depths of my heart. The feeling had been there for a long time, but I had never admitted to myself or acknowledged it.

Now I had everything to lose.

The same girl I loved was the one I had to track down and kill... because I promised her.

And this was not a promise I could break.

After the soup and canned carrots for dinner, we indulged in the stale crackers and honey for dessert. Amara and I sat around the fire, the only form of heat and light.

"I think it's time we talked." I leaned back in the chair. "You told me a little about Vadik. When did you start working for him?"

She looked up. "It was a year before he sent me to track you down.

161

He paid extremely well and provided all I needed. He took sex as payment and indulged me in every luxury. I thought I had it made. Eventually I saw I would not be able to leave without repercussions. But it worked all right for me then."

She gazed at me through her lashes. I ignored the insinuation. It was hard to believe anything that came out of her mouth.

Amara rubbed her leg, then tucked it underneath her. "I sensed more to his obsession than simply the stone—the way he talked about you, the anger and offense he displayed. If anyone else betrayed him, he would have them killed. You were different. I noticed mannerisms and expressions you both had. Also, there are some family... traits..." She stirred in her chair.

I bent over, placing my face in my hands. "Not sure I want to know this."

"Then there was a night I caught him talking to your mother's painting. He was drunk, and I didn't understand most of it. He was cursing her for hiding you from him and angry her death kept him from being able to find you. Through her magic, she kept him from tracking you."

I blinked rapidly and sat back in my chair. This was why my mother killed herself. Her gift to me was to let me live a life without him in it.

"I don't know anything more than that." We stayed quiet for a moment, the crackle and pop of the fire the only sounds before she spoke again. "Zoey has the stone, doesn't she?"

My chin jerked up in response before I could stop it.

"I knew it." A slow grin curved Amara's mouth. "I suspected in Peru, after she returned, but when you tossed your boots in the doors I knew."

Ahhh. Now I was beginning to understand why Amara might have helped me escape with her. At least one of the reasons. The stone.

"We have to get it. Vadik will figure it out eventually."

"We?" Whatever Amara wanted was only in her best interest.

"You can't do this alone. I will help you."

"Sure," I scoffed.

Her lids narrowed. "Did I not help you get away from Vadik? You'd still be rotting in the cell, bleeding to death if it weren't for me."

I folded my arms over my chest and nodded solemnly. "You're right."

She tilted her head, her eyes still tapered. "Really?"

"Yeah," I replied. "I wouldn't be here without you. And I need to find Zoey before Vadik does."

A glint flashed in Amara's irises. "So we find where DMG is holding her and retrieve her?"

"Sounds like a plan, but tonight we sleep." I rose from the chair, snatched a blanket off the back, and threw it on the ground.

"What? Right now? It's still early." Amara twisted in her seat, watching me. "Don't we need to strategize?"

"Get some rest. You'll be better use to me." I lowered myself onto the blanket, placing my weapon next to me. I laid back and threw one arm over my eyes, the other curled around the axe. On the run, I always slept with my boots on and one hand on my blade.

She sat for a moment before I heard a loud sigh. The chair creaked as she stood, her feet padding across the room to the bed. "We still could share." I heard the smile behind her words.

"Go to sleep, Amara."

She huffed and flopped back on the pillows.

After a while the only sound in the room was the crackling of the dying fire and Amara's even breaths.

TWENTY-TWO

I kept to the shadows, skating between untouched buildings and ones that were missing. The night defended me from being observed. I smiled to myself. It had been easy to sneak away from Amara. She wasn't the only one who knew how to deceive and lie to get what they wanted. Not that I really lied. She *was* better use to me asleep. My years with her taught me that when she did fall asleep, she was out. I also knew her sounds, like when she was really asleep and when she was faking it. She tried to pretend she was slumbering for over an hour, until eventually she succumbed. I waited another hour.

Slipping out unnoticed was effortless. Even if I didn't have my powers, I was still good at moving around almost undetected.

My memory wasn't clear on the location where I had found Zoey crawling out of DMG's air vent the night of the storm. My powers had led me to her the first time, now it would be the promise taking me to her. The oath was like a compass, moving me toward her. Before it had been something I could manage, almost ignore, because she was far enough away. Now every step I took forward challenged my control. My feet shuffled faster until I ran, like I'd been hooked on a fishing line and she was reeling me in.

Zoey. Zoey. My boots pounded the pavement. *Kill. Kill.*

I shook my head. I had to get her, but the closer I got, the more dangerous I became. Still, I would not leave her to be Rapava's test subject or Vadik's slave. I wouldn't let that man take someone else from me. Zoey was dying, but I would not let Rapava touch her. And whatever it took, I would fight the killing impulse till the very end.

I hobbled across the city, pain searing through the nerves in my body, even my axe felt heavy on my back. I tuned out the aching and pushed forward. *Keep moving.*

Electricity seemed to be sporadic downtown, available for the less affected and wealthier areas, leaving the dark night to the homeless and gangs. Almost all of the rubble had been cleared away, but holes gaped where buildings should have been. The empty spaces felt like ghosts. Even though nothing was there, you could still feel their presence.

Bonfires and makeshift settlements made from clothes, blankets, and parts of demolished buildings took over some of the vacant lots. But even with the growing homeless, the crumbling city I left was slowly rebuilding. Loss and devastation were giving way to hope and renewal.

The strength of humans sometimes astounded me. Even in the face of complete despair, they fought back, rose from the ashes, and kept going.

I had always put a division between humans and me, a barrier, thinking they were weak and simple. Zoey made me see them differently. Now I could see the communities they were creating and the intricate line between protecting, guarding, and depending on each other. This city would get back on its feet again, and even though they'd never forget, they'd move on.

Every nerve jumped and twisted the nearer I traveled to her... wanting her. My desire split down the middle between wanting to protect her and wanting to kill her. The yearning to wrap my body around hers and the feel of her heartbeat against my chest. The sensation of her hair sliding between my fingers and her breath against my neck. To touch her, know she was safe in my arms. These fought with the desire to slide my hands over her skin, cup her neck, and clamp down. Hearing air struggle to reach her lungs, the fight dying out of her body, before I snapped her neck. The crunch of bone, her body falling limp...

Stop! I shook my head, flinging out my violent cravings. I focused on my feet moving across the pavement. My body already felt fatigued and sore.

Finally the pull of her brought me to an area I recognized, where I last found her. The feel of her being near crawled over me like a dozen spiders.

I was surveilling the block when a black van backed into the alley alongside a very nondescript building, immediately turning off its headlights. A car was suspicious enough, but a black windowless van near where I felt her? Didn't take a genius. I slunk back and hid in dead brush. Burnt shrubs crackled underfoot as I slid down the side of the building.

The connection to her was fire in my veins. A promise was unbreakable until you completed the vow. It was why I had never made

165

one before. Ever. There were a lot of things I never did before I met Zoey. I thought I had been happy enough. Content. One tiny human completely unhinged my life, my rules, and my stability, making me see I had been walking around for centuries as a zombie.

The love for others was cut off the moment I lost my family, the girl I loved, and my unborn child. I never imagined I would experience it again. It was easy with Amara. She didn't ask anything more of me than I was willing to give. I was never in danger of losing myself to her. Amara was fierce and stubborn, but Zoey possessed a spark that ignited me. She awakened me and became the fire in my veins.

I took a breath, ebbing back the surge of blood lust. The oath twitching my muscles along my arms and shoulders. The need to touch her, to be inside her, still overpowered the other, darker desires. But how long before they switched?

I should have run the moment I locked eyes with the stubborn, green-eyed, feisty human girl. She challenged me and drove me insane from the first second. Most humans and fae had a natural fear of me and would not hesitate to do what I commanded. Normally, if someone didn't, I would bend them under my authority. I tried with her. She would not break. She literally *bit* back.

A door banging in the alley refocused me. I leaned over enough to peer down the lane. A man exited a pair of taupe doors, which blended in with the block-shaped structure almost seamlessly. Something you would never look at twice. A perfect front for a secret government agency. A security camera was bolted above the doors in the same color as the building and slightly behind an advertisement, cloaking it from notice unless you were looking for it.

DMG was watching, whatever went in or out.

The man strode toward the vehicle, two guns attached to either hip. Those I recognized from experience. One stun, one kill gun for fae. He waved at the two men slipping out the car, one tall and one short, and proceeded to the back of the van.

"Had to sedate this one," the tall man said as they unloaded a gurney. A sheet covered a form underneath. No doubt another fae subject to be examined. A growl rose in my throat at the thought of what they could be doing to her.

"You going back out?" the man from the building asked.

"Yeah, Peter and I are on a roll. Liam still thinks he can top us even by himself," the short man scoffed.

"All right, I'll take this one to the lab." The man grabbed the gurney and pushed it to the door. "And don't forget to check in with Kate when you get back. Ever since Daniel's death, she's been fanatical about it."

"Yeah, I know. She bitched us out last time. See you, Hugo." The short man waved and moved toward the passenger side door. The door to the building snapped shut, the man and the gurney disappearing.

On my earlier investigation I found the air vent Zoey used to get away was since sealed, locked, and guarded with sensory triggers and goblin metal. They lost her once before, they would not let her or Sprig escape again, and they didn't want anything or anyone coming to help her. For safety DMG probably had more than one entry, but they kept them well concealed. This secret branch of the government would be well protected—almost invisible and almost impossible to enter. My plan of sneaking in and breaking her out was dwindling before my eyes. It was my own arrogance to think it would be simple. With my powers gone I was even more useless against an assembly of guards.

"Dammit," I mumbled. I knew what I had to do. I rubbed my cheek and released a small sardonic chuckle from my throat. "God damn you, human."

The two men climbed into the van. The engine turned over and the alley blazed with light. The tires crackled and crunched over pieces of the building that had fallen during the big electrical storm. I exhaled before I stepped out of the shadows into the entry of the lane and blocked their way, my hands rose in surrender. My eyes squinted against the blinding glow of the headlights. The brakes squealed as the van came to a shuddering stop only a foot away from me. The front doors swung open, and outlines of the human men pointed guns at me. I recognized them. They were a part of the group that attacked Zoey and me outside the bank before we jumped to Peru.

"Don't move, fae," the one on the passenger side said. In the light I could see he was short but fit, the only thing remarkable about him. With his average build, brown hair and brown eyes, he was the type you would barely remember meeting. The driver was much more substantial: buzzed blond hair, brown eyes, and over six foot. He had the ripped muscles of a guy who worked out every day, and there was something in his perfect posture and clipped words which conveyed a military background. In my time, I had run across a lot of militaries from different time periods, but they all had a similar way of holding themselves. A rigidness in their stance and a controlled way of holding a weapon.

The driver unlatched the safety on his gun, sliding around the door to me.

"You don't need the weapon. I come willingly." I raised my axe and placed it on the ground at my feet.

"That's what worries me. We've never had a fae surrender to us." The driver walked toward me. His foot swiped at the axe, trying to kick it farther away from me. He grunted with pain when the axe didn't budge. I tried not to laugh when he stepped over it, pushing me back with the threat of his gun. If it took three huge fae to move it, I would love to see how many it took for mere mortals to pick it up.

"This doesn't sit right with me; I know who you are. We've had the pleasure before," the driver spoke again.

"If you want to call it that." It was hard to keep the snarl out of my voice.

"You're the Wanderer. The fae who kidnapped and polluted one of our seers." He pointed the gun at my head.

"Polluted?" I felt one of my eyebrows curve up.

"Putting your foul powers in her and your fae dick." His voice hitched with disgust. "I'm kind of glad my friend is dead, so he wouldn't have to live with what you did to her. But then again, he would have sliced you into tiny bits the moment you stepped out. Maybe I should do it in his honor."

Daniel. Even from the grave the guy plagued my life.

"Funny, she seemed to have no problem with my fae dick. Quite the opposite. She definitely enjoyed riding it," I taunted. Why did the mention of Daniel's name cause me to act like an asshole? Well, more of one.

His partner looked over at him. "We have to take him to Rapava."

"Do we?" Peter took a step closer. The gun dug deeper into my temple. The glint in Blondie's eyes told me he wanted nothing more than to shoot me in the head.

"Peter. Don't. He's trying to provoke you." The dark-haired guy shook his head.

"Go ahead." I pressed my head harder into the barrel, knocking Peter back a step. "I could break your neck and your boyfriend's before you pull the trigger."

"Peter, calm down. Daniel would not want you to avenge him like this." The other guy put his hand on Peter's shoulder.

Peter took a breath, relinquishing the strain he held on the trigger. "Why are you giving yourself over to us?" he probed, flicking his chin at me. The dark-haired guy moved close, patting me down, searching for more weapons.

"What the fuck does it matter?" I snarled at the passenger. His hands traveled along my inner thigh and over my ass. "All you need to know is you have one of the rarest Faes on earth. I am sure your boss wouldn't want to miss out on testing and dissecting me."

Peter didn't look convinced.

"He's right." The other fellow straightened and moved away from me. He grabbed for something on his belt and tugged off a walkie-talkie. "We need to let Rapava know."

"I don't trust this asshole, Matt." Peter stepped closer, pressing the gun into my head. The rage inside clenched, and I struggled to keep my breath even. "That you *want* to be captured makes me think you are coming for her. Let me assure you, not only will you not be able to break her out, but she will not want to go with you. She doesn't have to pretend to care for you anymore."

My eyes darted to him. A smug grin etched on his face.

"Zoey's a survivor. She did what she needed to do to live and eventually get away from you. Now she is back with us. She's happy not to have to act anymore, pretending to like fucking you."

I flashed on images of her naked body under and over mine, her groaning as I thrust in deeper, her nails skating down my back. "Sure." A grin inched up the side of my mouth. Peter's eyes narrowed as the knowing smile grew on my mouth.

Peter glanced over his shoulder at Matt, a smirk sprouting over his own mouth. "This fae was played, and he didn't even know it." He turned back to me. "Zoey turned the tables and wrapped you around her finger. Now she has you under her spell, and you're willing to turn yourself over to us for her."

Everything in me wanted to throw his theory back in his face. I thought of every touch, every time our bodies curled around each other, every time her lips met mine. But deep, deep down I felt a seed of doubt burrowing into my gut.

No. No way.

I didn't even realize I was shaking my head until Peter laughed. "You can deny it all you want. Won't be long till you see the truth, fae." He tipped his gun in the direction of the doors at the end of the alley. "Matt, tell Rapava we're coming back with an excellent test subject. I'm sure Zoey will also love to show the Wanderer how she really feels."

Matt clicked on the walkie-talkie and mumbled into it. Peter tried to lift my axe but left it where it was when he couldn't. Instead, he got behind me, shoving the gun in my back. "Move." Matt jogged to the door, punching his fingers at the keypad by the door. The clink of several bolts releasing rang in my ears.

I had no idea what lay in front of me. The only thing I was keenly aware of was that this might be the stupidest thing I had ever done.

TWENTY-THREE

We went through several more coded doors before I saw an elevator at the end. A structure, reminding me of an airport security scanner, stood framed about four feet from the elevator. The moment my foot crossed the threshold, the contraption beeped and lit up, a gate dropping over the door behind us.

Damn. A fae detector.

The blond prick yanked me into the elevator and pushed a button, closing the doors. We only went a few stories underground when the doors parted, and he led me down an underground concrete tunnel. Lights dotted the wall and guided our way. My eyes stayed alert, trying to take in everything around me.

The passageway led to another set of security doors, then another elevator, where they both had to insert a special security card. This time the descent went on and on, deep underground. The buttons on the panel were not numbered but were in some code I couldn't decipher.

Finally, the doors opened. A hand shoved me out of the elevator. I gritted my jaw, feeling the roar of anger wanting to respond. I could easily disarm him and throw both of them to the ground. The idea of doing it for a bit of fun crossed my mind, but I clenched my fist tighter and walked where they told me to.

My gaze caught the vast quantities of computers, machines, and lab equipment blinking, beeping, and humming in the open area we moved past. In a city where electricity was still scarce and only came on for a few hours a day, this place had conveniences and technology available to them. Zoey had mentioned they were "off the grid," which made sense for a secret government agency, especially one fighting against the threat of fae.

The two idiots forced me down a long corridor. I noticed a feeling of nausea crawling over me, making me lethargic. My anger dissipated. All I wanted to do was sit or maybe take a nap.

"What the…?" I glanced over my shoulder at Blondie. He only grinned smugly. I could feel the fury stir deep in me, but by the time it got to the surface, I felt more exhausted than upset. It was similar to when I had been sliced lightly with fae metal. Goblin metal could kill us, but in small dosages it caused fae to become tired, queasy, and sluggish. It dulled our magic. It was a perfect thing to have here. It was like castrating us.

Matt walked in front of me, stopping at a door almost hidden to the eye, and punched in another code. The door beeped and opened. Blondie forced me into a room within a room. The outer room was a cross between a medical lab and viewing room except blinds kept the inner room from being seen.

Peter hustled me across the room to the door, entered another code, and swung the door open. He pushed me in the smaller room and slammed the door behind me. I glanced around. This room was a lot more frightening. A retractable light hung from the ceiling. It took me a moment to see the room also had a robot arm with a needle. A single hospital bed sat below, and thick chains and cuffs hung from the metal rollers on the side of the bed. My eyes wandered the room, taking in every bit of information. I felt tired and wanted to lie on the bed and sleep, but I fought against the urge. I needed to be ready. Alert.

Easier said than done.

Hours passed, bleeding into more hours. My energy evened out after a while, but it leveled on the low to almost nonexistent side. The strength it took to stay alert dwindled and finally caused my legs to give way. I slid down the wall.

When the blinds along the inside window moved, it startled me awake. My eyes snapped open, and I watched them carefully. I didn't move off the floor, but I felt my shoulders rise in defense. My body stayed tense, and I felt eyes through the glass watching me like an animal in the zoo. I couldn't see through the darkened glass, and only my own reflection manifested in the window, but I knew Dr. Rapava was on the other side.

Examining. Studying.

I'd seen enough cop shows to know about the double-sided glass. They could see me, but I couldn't see them unless they turned on the light in their side of the room. With my background it was shocking I had never been inside a police station, but I wasn't stupid enough to get caught by a human. And they couldn't keep me even if they had tried. Now it was different. I was sure if I still had the power to jump, I wouldn't be able to escape from here.

"I want to see her." I stared through the glass, past my own likeness, my voice harsh and demanding. After a few beats, the curtains lowered back down.

Fury rattled in my gut, along with the sensation she was near.

Killkillkill.

No, fight it. You are stronger than the desire.

No, she must die.

I rubbed my face, dropping my head into my hands, and forced good thoughts of Zoey into my mind. Memories of her and me in bed. In the rain. Rolling on the ground of Machu Picchu. Laughing. Fighting. Fucking. But every recollection turned into me digging my fingers into her soft skin and crushing the life out of her. A deep growl tore from my gut. I wasn't strong enough to stay away, which would have been the best. I could give myself every excuse in the book for why I was here, under the pretense of wanting to protect her, but the oath was taking over and my desire to track her down and kill her was taking away my memories and my feelings for her.

I sighed, wrapping my arms around my knees, and blocked the lights above my head from my eyes. I drifted in and out of sleep, dreaming of her—her face, her voice calling my name. My fingers wrapping around her throat, squeezing till I crushed her esophagus.

A vibrating at the windows startled me from the dream, and I bolted to my feet. A strange zing in my blood purred through my arms, flexing my fists open and closed. Slowly the blinds lifted, retracting into the ceiling.

This time the intensity of the gazes from the other room slammed into my chest like a cannonball. I took a step back, crossing my arms. My reflection in a blackened window echoed back at me. A crackling noise sounded near my head, jerking my attention to the speaker above.

"Welcome, Wanderer." A man's Russian accented voice came over the speaker, but years of living in America had watered it down. I had come into contact with the doctor only once, at the bank in Bellevue, but I recognized his voice. "We are happy to have you here."

I didn't reciprocate the greeting and only stared back into nothing. The black space pulled me forward, and I stepped closer to the glass.

"I have to admit I am surprised to see you here," Rapava said. "The fact you got away and made it here undetected is impressive."

His voice continued, but it became background noise to me. The draw to the window drove my feet flush with the wall, and before I realized it, my hand went to the glass. I could feel her. Every fiber in me screamed her name. Two extremely different needs, both violent and consuming.

"I want to see you," I commanded at the glass.

"There is no one here but you and me," Rapava stated over the sputtering intercom.

A low growl caught in my throat, but I kept my focus straight ahead. "Don't. Hide. From. Me."

The speaker clicked off, but before it did, I heard low voices arguing. I stood unmoving for a while, staring at the same spot. Then a light flickered on in the next room.

My chest clenched along with my fists when her face came into view. She stood right where I had been staring.

Zoey.

Every time I saw her felt like I was being slammed against a wall by a giant. Emotions, of tremendous yearning and hate, clobbered me. The animosity didn't scare me like the overpowering knowledge that I was in love with the woman in front of me did. I felt weak and defenseless. I was the guy people feared, not the one who wanted to wrap myself in her arms and disappear from the world.

Her face held no expression; her jaw was raised in defiance. Cuts and bruises ran along her face, neck and arms, a canvas of purples, yellows, and deep blues.

Had they beaten her?

She took a step back, folding her arms over her chest. "You saw me." The ice in her voice could have cut the glass between us. "I really thought fae were smarter." Her chin jerked up higher and she swallowed. "You never detected I was playing you, deceiving you? The more I confessed, let you think you saw the real me, the easier it was. Both you and the stupid monkey. You should have stayed where you were. With your own kind."

My lids narrowed on her. Her words felt like a goblin dagger to my gut, but I searched her face, looking for something to tell me she was putting on a front for the doctor. I knew her better than anyone, and I could usually sense when she was lying or trying to deceive me. This time I couldn't. Her walls were impenetrable around her. She stood her ground, staring at me with a cold, unflinching gaze.

"But your blood might be the exact thing to save my sister's life."

"Sister?" I flinched.

Zoey's lips pressed together firmly before she nodded.

"Yes, my sister is alive. DMG took her before the fire and brought her here."

"Lexie is alive?"

"Neither she nor I are your concern, Wanderer."

The muscles along my shoulders tightened. Was this all an act? Was she being forced into acting this way? Why couldn't I tell? *Because you don't really care. You need to kill her.* I crunched my palms into a fist, trying to shove out this impulse running along my veins.

Zoey began to turn before she said, "But I guess I should thank you for making me the perfect weapon against fae—a human with seer and fae powers. I will grow more powerful, and you will die."

She turned away from me and moved to the door. Dr. Rapava moved closer to the window, so I could see him more clearly. "Because of Zoey, we know much more. We can now create stronger humans, ones who can fight and destroy fae. The playing field is even. And because your powers cured her defect only helps our progress. Sadly, you came too late for the other seer."

What? She wasn't dying?

Zoey stopped, her hand on the door. She glanced over her shoulder, and an emotion flickered too quickly over her features for me to make it out before she disappeared out the door.

Rapava kept talking to me, but my eyes were locked on the exit where the girl I promised to kill just left. I regretted the oath the moment it crossed my lips, but now it was too late. It was done. I didn't care how forceful the pledge drove me to act, I wanted Zoey next to me till the end. I would have fought the urge to kill her no matter how painful it became for me, till her last dying breath.

Now she wasn't dying at all. My power was killing me, but it had healed her.

"I don't think there is any doubt why you are here." Rapava's voice finally broke me away from my thoughts. "But Zoey is not who you thought. Her loyalty lies with me and with her sister. She is a Collector, a hunter, a seer. *My* warrior," he stressed, examining me. For several minutes he got caught up in analyzing me. "I've dreamed about researching a specimen like you. One of a kind." He got a faraway look in his eyes, then shook his head. "Vadik will be looking for you also. We are well guarded against fae here, but I will double our security. Now you and Zoey are mine. I do not want to lose either one of you.

"And I will get the stone as well."

ZOEY

TWENTY-FOUR

Please say this is a nightmare.

But every time my lids blinked, the figure of the man standing behind the glass didn't dissolve.

Ryker. My heart screamed. *No. No. This can't be happening. He shouldn't be here.*

He stood with his arms folded over his chest, appearing every bit like a ruthless warrior and unfazed by his challenger. The muscles twitched along his jaw and neck, showing he was ready to act at any second. His clothes were smudged with black soot; the top of his hair was singed. Fading bruises and cuts dotted his face and arms. He looked tired, pale, and thinner than I had ever seen him.

My heart strained against itself. *What happened to him? What had he gone through? How did he get away from Vadik?* I knew he would have eventually found his way to me. His character and the promise solidified this. Still I stared at him, not wanting to believe.

He said he would find you and he did.

Somehow he had broken away from Vadik and come here... for *me*. The need to reach out for him, to tear through the glass and feel his arms around me froze me in place. I didn't trust myself to move or speak.

There was no question of how he found me. I had made him promise to kill me before I died of the weakness in me. This was before I knew where I was headed and what danger he would be in if he came for me.

Dammit, Zoey.

"Remember when you said if you had the opportunity to retrieve certain information you would take it? Here is your chance to prove you're more than empty words." Rapava's voice poked at my heart. Rapava had purposely walked me into a trap the other day, called my bluff on Ryker. That's why he was so smug.

If I chose Ryker, Lexie was dead. And probably very soon after both Ryker and myself. If I chose DMG, I would be condemning the man I loved to torture, pain, experiments, and death by my hand. There was no way to win here. Whatever I did would hurt someone I cared about.

"Can you tell me why he simply gave himself over to my men?"

"I cannot, sir."

"Really, Ms. Daniels?" Rapava said with disappointment. "There are only two reasons a man would ever turn himself in: honor or love. Honor is not exactly high on the fae list, and it is certainly not why he is here."

I felt myself sinking again.

"I need to understand what he thinks of your relationship. And don't insult me. He is not here because you flirted with him."

"I cannot tell you why he's here. As you know, I was forced to do things to survive. I don't think he is capable of caring, especially for a human."

"There is also another option."

"What?"

"He thinks you have something of his... something he wants. Perhaps an artifact?"

I felt as though I'd just stepped in a deep fryer, sizzling and burning my insides into nothing, while making me crispy and hard on the outside.

Oh, hell, no, he won't. But in that instant I knew Ryker had. The strange pull... the silent voice that had been there the entire time, drawing me to it, keeping it close. Why I even slept with my boots on.

The stone.

It had been with me the whole time.

"You wouldn't have lied to me, Zoey? Failed to mention you hid this item somewhere?"

"No, sir." I forced myself not to look at my boots. Ryker crossed his arms, his feet shifting underneath him, his focus on me.

"Zoey?" Rapava's voice yanked my attention to him. "Are you feeling all right?"

Pop quiz.

"Yes, sir. Perfectly."

A knowing glint filled his eyes, but I ignored it and turned back to the window, turning off all emotion.

"I promise you, sir. I do not know the whereabouts of the stone," I lied easily, needing Rapava's doubt of me to ease up. "But I will find out for you."

178

"I know you will." He stepped to an intercom on the wall and pushed the button.

Ryker's head jerked up.

"Welcome, Wanderer." Rapava spoke into the intercom. Ryker tilted his head slightly, recognition fluttered over his face.

Ryker's head snapped back to the glass, and I felt his gaze burrow straight into me. He couldn't see me, but somehow he knew I was there. I could feel it. His eyes pinned directly to mine, taking my breath away again.

I barely heard the doctor talking to Ryker, my body and senses were captured in the power of his gaze. Ryker walked all the way to the wall, directly in front of me. His outline encased me in darker shadows, his stare piercing me. His hand came up to the window, lying flat against the glass. My heart thumped in my chest, rang in my ears. Heat flushed my body in a reflex of need. It took everything I had to not place my palm against his.

"Interesting." Rapava took his finger away from the button, speaking only to me. "He senses exactly where you are. His blood in your system must connect you to each other, no matter if he can see you or not. This is extremely fascinating." The way he said it turned my stomach. An idea was forming, one I was sure would not be good for either Ryker or me.

For Lexie's life you have to play this game.

"I want to see you," Ryker's deep voice was low and demanding.

The fight to keep my feelings in check was like shoving hot needles down my throat. A sob sat at the base, strangling me.

"There is no one here but you and me," Rapava spoke to Ryker. He was testing him, seeing if Ryker's presence was chance or something more.

Ryker gritted his teeth, a low growl vibrating in his throat, but his attention stayed on me. "Don't. Hide. From. Me." Every syllable exiting Ryker's mouth was a claim on me. The pull to him was so potent my mind had to retreat to my safe place, where I didn't think or feel. I couldn't let him in. If I let my feelings get the better of me, I would tear through every shard of glass separating us. Nothing would be able to separate us. And we would all die.

With a snap, I shoved everything down. I used to be good at pretending, being something I wasn't, before I met Ryker. Now, playing a role was no longer as easy as it was once. It was exhausting bullshit. But his life, my sister's, Sprig's, Croygen's, and most certainly mine were on the line.

I turned off my soul and became fighter Zoey. The one who would do what she needed to do to survive. I rolled my shoulders back and glanced over my shoulder at Rapava. "Let him see me."

"No." The doctor shook his head.

"He already knows I'm here." I shrugged. "If you want my help, we do this my way. He'll cooperate better if he sees me."

Rapava stiffened. "Do *not* presume to give me orders. We do this *my* way."

Shit.

"You already walk a thin line here. Being nice to a fae, even if you are playacting, could easily cause you to slide back."

"You don't think I can do it?"

"I want to think so... for you sister's sake."

My teeth ached the more I clamped down on them, but I gave Rapava a swift nod. "I will do it for both of you. I want you to be proud of me again."

His eyes softened and a small smile twitched his mouth. "Fine. I will oblige this request. Are you ready?"

"Yes."

No.

I turned back to the glass, Ryker stood in the same stance, his focus still on me.

Rapava flipped a switch, and the room burst with light.

Ryker sucked in air as his eyes took me in, tracing over my face and body. With me no longer hiding in the shadows, I felt even more vulnerable to his stare. I could feel it move over my skin like fingers. His gaze went over the bruises and cuts along my face, neck, stopping on my arms.

I took a step back and folded my arms around my chest, out of view.

Lexie. Remember Lexie.

"You saw me." I lifted my chin, my voice void of emotion. It was only an instant, but a muscle twitched along his jaw before turning back to stone. "I really thought fae were smarter. You never detected I was playing you, deceiving you? The more I confessed, let you think you saw the real me, the easier it was. Both you and the stupid monkey. You should have stayed where you were... with your own kind."

He shifted his footing, his gaze turning critical as he searched my face. I had to play this perfectly. I could see he knew something was wrong. If he knew about my sister, maybe he'd put two and two together. If anyone could see through to my core, it was Ryker.

"But your blood might be the exact thing to save my sister's life."

"Sister?" he balked.

"Yes, my sister is alive. DMG took her before the fire and brought her here."

"Lexie is alive?"

Rapava cleared his throat so softly only I heard it. It was getting too personal for him.

I pressed my arms firmer into my chest. "Neither she nor I are your concern, Wanderer." His back stiffened, his lips pinched together, his demeanor hardened toward me. Being this close to him was torture.

I can't do this…

Rapava's hand was off the speaker button.

"I'm sorry, sir, but seeing him has brought back a lot of painful memories." I didn't stop the tears building behind my eyes, hoping Rapava would believe they went along with my words. "I need a moment."

"Of course. Come back when you are ready." Rapava's unvarying tone made it hard to decipher how he truly felt.

My need to leave pushed me to the exit before I even realized it. I felt both Ryker's and Rapava's eyes on me. I nodded to the switch, and Rapava pushed on the speaker. I glanced back at Ryker. "But I guess I should thank you for making me the perfect weapon against fae—a human with seer and fae powers. I will grow more powerful, and you will die."

I walked toward the door, hearing Rapava's footsteps move to Ryker. "Because of Zoey, we know much more. We can now create stronger humans, ones who can fight and destroy fae. The playing field is even. And the fact your powers cured her defect only helps our progress. Sadly, you came too late for the other seer."

I halted, my hand on the door. This was the one thing I wanted to keep from Ryker—that I wasn't dying. It made it all much more complicated. I didn't need his guilt on me too.

I automatically looked back at him, trying to hide the anguish I felt. He stared at me; pain etched deep in his eyes. I couldn't take one more minute; sobs shoved their way up my esophagus. I flung myself out the door, slamming it behind me.

"Already done?" Liam leaned against the opposite door. I nodded, not trusting my voice.

Liam walked me back in my room, the temptation growing with each step to rip off my shoe and pull up the heel of my boot. The moment the door to my room shut behind me, I fell against it and slid down, sobbing. My hands went to my boot and tore at the laces, my fingers trembling trying to free the knots.

"Ahhh!" I screamed, my hands inept against the coiled tie. I slammed my heel into the floor, kicking at it with my other foot, like a wild animal. A deep screech resounded up, my nails clawing at the leather, but the boot stayed steadfast around my ankle. I gave one last tug, feeling my energy leave. My shoulders sagged, and a soft whimper puttered out.

I felt soft, damp fur curl on my chest, a hand stroking my cheek. My blurry gaze went to the red color matting his coat. His arms and body were covered with new marks and holes from testing. His skin blazed hot under his sticky fur. Everything outside of my best friend was forgotten. He became my only concern in that moment.

"Sprig…" I cradled him into my chest, the words I needed to express my heartache for him, for Ryker, choked off.

"It's okay, *Bhean*."

No, it wasn't okay.

And everything was about to get worse. I had to become a monster. A DMG soldier.

TWENTY-FIVE

The ten-minute reprieve Rapava gave me before demanding my return didn't give me much time to collect myself from my breakdown. I wasn't sure if I was disappointed or relieved I didn't get a chance to look inside my heel. Even if I had, most of me was afraid of what I would find—that it really was there. Ignorance had protected me. Once I knew the truth, the danger would escalate.

Ryker's presence almost pushed me to the brink. But I had taken a breath, seizing a moment to think about my impulsive reaction to touch the stone. I normally wasn't impetuous. I made decisions quickly, being a Collector and a fighter, you had to. But I was always strategic. Impulsive in my work, in my life, would have gotten me killed. Ryker crushed all logic, burrowing down on my impulse button.

I really wanted to place the stone in my hand and let it take over me. It would give me power to force this nightmare to go away—solve so many problems. Was the sacrifice worth it? I wanted to say "yes." However, I could hear his deep voice, see his head shaking. "Absolutely not, Zoey! We will get through this." Because if I chose the stone, everything could get far worse and my life would belong to the stone, and it was as dangerous as Rapava and Vadik. Its power might consume me, turn me evil and destroy me. Who was to say I wouldn't end up worse than what I was fighting and be devoured with greed, power, and anger?

I never told Sprig what had happened or that Ryker was here. I couldn't. The barrier I needed to erect pushed all emotion out. If I talked about it, the wall would crumble.

"What's wrong, *Bhean*?" Sprig asked as I set him on the table. Liam's knock on the other side told me it was time to go.

I softly touched his wounds, then shook my head. "Nothing."

"No. Not nothing. You are acting really strange. And not a hungry or needing-sex strange." He tilted his head, his face pale and chalky. Even his attempt at humor didn't reach his eyes.

The smile stretching over my face was full of pain and sadness. I straightened my back and pivoted around. "I'm ready," I said sternly to Liam when he opened the door. The trip back was a haze as I kept my focus on the back of Liam's head.

"You're back. Good." Rapava waved me into the outer room. A spasm in my chest fluttered at the sight of the inner room, but I quickly shut the gate to any emotion.

Ryker was strapped to a hospital bed, laid flat out on his back. His wrists and ankles were chained, which were probably made of goblin metal. He was bare chested, wearing only the issued gray pants given to the fae. His torso was covered with deep slash marks. A circular wound in his shoulder looked like a bullet entrance, and he had a gash in his side. The long, raised scars traveling from his stomach around to his back looked the worst. Against my will, sickness crawled up, dipping my knees. I could feel my body wanting to curve over.

I can't do this... I can't do this.

"Zoey, you look pale. You are not backing out of our deal, are you?" Rapava watched me.

Morality switch. *Off.*

"No, sir." I straightened, rolling my shoulders.

Ryker's head fell to the side, and his lids blinked rapidly, as if he were trying not to fall asleep.

"I gave him a little dose. To keep him calm," Rapava responded to Ryker's movements. "I won't lie and say this is not exciting for me," Rapava said, his toe tapping excitedly against the tile. "This is such an incredible day. We have one of the most unique specimens in the fae world. He is how you got your powers. He'll help us to discover how they cured you and how to obtain the knowledge of one of the most powerful objects earth or the Otherworld has ever known."

Rapava actually grinned as he ran his palm down Ryker's chest. I had never seen Rapava show much emotion. He was practically giddy with anticipation.

To torture the man I loved, I needed to control the rage consuming me.

"Let's get started." Rapava glanced over at me. It was like he saw the hesitation in my eyes and my soul. "I don't think I need to remind you what is at stake."

Lexie.

"No," I replied. "What would you like me to do?"

He strolled to the door of the inner room and punched in another access code to the entrance. "While I am examining and testing this specimen, I would like you to find out anything you can about the stone and also anything he might know of possible fae attack, even Vadik's plans."

"Don't you work with Vadik?"

Rapava clutched the door, his blue eyes narrowing. "I do not work with fae. We found self-serving opportunities at times, which helped the cause. A cause you once believed in. Lost your partner, too." He pushed the handle down, popping the door open. "I was never foolish enough to think Vadik was not doing the same. You will learn. You keep your enemies close."

No, sir, that's a lesson I understand well.

Rapava led me into the room, my feet growing heavier with every step. It was hard enough with a plate of glass between us. Now there was nothing to protect me from my feelings.

Even over the smells of bleach and rubbing alcohol, my nose recognized his scent. It crawled up my nose, down my throat. It stopped at my heart, tapping at the door, trying to get in. The ache in my bones to run to him and crawl into his arms was almost impossible to ignore. But even without these obstructions, could I run into his arms? The oath I made him take remained. I had no clue how strong or controlling it was for Ryker.

I was about to see.

"Wanderer." Rapava walked around to Ryker's side, pulling on his latex gloves. The rubber snapped around his wrists. "I've been looking forward to this for a while."

"Where is she?" Ryker ignored him, his head tilting to look around the room.

"Come, Zoey. I think your fae lover wants to be reunited."

I steadied myself and took a step to the other side of Ryker.

His white eyes latched on to me. His nostrils flared, like he was taking in my scent as well. The intensity in the room swelled. Fire raged between us, a magic that produced a craving for him and shook my legs.

His pupils widened and then a thick haze brewed, clouding them. He grunted and metal clashed against the bars as he strained against the refrains, his hands reaching for me. He bellowed loudly, rattling the windows as he lurched again, the gurney skidding over the floor. I leaped back as he banged his head against the bed, trying to free himself.

"Whoa." Rapava grabbed for a needle lying on a tray near the table.

"Calm down."

"Fuck you," Ryker snarled at Rapava, but his gaze never left me. Determination was the only thing I saw in his eyes. I knew, with a sickening contraction of my stomach, he did not see me, but an object he needed to kill.

My heart thumped in my chest as he struggled and kicked at the restraints. He flailed with the primal need to free himself, like a wild animal.

Rapava shoved a needle into Ryker's neck and he stopped thrashing. As he slowly stilled, he kept his eyes on me. In a blink, the fog in his eyes cleared, and he glanced around as if he didn't know where he was.

"Human," he muttered. This time when I saw his fingers reach for mine, it was not in hate but in longing.

My eyes flooded with tears. I blinked, looking away from his outstretched hand. I ignored him. It was one of the most painful things I ever had to do. That I was able to do it made me hate myself with an unfathomable force. I was almost ready to unchain him from the bed and happily let him take my life. It was something I could live with, except Rapava might take my death out on Lexie. Other lives were on my shoulders.

"I might have been wrong on my estimation of your relationship with this fae, Zoey. I apologize." Rapava blew out a breath, placing the syringe back on the tray. "He only wants to kill you."

I tried to still my shaking body.

Rapava selected another needle, this one meant to extract fluids. "With his high emotional response to you, you will have to double your efforts to get the information we need."

Ryker's arm twitched, his focus still on me. I couldn't bring myself to fully look at him yet.

"I only gave him a little morphine. It should go through his system soon. Then you can begin." Rapava turned to get a few items from another table.

I was close enough to feel the tips of Ryker's fingers brush my hip. My teeth sawed into my lower lip in anguish. Again his hand grazed me. The struggle to look at him was out of my hands. My gaze instantly went to him. I tasted the copper and salt of blood on my lip as I bit down deeper.

He stared at me. It wasn't with confusion, anger, or coated in blinding need to kill. To an outsider it might appear like nothing more than him watching me, but I could see past the wall he erected for everyone else. It was like he was telling me, *Do what you have to do. Whatever it is, do it.*

Rapava whipped back around, drawing my attention away from Ryker. He handed me a scalpel the size of a chef's knife, the blade lined with serrated edges like shark's teeth. He dosed Ryker with another shot.

"What was that?"

"Oh, it's a little concoction I've designed here at the lab. It will push the morphine out of his blood system and enhance the sensation in his nerves."

"What?"

"A tiny nick will feel like his flesh is being burned. The drug reacts to the metal of the blade; it sears the skin and makes it harder for fae healing powers to work properly. It seems he has been previously tortured. We'll reopen those wounds. It will be more painful and easier to get information from him."

Dizziness spun my head and clogged my throat.

At my slight hesitation, disappointment seemed to settle onto Rapava's shoulders. He grabbed the intercom phone off the wall, mumbled something I couldn't hear, and before he even hung up, the outer room door opened.

My limbs went ridged, torquing my body as I jerked with surprise. *No.*

Liam carried Lexie in the room and set her in a chair. Her dark eyes appeared distant but curious as she glanced around the room.

Oh god, no. Her presence made Rapava's threat more real. Hurt Ryker or hurt Lexie.

Lexie slanted her head, swinging her working legs back and forth on the chair. I could hear her humming to herself, appearing young and childlike. Innocent and sweet.

Drugged.

Rapava went silently back to Ryker, watching me through his lashes. "So... shall we began?"

I gave myself one more minute, glancing from Lexie back to Ryker. Then I dropped the blade... slicing Ryker's chest.

A scream of anguish tore from his throat.

"Now tell me where the stone is." As the words rolled icily over my tongue, the last of my humanity turned its back on me, leaving me completely alone.

187

TWENTY-SIX

I went back to my room covered in blood.

"What the flaming goat's nuts happened to you?" Sprig climbed out from his cage the moment the door closed behind me.

Normally I would want a shower, but I walked to my bed and sat on the edge. I was numb and detached, barely aware of the blood drying on my clothes and skin.

"Bhean?" Sprig jumped down on the bed, then scaled my leg.

I didn't move or acknowledge him. I only stared straight ahead.

"Talk to me," Sprig's voice sounded quiet and soft.

I could not speak.

"Okay, tell me whose blood this is." Sprig slid off as I stood.

"Ryker's."

"What? Ryker's? Viking is here? Why is his blood all over you? What happened?" His questions kept coming, but I tuned him out.

I stood, walking to the corner of the room and slid down, turning my face away from the room. I wrapped my arms around my legs and stared vacantly. I went to a faraway place where no one or nothing could touch me—not even emotions.

I sensed Sprig making a fuss for a while, but he went silent when the lights clicked off. DMG was putting us to bed.

Sprig always brought me comfort, but he wouldn't be able to comprehend what I had done to Ryker. He didn't have a mean bone in his body. Sprig would listen, but he'd be aghast. He would never even consider torturing a friend or someone he loved. Deep down, he would never think me capable.

I was.

Time was a weird thing, or at least one's perception of it. Time didn't actually slow down or speed up, but without being tethered to the world, it jumped, skipped, and stopped at its own discretion. It must have done a few cartwheels, because to me, it was a blink of an eye, a lifetime, when I felt a hand on my shoulder.

"Zoey?" Croygen's distinct voice whispered in my ear. "Hey."

I didn't move.

"Zoey, what happened?" Croygen sat next to me. The warmth of his palm rubbed my back, splintered my numbness, pulled me back from the depths. Like a life raft.

He could accept and understand what I'd done, like Ryker would have. I turned, crushing myself into his chest. His arms wrapped around me, holding me. I didn't cry, but my body shook so violently he rocked us back and forth to calm me.

"Tell me," Croygen said. "The monkey was not making any sense and told me to get my ass here. Said something about the Viking being back? What is going on, Zoey? Is Ryker here?"

"Yes." It was only one word, but it broke the dam for the rest to follow. "He came back for me."

"Is that his blood?"

"Yes." I recounted the events of the whole day in a monotone cadence.

Croygen listened, his face not giving anything away. Sprig uttered comments, until I got to where Ryker was strapped to the bed. I glazed over the torture part, but Sprig still crawled away, hopping back into his cage and shutting the top.

He hated me too. He teased about disliking Ryker, but Sprig cared about him, and he wouldn't understand my cruelty. I couldn't understand it either.

"You had to." Croygen brushed at the hair sticking to the dried blood on my face. "You must do it for your sister. Ryker, out of anyone, would understand this."

"Doesn't make it better."

"Probably not." Croygen hands dropped. "If it was Ryker's sister, he would do it for her."

I lifted my face. "You know about his family?"

Croygen nodded.

"Yeah. One night when Amara was working, he got drunk and told me. I don't think he remembers he did." Croygen leaned his head back against the wall. Both of us still huddled in the corner. "But I know there is nothing he wouldn't have done for Madi, to save her life. You have a second chance with Lexie. He would never forgive you if you didn't take it."

Croygen was right. I knew Ryker would want me to save her. But taking the life of a man I didn't want to live without, for a sister I couldn't survive without, was my own ruin. Either way, I couldn't live with the outcome.

"I can see him resisting the oath." I let my head slide till it was on Croygen's shoulder.

"He's incredibly strong. He'll make it through this."

"No, he won't." I sighed. "He's dying. I can see it."

"Then even more he'd want you to fight for your sister."

"I know. It's what makes this harder."

"This is a perfect example why I don't let myself love." He pulled me tighter into his chest, contradicting his words.

"What about Amara?"

He tilted his head against mine. "We both know that isn't love."

When the tips of Croygen's boots slipped through the vent, disappearing back in the direction of his room, I wandered over to Sprig's cage.

"Hey, buddy?" I peered in. In the dark, I could see him curled in the corner, his rhythmic breathing moving his tiny body up and down. My hand traced over his back, which felt hot under my fingers. Fae didn't get sick often. Not unless something was really wrong, like an overdose of goblin metal. His hummingbird metabolism should work through it fast. I hoped he would be better in the morning. The testing, drugs, and lack of sugar had to be affecting him.

"I'm sorry. For... everything," I whispered, before drifting over to my bed. Guilt consumed me for bringing him back here. Neither of us came willingly, but the only reason he was here again was because of me. I plopped onto my cot, exhausted from the day. The dull reflection off my boots from the emergency light above the door took my full focus.

Please say you didn't, Ryker...

I could hope all I wanted, but my gut knew the truth. Still my stomach twisted around as I unlaced my right boot. Instinct picked that one first, luring me. With a tug, the boot slipped off my foot, falling to the floor. I leaned over, cupping the heel in my hand. Air stopped in my lungs as I tugged at the insert. It peeled away, the dark shadows disguising the depths of the hole. I tilted the shoe.

A stone rolled out on to the side. Oxygen flooded out of my lungs. *Hell.*

The smooth gray stone easily fit into a palm and looked nothing more than a rock you'd find on the beach. But I knew the truth. Without even knowing why, you were drawn to it. Its power was subtle and unassuming, calling you to pick it up, to curl your fingers around it, and to keep it forever. It was strange, but I felt it had been patiently waiting for me to finally acknowledge it was there.

It was alive like most fae-made things, and the stone knew the taste of my skin, my soul. It understood my weaknesses, my desires, the things that made me tick. It had known even before I did what I most desired.

And it could give it to me…

I lifted my hand, reaching out.

"No." I jerked my arm out of reach, shaking my head to clear it. I dropped the boot into my lap; the stone rolled back into the dark hole of my boot.

A sound escaped from the rock, a whisper of my name. *Zoey…*

No. You are not getting me, I replied in my mind. But the idea of taking hold of it was incredibly enticing. It sounded like a great idea to get all of us out of this mess... screw consequences. Except the outcome might be worse. I was scared enough of the deep anger I carried inside. It would use this rage and turn it against me, resulting in worse circumstances than I started with.

I was selfish but not arrogant enough to think I could let the stone take me without horrific effects. The last time I held the stone I saw how easy it could turn my mind, twisting my good intensions.

I tucked the insole back and dropped the boot to the ground, shoving my foot in. The weight of my awareness tripled the heaviness of the shoe. My attentiveness created anxiety and grappled with my nerves. *Would people notice?* Now that I knew, I felt everyone else would.

My head hit the pillow as I fell back, my hand rubbing at the tension across my forehead. Ryker did the smart thing keeping it far from Vadik or even Amara, but now the burden was mine. I crossed my arms and legs, closing my eyes, letting exhaustion override my mind. Sleep pulled me away from the world.

Zoey, you can't fight me forever. It's supposed to be you and me.

Together. I will take your pain away, give you everything you've ever desired.

The words wrapped around me and flooded me with images and feelings of happiness.

Would it really be that bad?

The lights blazed on, tearing me from dreams of Ryker, us relaxing on a porch with a beer, watching Lexie and Sprig play on the lawn together.

I swallowed the lump in my throat when reality flooded in. The realization of the truth of my life constricted my lungs. Ryker was below me, waiting for another round of torture and tests. Lexie was drugged beyond thought or feeling. Croygen would probably be used for parts, and Sprig and I were lab rats, forced to create a new line of superior humans and primates.

My gaze returned to my boot, and I sat with a snarl. The stone was no better than Rapava—a passive-aggressive bully, twisting my mind and emotions so much I didn't know which way was up.

My legs lifted me from the bed, Ryker's blood still covering me, and I strolled over to Sprig's crate. "You awake?" I asked, lifting the cover.

He was sound asleep, his body in the same position I left him the night before. I petted him, his skin still burning.

Hell. My stomach sank.

The door unlocked, swinging open. I jumped, turning to see Delaney strolling into the room.

"Good morning." She walked to the side table, setting down her tray of needles and fabric. "I brought you a new set of scrubs. I was told you needed a shower and new clothes before starting out this morning."

I nodded, walking back over to the bed. *Play the good soldier, Zoey. One more day.* I hoped this wouldn't be a phrase I would be saying months from now.

"He doesn't look well." I motioned back to the cage. Delaney uncapped the syringe and stabbed it into my neck.

"I will look at him later," she replied, not sounding at all concerned. She pulled out the needle and placed it back on the tray. "Let's get you cleaned up, some breakfast. The doctor would like you downstairs in an hour."

My molars ground together. Today was going to be difficult. That was probably a huge understatement. I stood and followed her down the corridor.

The shower washed away the red stains, but the clean top and pants only provided a new canvas to the abstract art I would be painting in fresh blood today.

At breakfast I stole extra honey, stuffing it into my sports bra. I needed to give Sprig some happiness. I didn't realize how much I counted on his innocence, humor, and joy to get me through. Without it I felt even more lost and defeated.

Delaney stayed with me till Liam came into the cafeteria to claim me. I followed him out at the same time Kate was coming in. Her eyes locked on mine. She kept her head down, letting her long white hair hide her full face. I couldn't read anything from her face, but the intensity of her gaze gave me a strange sense of security. Someone else was on my team.

"More testing today?" Kate stared at Liam instead of me.

"No, Rapava has her extracting from a fae instead. Kind of jealous." Liam smirked.

Kate's gaze darted to me, then quickly back to Liam. "Really?"

"Yeah. Surprise, surprise, but she's actually good at something." Liam tilted his head toward me.

"Zoey was exceptionally well trained." Kate's eyes found mine. "Daniel was good. One of the best." I felt the underlying meaning of her words wash over me.

Liam snorted. "So good he got killed."

"Do not speak of a fallen Collector that way." Kate's mouth pinched together. "You should understand what it feels like to lose a partner."

Liam took a step back, the truth of her words hitting him.

"Plus, it only adds to the nasty things we'll say about you when you're gone." Kate spun around and walked into the cafeteria, leaving both Liam and my mouths agape.

Holy shit! Did she just say that?

Liam's lids narrowed. "Crazy, bitch." He turned and stomped down the hallway.

I wanted to cheer, to clap, but I kept it inside. *I always liked her.* A sly smile peeked out of my façade. My smile quickly disappeared as Liam led me to the elevator. The doors opened at the bottom. Lexie and Rapava stood at the end of the hall.

A spike of joy at the sight of her rapidly plummeted when I realized why she was there. She was my cautionary tale. A tale where happiness would only ever be a faraway illusion while bits of my soul were ripped from me.

TWENTY-SEVEN

My eyes lifted, needing to see Lexie again. Her face was void of emotions; her eyes unfocused. Liam stood behind her, his hands on her chair, but his smug smile through the window told me those same hands could easily squeeze the breath from her throat.

I carved into Ryker's chest, going deeper into a cut that had almost healed. "Tell me, fae!"

Saliva dribbled out the side of his mouth, hatred burned in his eyes as he snorted and huffed through the agony.

"FUCK. YOU."

"Try again." I pushed the blade deeper. He was slipping from me, I could feel it, with every slice of my blade. His eyes became more and more distant as the blood oozed from his wounds. The killer in him was taking over.

Shards of pain shattered in my soul as my knife deepened. What was I doing to him? How could he ever forgive me? Would he? Or in my quest to save my sister, I'd lose him, both his life and his love?

He grunted in pain, spitting at my face.

My hand shook as I lifted it to my face, wiping it away.

"Are you all right, Zoey? You seem out of sorts today," Rapava said from across the table.

"I'm sorry if this bothers me," I snapped at him. "I was a seer, a Collector, not a torturer."

Rapava straightened up, his gaze moving over me.

"I am sorry you feel that way. I thought you would want to take revenge for what this... thing has done to you. Assaulting you. Demeaning you. Didn't he emotionally and physically abuse you? Mess with your mind so much you forgot who you were for a while?"

No, that's you, you bastard, I screamed in my head.

"And what are *you* doing, Doctor?" Ryker snorted, getting the irony as well. "You think your psychobabble is going to get her to stop pansying around with her baby nicks any more than it's going to get me to talk?" A gruesome smile crept over his mouth. In this moment, he was the Ryker I knew. Most of the time all I saw was the version of him that wanted to kill me. "Your hard-on for the stone is the only thing you will have in your hand tonight. Jacking off, alone, to another failed attempt." Ryker sneered with a strange chuckle. "How's the research going? Find the connection yet? Wonder why all the other subjects keep dying?"

Rapava rolled his jaw.

"Oh, did I hit on a nerve? You stupid fuck. You think you're so smart," Ryker mocked. "But you can't figure it out, can you? And you can't get me to talk. Pisses you off to no end, doesn't it? *Doctor*."

Rapava reached over and yanked the knife out of my hand. His eyes were wild with abhorrence. He jammed the blade into Ryker's side. A cry tore from my throat as blood spurted like a fountain and splashed my face. Ryker's roar rattled the room, slamming my heart faster in my chest.

Then Ryker started to laugh. The chilling, hollow guffaw drove into my heart, rippling goosebumps over my skin.

Rapava yanked out the knife with a zealous movement. Ryker's head fell back, his eyes fluttering shut.

"Wake up! You will tell us where the stone is." Rapava's face turned a deep shade of purple, holding the knife to plunge it again. Blood dripped along the blade, running in streaks down his lab coat.

High, pierced screams broke out from the other room, slamming further fear into my system.

Lexie!

My eyes darted to the other room. Lexie stood, her gaze going between Ryker and the bloody knife in Rapava's hand. Her eyes were wide, clear, and full of horror. She was awake. I could see the girl I raised, her true emotions not hiding behind the drugs in her system.

"Shut up!" Liam tried to push her back onto the chair, but she didn't seem to notice him, her focus fully on us. Lexie's legs couldn't hold against Liam's strength and buckled, banging her back into the chair, ceasing her shrill shrieks. The sudden silence filled the rooms with an unnerving sensation. Adrenaline, fear, and panic thumped in the air.

I took in a shaky breath.

"Get her out of here," Rapava yelled at Liam, dropping the blade on the table. He peered at the blood dripping off his lab coat and took in a controlled breath. "I will return." The doctor stiffly turned, heading out of the inner room. "Pick her up," Rapava ordered Liam, pointing at Lexie, his usual cool manner dissolving.

Ryker got to him like no other I had seen. Rapava never lost his temper. But Ryker hit the doctor's weaknesses. Rapava wanted two things, and neither were panning out. He was growing impatient and reckless.

I watched Liam pick up Lexie like a baby, her gaze on Ryker's form as he carried her to the door. Just as Liam took the corner, her eyes flashed to mine. Awareness and intensity showed in them. Then they disappeared around the corner.

Like a hawk, I tracked Rapava walking out the main exit, the door closing behind him.

I was alone. With Ryker.

I leaned over him, gently touching him. My heart needed to see if he was okay.

"Ryker?"

He stirred, his eyes blinking open.

"Ryker, I—"

His wrists were bound, but he was able to grab the bottom of my shirt, yanking me so hard I stumbled into him. He grabbed the collar of my top, bringing my face only an inch from his.

"When I'm free…" His voice was husky as his lips brushed against my earlobe. My lashes fluttered closed. Feeling him close made me forget everything outside of us. The danger only triggered my desire for him. "I am going to fuck you so hard." His hot breath billowed down my neck, between my breasts. I sucked in a sharp breath. "You want it, huh?" he whispered hoarsely, noticing my reaction. "You will be crying and begging me for more... to go deeper... you will be about to climax…" He nipped at my ear. I felt myself tightening, wanting to feel him inside. "And then…"

"Yes?" I whispered so quietly I barely felt my mouth move.

"I. Will. *Kill*. You."

I jerked back. His fingernails scraped my neck as he reached for my throat. Ryker's face only held disgust, his eyes distant. My feet backpedaled, stepping clear of his grasp.

"Human. You are *dead*," he barked, his head raising off the table. The restraints labored as he fought against them. He seemed unaware that every move he made only opened the wound on his side more. He grew more feral, saliva spraying from his mouth. But at the same time, he

197

moved like a robot—programmed.

Emotion I kept hidden all day bucked against the walls I constructed, cracking small holes. I turned and walked out of the room, tears edging the rims of my eyes.

"I. WILL. KILL. YOUUUUU!" Ryker bellowed. The determination in his words skated along my spine. I locked my teeth together, not wanting to let my emotions out.

I went through the main door, my body shaking.

The bell of the elevator rang, the doors opening. Liam stepped out, his gaze landing on me. "What are you doing?" Liam came out, walking toward me. "You can't leave. Dr. Rapava is coming back."

"I'm done for today." I stepped around him.

"That's not up to you." Liam grabbed for my arm. I swung around with a snarl, halting him in his steps.

"I. Am. Done. For. Today."

I leaned closer to Liam, stressing each word. He seemed to sense my seriousness and let go of my arm.

I whipped back around, walking into the open elevator. He moved alongside me. Without a word he returned me to my room, locking me in for the night.

I proceeded toward Sprig's cage, needing to see the little guy. The lid of the container squeaked and spilled in fluorescent light when I lifted it, peering in.

My heart sank to my knees. Sprig was still in the corner and appeared like he hadn't moved an inch. His form was curled in a ball, laboring in and out as he breathed.

"Sprig?" I reached down to touch him. "Buddy?"

The skin underneath his thick fur blistered with heat.

"Sprig?" My throat closed, trying to swallow the dread piercing my lungs like a dartboard. "I brought you honey." I tugged the packages from my bra. Maybe sugar would help him. I tore into one of the containers, placing it under his nose.

His nostrils flared and twitched, but he didn't open his eyes. Oh my god. My stomach plummeted like a roller coaster, then rose with nauseated panic.

I squirted the honey on my finger, pressing it to his mouth. Nothing. There wasn't anything that would keep Sprig from his honey. Zero.

"Buddy, come on." I lined his lips with the sugary substance, trying to entice him out of his deep slumber. When Lexie first came to us, she wouldn't eat. I rubbed applesauce along her lips to get her to lick it off and start eating. It had worked.

I hoped it would again. Seconds ticked by and Sprig did not respond to the honey. His breathing only grew more forced.

"No!" The word discharged from my mouth, my panic building to anger. "No, you have to be all right. Get up!" The blast of anger rapidly fizzled, plucking tears from my eyes.

"I can't take you too... please, Sprig."

His chest went up, faltering, before he breathed out.

Oh my god. He was dying.

My knees buckled and I slumped to the floor. "I can't lose you too," I whispered, the pain in my chest making it difficult to breath. "Please don't leave me."

The lights above my head flickered off, plunging me into obscurity. I looked at the dark lights. My chest filled, sweltering with fury. The switching off of the lights turned on my anger.

Fury at Rapava billowed inside me like a hot-air balloon. Rage at this place, at Ryker and Croygen for following me here, Sprig for getting sick, Lexie for going behind my back to contact DMG. Everything. But most of all myself. For letting it all happen. For being a victim again...

No. More.

I grabbed my foot, ripping off my boot with a lurch. My nails shredded as I dug at the insole, ripping it out of my shoe. The rock sat in the heel of my boot, looking innocent and docile.

"You want me?" I growled at it. "Fine. You can have me."

The rash stupidity of this nibbled at my conscience. A voice told me to stop, that I would only make it worse. But I shoved the thought back, tired of listening and playing the game. I was ready for recklessness. Anything to get us out of here, to stop the loss of all the people I loved.

I tipped the shoe, the stone rolled to the edge.

Zoey, stop! My gut screamed at me.

No, Zoey, this is what you want, the stone called.

There was no doubt who won as the gray rock plopped in my hand. The moment it touched my skin, it grabbed hold of me. I felt my head hit the floor.

"Zoey, I knew you'd come back for me. I felt our connection. I like you. You and I will do amazing things together." The stone's deep, soothing voice spoke into my head. "Do not doubt yourself. You made the right decision to say yes to me."

"But I haven't said yes."

"Yet," it responded. "But you will."

Flashes of images assaulted my brain almost too quickly to decipher. Finally it landed on one.

I stood off in the distance with Ryker, Lexie, Sprig, and Croygen beside me. The DMG building was on fire. The ground exploded and erupted as the surface below was bombed. Experimental animals ran off, escaping the blaze and running free. The prisoned fae fled for higher ground. Happiness filled me as I watched it burn. Every last paper, test tube, needle, piece of lab equipment, and document was destroyed. Rapava sat on his knees in front of it, his head in his hands as he screamed.

"Excuse me." I left my group, walking over to Rapava. He glanced over his shoulder at me, fear buried deep in his eyes. "It is done. You are done."

His lip curled. "You think so? I will start over, and I will only come back stronger. This war is not over."

"Yes, it is." I grabbed the sword at my waist, holding it how Ryker showed me, and swung. Rapava's head was sheared off his body in a spray of blood. I flung it into the dirt where it rolled away.

The image went black, the stone's voice coming back to me.

"But if that is too quick for you, Zoey, you can torture him like he has done to you and those you love."

"That option sounds good too."

"But he is only a drop in the bucket. We have far more to accomplish and do together. This doctor is nothing and only a bump in the road to our greatness."

More pictures of me emerged shaking hands on stage, accepting an award for advancements in the cure of disabilities and diseases.

"You can have a medical research hospital named after you. Think about all the lives you will save and the children and their families you can help."

The image changed. The ranch-style home with the pool it showed me once before came into view. The parents I never had, the friends, and kids were all back. This time Ryker was the one next to me, rubbing my belly with his baby inside. His arms wrapped around me as we watched Lexie play in the pool. Sprig sat on the patio table eating a bag of honey-coated mango chips, with a jar of honey next to him so he could dip them. Croygen lay on a raft in the middle of the pool, a beer in one hand, frowning as Lexie's splashes fell inside his drink.

It was everything I wanted. This was the picture which touched my heart the most. The stone pressed deeper into the fantasy, creating every detail so real and perfect it was like I was really there.

"One word, Zoey, and all the hurt is all forgotten. You will have everything you've ever wanted. You will never remember the pain or despair."

"Holy shit, Zoey!" A voice came from outside me.

I growled at the intruder. *No, not this time.* No one would take this away from me.

"Fuck! What is wrong with you? Wake up!"

The stone bored deeper into me, holding tight, flashing more perfect images of my life. Then suddenly I saw fire and destruction, watching the world burn, laughing. But before I could latch on to them, they were gone. The film flicked by faster and faster.

I felt a sharp sting to my face, my body being shaken. Then a pain crushed my hand.

I screamed and my hand unlocked, the stone falling away. My lids tore open, and I sucked in a gulp of air. Croygen stood over me, his foot on my wrist. The stone lay only a few inches from my fingers. My hand uncurled, automatically reaching out for the object.

"No." Croygen pressed his boot harder into my hand. Insert Viking instead of pirate here and I was having a full *déjà vu* moment. These guys always came and prevented me from saying yes.

"Get off me," I snarled, tugging at my arm.

"No," Croygen said again, shaking his head, his black eyes glowing enough they reflected. "Is that what I think it is?" He wasn't really asking a question, so I didn't respond.

"Fuck, Zoey, you had it this whole time?"

"Yes."

Croygen waited for me to continue.

"Ryker must have put it in my boot after I returned from Seattle," I said. "I didn't know I had it till the other day."

Croygen snorted. "That bastard is smart or plain lucky. He kept it safe and close and still concealed it from Vadik."

201

"Are you going to steal it now?" I retorted.

Croygen watched me, his head tilted. "Is that what you think?"

"You're a thief, aren't you?"

"I steal to sell for money, not to use it myself." Annoyance constricted his vocals.

"Really? You don't want it at all? Have all the riches and wishes you ever wanted granted?"

"It's not a genie in a bottle." He slipped his foot off my wrist but grabbed me under my arms, bringing me to my feet before I could react. "I grew up hearing the legends and cautionary tales of the four treasures of the Tuatha Dé Danann. They are not to be messed with. Their powers go beyond anything we could ever know... and not usually for good. They were hidden for a reason." He kept a tight grip on me, his gaze turning to the lump of rock on the floor. "I can't deny the draw of it. To have something that powerful in my grasp..." Croygen pulled away from me, rubbing his head. He swore under his breath. "Get it away from me now."

"What do you want me to do with it?" I tossed my arms up. "I am obviously no better with it than you."

"But you are." His head came up, looking at me. "You've carried it with you for months now. I've been near it five minutes and already want to cave. I don't have willpower like you do. You are stronger than you think."

"Ryker had it for years. In his boot. Every day," I replied. Both of us stared down at the rock.

"Yeah, we all know he's a god with steel nuts." Croygen rolled his eyes.

Thinking on how long Ryker carried it, was able to say no, and not give in to temptation gave me strength. He'd be pissed at me right now and tell me to suck it up and be strong. I rolled my shoulders back. Using my shirt, I picked up the rock and dropped it back in my shoe. I laid the sole back in and shoved the boot on my foot.

"There." I laced them tight, triple knotting them.

"Thank you," Croygen breathed out, collapsing back on my bed. We both continued to stare at my boot.

"It would be so easy," I whispered.

"Yeah. It would," he agreed.

Silence.

"Would the costs be that bad?"

"From what I've heard." Croygen leaned over his legs. "Yes, more than the benefits. The four objects were not designed for good. The weapons, like the spear and sword, are supposedly neutral and are only influenced by the owner's intention. They were made from light magic. The stone and the cauldron are not. They have their own agendas and were made from dark magic. They want to take and destroy. Whatever you think the benefit is, it will never outweigh the bad they bring. It is the one truth we fae are raised knowing. Whatever it has been telling you is a lie. Its willingness to help you is only for its own benefit. It will take your energy and use it against you, making itself even stronger. And you will die a horrible death."

He slid his fingers back through the sides of his temples, his hair slicked back in a bun. He and Ryker were the two men who could get away with a look like that. The style fit them, and they were even sexier with it.

"As a kid you think it's your parents trying to keep you in line." He clasped his hands together, his elbows on his legs. "The older you get the more you realize they should have made the tales even scarier." His gaze went to my feet again. "Fuck, I can't believe I am sitting in a room with the Stone of Fál. I grew up hearing about it but always thought it was more a legend. It's a little surreal and uncomfortably tempting."

"But you knew it was real. Ryker had it."

"Truth?" Croygen lips hitched up. "I thought he was full of shit, had something he thought was the stone, or was passing it off as the stone."

"I think he would have preferred that." I sighed, my mind wandering to the man only floors under me.

We both went quiet before Croygen flicked his head to the cage. "So why is he so quiet tonight? Don't think I've heard him this silent for so long... even when he's sleeping."

It was as if someone came up and wrapped their hands around my throat. I pushed myself up and walked to the table.

"He's sick." The words caught in my throat. I stroked his fur, his breathing still strained and uneven. The honey glistened on his mouth, left exactly where I put it. Tears tickled the back of my lids.

Sprig is dying.

Ryker was too, and the more he fought Rapava, the weaker he grew. Each stab wound, cut, and metal poisoning took him away from me, and my possession of his powers was doing enough on its own. I felt helpless. Any choice I made was the bad one. I loved him—more than I thought myself capable. But to sacrifice my sister? No, Ryker and I would never be, if that was the choice. If we survived this, he would probably want nothing to do with me anyway.

Lexie. Ryker. Sprig. Croygen. Me. All our lives were on the line.

"Croygen, I can't take this anymore. We need to get out. All of us."

The pirate lay back on my pillow, shoving his arms behind his head, and stared at the ceiling. "And how do you suppose we do that?"

I licked my lips, my feet shifting with frustration. "I don't know, but Sprig can't take any more testing... and Ryker... I can't hurt him anymore. He is not healing. And he is too fucking stubborn to stop provoking the doctor."

Croygen's head turned to me, one eyebrow crooked up.

I rolled my eyes.

"A mule does come to mind when I think of you two." He smirked. "Actually, I'm surprised you even got together. Like knocking blocks together."

"Croygen."

He swung up, thrusting his feet back on the floor. "What do you want to do? You tried to escape once before. Want to recall that major fail? Took you weeks to earn some sort of trust here. And look what you had to do to earn their confidence back. Dissect your boyfriend."

I rubbed my head at the cruel memories. The side of me which could turn off emotion and do what I needed to survive used to cause me pride. Now it scared me. What else could I do? How far could I go?

"Now the asshole is totally fucked up, physically and mentally... wanting nothing more than to kill you and is too hurt to help with the escape. Sprig is useless, and even if he were all right, his jailbird antics don't work against the goblin metal. Your sister can't run or even walk fast." Croygen held his arms up, swinging them like a conductor. "Say it with me, Zoey. We. Are. Screwed."

The truth of his words weighed me down. I hit the wall and slid to the floor. I let my arms and legs flop with defeat. I was trying hard to keep up hope and strength, but every day a little more was taken from me. Realizing the stone was not even remotely an option only stole the little breeze I felt in my sail.

I heard a sigh from Croygen, and I lifted my head to peer at him.

"I mean, *I am* known as the pirate ghost for a reason..."

A speck of hope flared in my heart.

"Ruthless, unbelievably handsome..."

I tilted my head to the side.

"Nightmare to my enemies, fantasy to wome—"

"Yes, we get it," I interrupted.

"There's no way out of the injections. Even without our powers we need to think of a way to escape." He stood and paced. "We at least have a card for the elevator."

I pulled my knees to my chest. "Ryker is being held on the bottom floor. The door is secured by an eleven-digit code. All I've been able to pick up is it ends with a four and nine."

Croygen stopped walking. "You're making this sound easier and easier," he huffed. "You sure we can't leave his ass here?"

I glared at him.

"Damn, the sex must be good."

I smiled in response.

"Please don't ruin my theory that at least he has a small dick. No one, not even a fae, should be as lucky as that bastard."

My smug grin only grew more.

"Fuck. Now I really want to ditch his ass." Croygen shook his head. "What women do for this fucker amazes me. Amara. You. I mean, this guy wants to kill you, and you still will do anything for him."

"I don't know if he *wants* to kill me."

"Don't fool yourself. I have never made a promise, but the obligation I felt toward him for decades was strong enough. I've heard the longer it goes unsettled, a promise becomes almost unbearable until you fulfill it."

I pushed myself into a standing position. "I am not leaving him, Croygen. That's final."

He sighed and rubbed his face. "Fine, but don't say I didn't warn you."

"Warning received. Let's move on to the plan."

Croygen crossed back to his bed and fell on it, the springs squeaking with the force. He leaned back, his shoulders against the wall, and pulled one foot onto the bed. "The plan, sweetheart, is for *you* to get the code... then we'll go from there."

"But it could be weeks," I retaliated. "He will die by then."

"He's a lot stronger than you think," Croygen said. "I've seen him come back from injuries in days that would disable other fae for years. He will come through. And if not, we have one less body to carry." He grinned.

Croygen was mostly talk when it came to Ryker. He might say he would leave him, but I knew he wouldn't. He would rather save Ryker and force him to pay through an obligation for the next several centuries.

"Okay, I will work on getting the code. You try getting another key card, in case we need to separate."

"Won't be too hard. The nurse, Delaney, has taken a slight liking to me. Slip one off her easy enough."

"Really?"

"Don't sound surprised. Human or fae... they all eventually succumb to my charms."

I snorted.

"What? You don't think I can seduce her?" He jumped off his bed and strolled to me. "There isn't a woman on earth I can't seduce."

"Really?" I taunted. "Me. Amara. Naming two."

"Amara is a work in progress." He put one hand by my head and leaned in, his face getting an inch from mine. I would be lying if I said my heart didn't jump a little. When he wasn't being "Croygen," he was an exceedingly sexy man, smoldering with bad-boy antics.

"You consider decades a work in progress?"

"Yeah, in fae terms, it's a short time."

"And me?"

His dark almond-shaped eyes became serious as he searched my face. "You...?" He inclined until his nose brushed against mine, tipping my head back. I stayed still as lips brushed against my jaw. "Let's see..."

Ryker had awakened something in me, a sincere pleasure to be touched, to let my walls down, which now would not go back. To let go.

The man in front of me was not the one I wanted, but I also wasn't dead. We'd been here more than a month, and the only touch I had received was either cold or violent. I swallowed as his finger traced down my neck. I couldn't deny it felt good. He was affecting me, but I was no fool. I understood this was only a challenge for him. A point he wanted to prove.

I had my own point to demonstrate.

I cupped his face and pulled him to me, my lips at his ear. Breathing heavy, I nipped at his ear. I could feel him lock up, his heart pounding as my mouth barely grazed his jaw. In his scrubs it was easy to see I was affecting him. I let my lips slide up his neck, back to his ear.

"If this is you trying to show me your skills, I might have to seduce the lab technician myself."

Croygen sucked in his breath. "Can I watch?"

"Ugh." I pushed him back. "Nice try."

"Worth a shot." Croygen shrugged, his smoldering expression falling from his face, replaced by that of the bored pirate I knew. "Can't deny it would be nice to have sex with someone besides myself in here... and stealing Ryker's girl would be a bonus."

"Such a pig."

"Pirate."

"Same difference."

TWENTY-EIGHT

The plan for the next day was set. Solid? No. But set. It was the lifeline I needed to hold on to. Action. Getting out of here.

I couldn't wait weeks to learn the code to Ryker's cell. It was time and options I didn't have. Only one person was on my side here who could possibly help me. There was a good risk I wouldn't see her, she wouldn't help me, or we'd get caught. None of it deterred me.

I proceeded to breakfast with resolve and a huge knot in my stomach. Sprig had awakened and eaten one of the honey packets but then fell back asleep. Very unlike him. Seeing his eyes open relieved me a bit, but he wasn't behaving like the Sprig I knew.

Delaney walked me to the counter where I got my usual coffee and bowl of oatmeal, stealing more honey, before sitting down. The staff was getting used to me being there and ignored my presence instead of staring.

My gaze was glued to the door, but when you wanted someone to come, they didn't. I pretended to eat. Each spoonful held a morsel of oatmeal and every bite I chewed slowly, hoping for Kate to walk in. I glanced at the wall clock, the ticking pounding in my ears. My eyes went back to the door, my breath caught as a woman walked into the room. Disappointment washed over me as the tall platinum blonde headed for the coffee machine.

"Come on, finish up. Rapava wants you downstairs in five." Delaney stood tapping at her watch. She took her tray over to the garbage.

Anxiety circled around the lump of oatmeal in my stomach. This was it. I was going to miss my chance to talk to her.

"Zoey, come on." Delaney walked to the table. "We need to go now."

Come on, Kate... please...

It was like my pleas went down the hall and dragged her back. She stepped around the corner, moving into the cafeteria. I straightened, wanting to leap out of my seat in excitement, but held myself back. The timing of her entrance with my plan had to be perfect and unnoticeable.

Her white hair was pulled in a messy bun, her glasses stuck in the mass on top of her head. She fluttered in, looking scattered. She moved to the coffee machine. I picked that moment to throw my breakfast away, tripping into her.

The tray crashed to the floor, spilling the leftover liquid from my paper cup on the floor.

"Oh, sorry." I grabbed her elbow, squeezing it. Then bent to grab my stuff.

"Let me help you." Kate followed me down. The eyes of the bystanders turned back to what they were doing.

"I need the code to where they are keeping Ryker," I whispered under my breath.

"I don't know those. Rapava doesn't trust me with them." Disappointment strangled me. It must have shown in my eyes. Kate pressed her lips together, pity flowering out of her face. "Okay, I'll get them for you."

"Tonight?"

She paused, taking in my expression again, then nodded. "I will do what I can."

"Where are they keeping my sister?" I muttered.

Kate grabbed some napkins, spotting at the coffee on the tile.

"She's on this floor. Opposite end. Near where Sera was kept."

I grabbed for the piece of trash in her hand and clutched her fingers in appreciation, taking it from her grasp.

I stood up. "Thank you," I said for everyone to hear. The audience never knew our conversation had dual meaning.

She nodded and rose. "You're welcome, dear." She walked around me to the coffee machine, never giving me a second glance. Delaney came to my side, ushering me out the door. The plan was taking shape. It felt good to do something. Even if it was minimal, it was something.

Again my elated mood only lasted till Liam met me and took me to the torture room. Ryker was black and blue from head to toe. Dried blood, deep cuts, and bruises covered his face and body.

"What happened?" I exclaimed. He had not been in this condition when I left the night before.

Rapava looked up, his face pinched. "The fae and I had a private little chat last night after you left."

So Rapava had beaten and tortured him relentlessly. I crammed back the piercing hatred I felt for the doctor. "Did you get anything from him?" I tried to keep my voice even, but my legs wobbled while strolling over to the bed.

A snarl crinkled Rapava's nose. "No."

Ryker was mostly unconscious, but Rapava still made me stay and watch him cut and take more blood from him. I think he either wanted me to see Ryker as a piece of meat, or he enjoyed the idea of forcing me to watch. I never let on it bothered me.

"Sir, I was hoping you'd let me have some time with my sister today."

"You've seen her every day," he replied, keeping his attention on the task.

"Yes, sir. She's been in the other room." *As an incentive for me to behave, you sick bastard.* "But I was hoping to have some time with her. Talk."

"Talk?" He laughed. "What would you need to talk about?"

The true bafflement in his voice made me realize he had no idea what a friend or confidant was. To talk, relax, or laugh with someone was a foreign idea. Did he really have no idea what it was to have friends? Did losing his siblings so young cause him to forget what it was like?

"Sir, she is my sister. I miss her. I simply want to see how she is."

"She is fine. You clearly can see she is well."

I took a long breath through my nose.

"Fine. You can have ten minutes with her."

"Is now all right?" I motioned to Ryker's motionless body. "I feel I am only in the way here."

Rapava dropped his arms to his side and his back went rigid. He stared at me for a long time, then nodded. "Yes. Go. But if he wakes up, I will have you come back."

"Yes, sir." I tried not to respond with the eagerness I felt to be able to talk with Lexie. "Thank you."

Liam did his duty, shepherding me to a neutral room to visit Lexie. I wasn't sure if they were keeping me from her room on purpose or didn't want me to know the location, probably both. But thanks to Kate, at least I knew the area where Lexie was being held.

Liam locked me in a room, returning a little bit later with a drugged-looking Lexie.

"Ten minutes," Liam said sternly and stepped from the room. The door wasn't fully shut, but I'd grab the slight privacy he gave us.

Lexie stared at the floor, lost in her dream world. She clung to her arm crutches, her legs bending more than usual. I wrapped my arms around her. She tottered to the side, and I steadied her.

"Are you all right?" I stepped back, looking her over again. Either she was dosed higher with drugs or her legs were hurting her.

"Yes." She nodded, her eyes remaining on the floor. A twitch flicked across her face.

"Lexie? Look at me." I cupped her chin and pulled it up. "What's wrong?"

Her dark eyes went back and forth, not able to fully land on me. "I am fine. Thank you, Zoey." So formal and distant. Not her words or her voice.

I was sick of this. Here stood another person Rapava was taking from me. She was in there, but the drugs wouldn't let her out.

"Lexie?" I didn't know what to say, or how much I could say. What if Rapava asked her to repeat what I said to her and she had to obey. "Remember when we'd go shopping for sneakers?"

Lexie stared at me, then she nodded so slight I almost didn't notice it.

"You liked your pair of sneakers, huh?"

Her lids blinked, but I felt there was something in her eyes. I wanted her to understand, to get my meaning. When I was fifteen and she was six, I tried to be out of the house as much as I could but felt bad leaving her behind. On the nights I let her come, I'd tell her it was time to go sneaker shopping. Joanne probably wouldn't have cared, but I liked the idea we were getting away with something. We'd go to bed dressed and fold her wheelchair and toss it out the window into the bushes, then sneak out for the night.

A pair of sneakers. It was silly, but when I let her tag along, it always made her happy. Lexie's smile was worth the eye roll and heavy sighs from my friends when I brought her.

She gripped her leg braces. "Sneakers?" Her face gave nothing away. I didn't know if she understood my true meaning or her robot-self was asking the question. Her legs bowed and she fell to the side. I grabbed her and balanced her on her feet.

211

"Lexie?" Something was wrong with her; I could feel it. She could barely stand.

"Pair. Of. Sneakers…" She turned her face to mine and whispered, her eyes wide. "Zoey, he—"

"Time's up." Liam swung the door open, sauntering in.

"No," I blurted out. *What was she going to tell me?*

"Yes. Rapava said ten. It's ten." He motioned at Lexie. "Come on. It's time to return to your room."

Lexie's mouth pressed together, and she glanced between Liam and me before nodding. Liam led her out.

Ten minutes. That was the extent of Rapava's mind-controlling drug. It was why he wouldn't let me be with her any longer and why every time, right as she was taken away, I could see glimpses of Lexie underneath the haze.

After tonight, I would get more than the ten minutes.

For good.

TWENTY-NINE

Rapava did not request my return when Liam came back for me, and I was all for returning to my room. Seeing Ryker in his weakened state generated an ugliness in me. Instead of wanting to be near him, I wanted to be the farthest away from him I could. Loving him only compelled me to hate myself more.

"Liam," a woman called from behind us as we strolled down the hallway. We both glanced back. Delaney jogged up, her pink shoes flashing brightly against the stark white tile and the blue scrubs she wore. "I think I heard Peter was looking for you, something about training, and finding you a new partner."

Liam's expression darkened before he cleared it away. New partner? No matter how much I hated Liam, losing Sera had to be hard on him.

"Do you know where he is?" Liam asked.

"Uh... I think... the training room." She shrugged. "Sorry, I heard it from Kate."

My head jerked up hearing her name.

"Ah." Liam nodded in understanding. "Okay, I'll find him after I return her."

"I can do it," Delaney volunteered. "I was heading to check on PE-One anyway."

"Cool. Thanks." Liam stepped away from us, probably happy to get away from babysitting me. Delaney and I watched him disappear around the corner.

The moment he disappeared, her mood shifted. She grabbed my arm, her body curving closer.

"In case anyone is watching, keep your head straight and do not react."

Adrenaline filled my veins, like an IV drip. My mouth dropped open to speak, but I quickly snapped it shut.

"Good thing Kate is known to be flaky and scattered. Liam will never question it when he finds Peter was never looking for him."

A new player in the game just stepped on board.

"Are you—?"

"Shut up, Zoey." Delaney's nails dug into my arm. "Wait till we are back in the room." We walked stoically back to my room. She unlocked the door, walking me in, and shut it behind her.

"Wha—?"

"I'm with Kate," Delaney interrupted, answering the question on my tongue.

Trust was still a dicey thing for me. My face must have given away my doubt because Delaney dug in her pocket and pulled out a piece of paper. "She told me you wouldn't believe me unless I showed you this." She held out her hand.

I stepped hesitantly forward, snatching the bit of paper, my gaze staying on her till I had the document in my hand. My eyes drifted from left to right. On the paper was written: 54267790149.

"Memorize it." She shifted on her feet nervously. "I will be destroying it before I leave here."

"Is this…?"

"The code to get into the room downstairs? Yes. The number backwards gets you into the inner room."

A mix of hope, joy, and fear danced a jig on my chest. *Kate did it. She got the code for me.*

My happiness was crushed by paralyzing terror. We'd eliminated one hurdle, but many huge ones still lay before me.

"I've been with Kate since the beginning. I may not care for fae, but I do not believe in the practices Dr. Rapava is carrying out. The treatment of Sera, of you…" Delaney folded her arms over her chest. "Even of that one." She nodded toward the cage on the table. "I gave him an injection to flush out the toxins. He should be better."

"Sprig?" I turned and rushed to the cage and lifted the top. I sucked in my breath, fearful of what I might find.

He sat in the same corner, but his eyes were open. He hugged his tail like he used to do with Pam, when he needed comfort. I didn't check my reaction, only scooped him up, and held him next to my heart.

"Sprig…" I cuddled him, kissing the top of his head. "You scared me."

He nuzzled into me, rubbing his head against my top. Plastic crinkled and he stopped, pulling away. His finger poked at the top of my sports bra. "Honey tits?"

I burst out laughing. "What did I tell you?"

"Sorry. Is honey melons any better?"

"No." I shook my head.

"Nectar juice boxes."

"Stop."

"Sugar suckies."

"You're feeling better, huh?"

"I will." He stabbed at the hidden packages again, his eyebrow lifting.

I tugged them out, setting him back on the table and opening one for him. He snatched it from my hand and curled around it, sucking the honey out of the top.

I spun back around. Delaney's nose was wrinkled, her face repulsed by what she saw. She noticed me staring at her.

"I'm sorry." She cleared her face. "I'm not used to seeing *us* interact with *them* like this."

"I am one of them."

"You know what I mean." She watched Sprig lick the honey out of the container. "I hate what Rapava is doing, but I still don't feel comfortable around fae."

I could understand the notion, or at least I could remember the feeling. Once upon a time. I couldn't believe I had ever felt strange around Sprig. He was home to me. My world could not exist without him.

"I understand, but against whatever DMG tries to shove down our throats, fae have feelings. They have families, they love, laugh, get hungry, and have addictions." I motioned back to Sprig. He was trying to tear open a new honey packet, his tongue between his teeth, struggling. I knew honey would end up on the ceiling and all over him. I walked backward to the table, my attention still on Delaney, as I took the item from him, ripped it open, and set it back in his hands. "Just like us."

A smile hinted on her lips. She tugged at the badge holder around her neck, pulling it out from underneath her top. Her tag and a key card were clipped onto it.

"Give this to your friend." She handed me the card. "I think he was trying to get it from me earlier today."

I pinched my lips together and tried not to smile as I took it. Croygen failed to seduce and steal it from her? The infamous ladies' man and legendary thief? *Oh, I will never let him live this down.*

"Kate told me to be watchful of him. He was a devious one."

215

"You could say that."

She glanced at her watch. "I better go. I'll need the paper back. I need to know it's destroyed." She held out her hand.

I repeated the number over and over in my head, locking it in my memory, and handed it back to her.

She crinkled the paper in her fist. "Kate wanted me to tell you good luck. She wished she could do more."

"She's done a lot. Thank her for me." I paused. "If I need to contact her again?"

"She'll find you." Delaney turned for the exit. Kate knew more about the fae world than anyone, but I still didn't like leaving without knowing how to communicate with her later if I needed.

"Oh, I forgot." She dug into her pocket, pulling her hand out. "Here." I opened my palm as she dropped a couple of pills into my hand. "They are the highest potency you can get. You should not take more than a half... or a person can lose all bodily control." Her eyes were set with underlying meaning.

"I understand." I rolled my fingers around them and shoved them into my sports bra.

She curved back for the door. "Be careful."

"I will," I replied. "And thank you, Delaney."

She looked back at me, gave me a nod, and walked out. Her footsteps moved away from my room. She never relocked the door.

"Are there more?" Sprig licked at his fingers, the empty packages strewn around him.

"No. Sorry." I went over to him, rubbing his head. The dose of sugar didn't drive him into a tailspin sugar rush, which worried me. He still didn't look well. His eyes lacked spark, and his skin was still warm under my touch. But it was better than before; I would take it.

"I'd feel loads better if I had about ten more of those and Izel's pancakes." He blinked, staring at me with hope.

"Sure, I'll be right back."

"You're intercoursing with me again, aren't you?"

216

THIRTY

When the lights went out for the night, I put Sprig on my shoulder and went for the panel in the ceiling. Croygen's room was closer to where we needed to go.

The eerie dark coated us, tensing my muscles as I slipped silently through the vents, Sprig holding tight to my neck. He was still not himself, staying quiet and holding on to his tail for security. I needed to get him away from the testing and injections. His little body couldn't handle the constant examination and doses of goblin metal.

If anything happens to him. I shook my head, not letting myself think past that.

"Feels strange tonight," he mumbled next to my ear.

I bit my lip. He was right, the space held a density, a peculiar vibration in the air, like it knew something was going to happen tonight. My nerves rubbed against my skin, feeling raw and exposed.

We both stayed silent after that, scooting in and out of vents, making our way to Croygen's room. I opened the last vent, letting my legs shimmy down from the opening, touching a ceiling rafter.

The moment I dropped from the flue, I sensed a figure behind me. A gasp burst from my lungs as a large hand went over my mouth, clogging the cry in my throat. A body pressed into mine, an arm slipped around my stomach, pulling me in. My heart slammed in my chest as hot breath went down my neck.

"Rendezvous in the rafters. Kinky. I like it."

My elbow went back into Croygen's stomach. He stepped back with a heavy exhale, his arms dropping from me. "Figures you like it violent."

I whirred around, whispering hoarsely. "You scared the crap out of me."

"Now that is a level of kinky I never got into."

"Croygen," I sighed.

"Guess we should have set which room we were going to meet in." Croygen straightened, still rubbing the spot where I hit him. "Need to work on our organization skills."

"So, we probably shouldn't open a party planning service together yet."

Croygen snorted. "There are a lot of things we should never open together."

I could feel the underlying meaning soak his words.

"How did getting the card key go for you?" I lifted my eyebrows. "How fast did you seduce the nurse? Minutes? Seconds?"

Croygen folded his arms, his chin dipping to the side. "Uh, let's say her hatred of fae made it a tiny bit harder than I thought."

"You didn't get it?"

"Not exactly."

"It's a yes or no."

"Then... no."

"I know." I smirked, digging into my waistband.

"You know?" A shocked look of fear flickered over his face. He was probably worried I had found out he wasn't the stud he praised himself to be.

I tugged out the two cards from my pants, holding them up. "It seems I did better getting them from her than you."

"Oh, I get it. She *likes* you." He nodded as if it confirmed why he lost.

"No." I shook my head and smiled smugly. "I'm simply better."

His lids narrowed, snatching the card I held out to him. "I had a lot going against me."

"Sure." I winked.

Croygen huffed, irritation shifting his feet on the beam. "Where's the hamster? You leave his ass behind?"

"Screw you, ass bandit," Sprig mumbled from under my hair.

I automatically reached up, stroking his fur soothingly.

"He's not doing well. Unusually quiet. It's another reason I have to get all of us out of here."

"You mean there's a volume switch on him?"

I almost wanted to laugh. Croygen sounded so much like Ryker then. Of course, the thought of the man downstairs only inflicted sadness that weighed my limbs down.

"What happened there?" Croygen's voice was low, pointing at my face.

"Nothing. Let's get our plan set and go. We have no time to waste."

"Okay, boss, what's the plan?"

"First we go get my sister." I placed my hands on my hips. "She's near where Sera was." Croygen didn't know where that was, but I was saying the plan out loud more for me than anyone. "There are a couple of fae security scanning machines to watch for."

"When they were bringing me down here, we went through a huge one at the top level." Croygen nodded. "To stop it from going off, they punched in a number before I went through and after. Turning it back on."

Frustration gurgled from my throat. "We have no way around it. Our only exit is up the elevators and out the main doors."

Croygen rubbed his face.

"We go out together. Let it go off." I shrugged.

"I'll go with you to get your sister," Croygen said. "You guys go up and hide. I will go get Ryker and bring him back. Then we run."

"Sounds so easy."

"Not even close."

"I feel I should go with you to get Ryker. I know the code to get into the room."

"Then tell me, because you aren't getting anywhere near him. He wants to kill you."

"There are times Ryker, *my* Ryker, was present."

"I am not taking the chance."

Finally I consented. "Fine. Sprig will go with you."

"What?" Both boys responded.

"Sprig, Croygen needs eyes and ears getting Ryker out." I grabbed at his tail, petting it. "Don't you want to help Ryker?"

Sprig sighed, laying his head on my neck. "Okay, only so I can annoy the Viking again. I miss that."

"If you help Croygen, and we get out of here, I am sure he will let you annoy him anytime you want."

"But he can't like it." Sprig sat back on his heels. "That will take all the fun out of it."

"I have confidence you will be sure he doesn't," Croygen said snidely.

"The buttaneer will be leaving us soon, right?"

"Why?" A grin hinted on Croygen's mouth. "When I bring you so much happiness."

"Happiness?" Sprig sputtered.

"Oh right, that's mine." Croygen winked. "Your irritation is *my* joy."

"All right." I twisted on the flashlight beam, heading for the venting system, which would lead us to Lexie. "Let's go."

Croygen followed, lifting me to climb into the duct.

"Whatever's ahead of us? Thank you." I looked back at him. "For being here. For saving my life."

"I haven't saved it."

"Yes, you did." I glanced between him and Sprig. "Both of you did."

The unknown before us was staggering, as was the amount of danger we were stepping blindly into. The peril gripped me, almost forcing me immobile. But the strength of the two next to me and the love for the others kept me moving and led me down this road of jeopardy.

I now understood what it felt like to have family. To truly love. People you would fight and die for no matter the outcome.

Croygen let go and I dropped to the ground, Sprig's tail wrapped around my neck. The nightlight in the corner flushed the room with distinct silhouettes.

"Lexie?" I whispered her name as I walked to the bed. A sick feeling formed in my stomach as I replayed how I had walked to Sera's bed in the same fashion. Lexie's thin frame was lost under the covers in the same way. She lay on her back, stone still. The only indication she was still alive was the slight rise and fall of her chest under the blankets.

Croygen's weight landed in the spot I just vacated.

"Lexie?" I called softly again, my hand urging her awake. She didn't move. The dread in my gut only amplified. I shook her a little harder. "Wake up."

Lexie had never been a heavy sleeper. I learned that from the many times I snuck back into our room late. She was a pain to get out of bed, but she usually woke easily, then would grumble and turn away from me.

I jiggled her more forcefully. "Lexie, get up." Her lids didn't even flutter.

My gaze shot nervously over my shoulder to Croygen. He stepped to the bed, taking over trying to stir her.

Nothing.

"What is wrong? Why won't she wake up?" My heart thumped

loudly in my ears.

Sprig leaped down beside her, poking at her cheek. His nose tipped up and wiggled, like he smelled something.

"Calm down." Croygen moved me out of the way, inspecting Lexie closer. He prodded her lid open, looking at her eyes. Sprig leaned over waving his arms in front of her eyeball. "She's severely drugged." Croygen clicked his tongue. "I mean elephant tranquilizer drugged. The kind you find yourself naked and tied to an anchor."

I didn't want to know.

"Why?" I asked out loud, but it was more my brain trying to understand. Was this something they did only tonight or something they did every night?

"What do you want to do?" Croygen turned to me.

"What do you mean? We're not leaving her." My voice rose an octave.

"I wasn't saying that." He placed his hand on my arm. "I was thinking you can't carry her, unconscious."

Lexie's comatose body hindered our plan. She was thin but taller than me. I knew I wouldn't be able to get her out on my own and if anything happened, we'd be doomed.

"You take her. I will get Ryker."

Croygen moved his head back and forth. "No way."

"It's the only way."

"The man wants to kill you, Zoey."

"I'll simply have to make sure he doesn't." I touched Lexie's hand, her skin clammy. "The real Ryker is in there. I've seen it, and I know the setup."

"Zoey, you're being stupid."

"What do you suggest?" I hissed. "We don't have another choice. You get Lexie out of here, no matter what. She is my priority. I will deal with Ryker." Croygen opened his mouth, but my expression clamped it shut.

"Wow, he can be trained not to speak." Sprig crawled back up my arm, sitting on my shoulder.

"Like you should talk. You're like the Energizer Bunny with a mouth."

I shot daggers at both, silencing them. "The plan is still the same, except it's me getting Ryker." I tapped Sprig's tail. "Sprig will be my lookout. You use the key card and get Lexie as far as you can. Get her to the upmost level next to the security alarm. But if you hear anything, or sense anything, you take her and run."

"I'm not leaving you."

"You. Take. Her. And. Run. You got that?" I practically growled.

He exhaled through his nose with irritation but nodded.

I turned back to Lexie and pulled the blankets off her body, preparing to let Croygen pick her up.

I ceased breathing.

"Holy shit." Croygen jerked back, and Sprig emitted a high squeak.

Horror curdled in my stomach, screams stacked on my tongue. My eyes did not want to believe what they were seeing.

From the knees up, she was the girl I loved and raised. Wild curly thick hair, dark creamy skin. She always looked like an angel. When she slept. Awake was a whole other story. The girl had a mouth and personality on her that was vibrant and unfiltered.

Now everything below was not the same girl. Where her crippled, twisted legs used to be were now someone else's. The legs were pasty white and more muscular than Lexie's twelve-year-old frame. They started just below her kneecaps. The deep caramel tint of her skin opposed the pale color of the foreign legs.

"That's fucked up." Croygen stretched out, touching Lexie's new toes.

I wanted to throw up. I always thought when Rapava wanted to cure diseases and disabilities it was with shots of magic or medication extracted from fae. Sprig was my first notion this was not the case. Rapava did not care about healing. He was making, with bits and pieces, his new human race.

"They're not fae." Croygen touched the attached legs.

"What?"

"They're human."

"Are you sure?" My seer gift was picking up a very dim glow from Lexie.

"Yes."

"He's right. I can smell human." Sprig leaned over, sniffing again. "But there is magic in her blood system." That was why I was getting a faint glow.

I stared at the legs. He was using human parts? Not fae? In his mission to save the human race, he was now sacrificing them. He would say it was for the greater good.

222

Sacrifice a few for the many...

My eyes caught on a tiny mark on the snowy-white ankle. I leaned in, my fingers sweeping over a small *SG* tattoo by the heel in blue, yellow, and red. *Super Girl*. My memory flashed to the cape in the closet I found, when Croygen and I were hiding. I swallowed back bile creeping up. A thought blistered in my mind. *No.* I looked back to Lexie's face. I didn't have time to think about anything but our escape. All of this would take some time to sort out. Time we didn't have.

"We'll deal with this later." I nudged Croygen and wrapped Lexie with a blanket. He stepped up, sliding his arms under her body. She draped limply over his arms.

"She looks like a soggy burrito." Sprig snorted, then covered his mouth when I glared at him.

Croygen tucked her into his chest, and I ran ahead of him to open the door. I peeked out. The silent hallway felt like it was strung with watching eyes and traps.

"Okay. I'm heading down. Please, don't come for me... get her out. If the pledge means anything to you, save her life. Not mine."

"Doesn't work like that."

"Please, Croygen."

He stared at me. Then suddenly he leaned over and kissed me. Surprise whisked the air from my lungs. His lips were tender but ardent against mine, capturing the intensity of the moment. He pulled back a breath, his dark eyes sternly looking into mine. "Get out. Whatever it takes. Even if you have to leave him."

"Doesn't work like that."

"Now you understand." He smiled and whirled around, jogging for the elevator. Lexie's limp form bobbed up and down.

I watched him round the corner and sucked in my breath. "Hell." I turned the opposite way, heading for the other elevator. Croygen and I had been through a lot together. We had built a friendship, a bond no one could break. And this was probably more than he had ever let himself feel for a woman in a long time. If ever.

"The scally-wanker better keep his mouth and other body parts to himself from now on," Sprig griped in my ear.

I ignored him, reaching the elevator doors. I took in a shaky breath.

"You ready?" Sprig asked.

"Are you?"

"For hell?" His tail circled my neck. "Eye, Matty."

This could end badly in so many ways. More ways than it could end well.

"Let's go get our Viking asshole." He lifted his arm in a battle cry.

"Shhhh," I hushed.

"Let's go get our Viking asshole," he repeated in a whisper this time, raising his arm with less gusto.

Every step I took I tried to ignore the growing anticipation a net was about to come down on me, that I was walking into a trap.

As a human or fae, I was a fighter.

And this fight I had to win.

THIRTY-ONE

The elevator doors opened. Through the darkness the lights of the lab equipment and monitors sparkled like alien stars. I slipped against the wall and walked as quietly in my boots as possible down the hallway. My neck was damp with nervous sweat, while the code numbers continuously looped in my head.

A panel next to the elevator lit up, sensing motion. Hell. This was probably another trap. A way to monitor people coming and going. I filled my lungs and held my breath. It was too late to turn back now.

"When I go in, I need you to stay out here and keep guard, okay?" I whispered to Sprig.

He held up his thumb and hopped off my shoulder onto the ground, keeping to the shadows.

Okay, this was it.

I punched in the eleven-digit number. The panel blinked in response.

I cringed when the door beeped. The lock releasing sounded like a ton of bricks falling into a metal dumpster in the silent corridor. Giving Sprig one last nod, I opened the door and slipped into the room.

The outer room blushed an eerie yellow from the emergency lights along the floor base. The code to Ryker's cell was the same code backward. No sooner had I hit the last number than the green panel beeped, releasing its hold.

Nerves in my stomach twisted. I hadn't let myself think about actually being alone with him. Croygen warned me, but circumstances and my stubbornness won out. Again, I was far too deep to turn back now.

I crept into the inner room, shutting the door behind me. If someone came, I'd hear the door beep, giving me a little warning to hide.

It took me a moment for my eyes to adjust to the solid blackness of the inner the room. Eventually the glow from the emergency lights from the other room bled, giving an outline to the objects in the room. There wasn't much here, only a bed and some medical equipment. The darker mass of Ryker on the gurney loomed in the middle of the room. His labored breath, like someone in pain, reached my ears.

Emotion took hold and I rushed to his side, my fingers finding his face. Tears filled my eyes as I touched him, my heart slipping into my gut, thrashing around like a wounded bird. "Please be all right." What if we went too far? What if today was simply too much, and I had killed the man I loved?

By having his powers, you already have, Zoey, I thought.

"Ryker, open your eyes." My hands slid along his jaw, cupping his face. His grown-out stubble scratched my palms. Touching him now was different. Before, I had only been a husk, not letting myself truly experience what it felt like to have him near again.

He stirred under my hand, a slight moan coming from his throat. I leaned in closer and saw his lids blinking, trying to open.

"Ryker, wake up. We need to get out of here." Not thinking, I unhooked the cuffs on his arms. Freeing him. His eyes opened, his white eyes glowing in the darkness. Absent eyes landed on me like we were strangers.

He sat abruptly. My arms dropped, and I took a step back. He still only wore the gray scrub pants, and his chest continued to leak blood and pus from both new and old gashes. Wounds I gave him.

"You come back for more, *human*?" Disgust twisted the words, his eyes cold and remote. "Carving me up in the day isn't enough for you?"

"Ryker, it's me."

"I know who you are." He swung his legs down and stood up, his body moved like a coiling snake. "I've been waiting to be alone with you for a while."

This man wasn't Ryker. A shiver ran down my back. *Shit.*

"Ryker. It's me, Zoey." I focused on linking our names, making a connection. Deep down, I believed in those rare moments we had shared, the times his eyes cleared. I felt if he really saw me, he would be able to override the promise.

I was extremely wrong.

"Your name will mean the same to me dead or alive." His voice was void of feeling. "Nothing." He fisted his hands, taking a step.

"Fight it, Ryker. I know you are under there somewhere." I backed up, while out of the corner of my eye, I saw Sprig peek through the gaps of the blinds, tapping the window.

Ryker didn't even flinch. "All that's in here." He pointed to himself. "Is a demon. Well, half—on my father's side." He took a step, drawing my attention back to him. For every step he took, I took two back.

Father? Demon? What was he talking about? He didn't know who his father...

Oh no. No. No. No. An image of two blond men came into my mind. How did I not see it before? The similarities between them became glaringly obvious. The body frames, strong jaw lines, the Nordic likenesses.

"Vadik?" My mouth dipped open.

A gruesome smirk turned up Ryker's mouth. "And this half-demon has made a promise to kill you, human."

We moved at the same time. I went for the door. He bolted for me, reaching me as the door handle rolled in my hand, slipping through my fingers. His hand wrapped around my throat, and he threw me back against the wall next to the door.

"Ryk—" My mouth opened to speak, but he squeezed down, cutting off my words. With a grunt he slammed me again, ripping the air from my lungs. My fingers went to his hands, clawing at them. *"Ry-ker..."*

His lids fluttered, and his glassy eyes sparked with life. His hand loosened around my throat, giving me a gulp of air.

"Zoey." He blinked, his voice low. He dropped me to my feet, his hand falling to the dip at the base of my collarbone.

"Yes," I whispered hoarsely, ignoring my burning throat. "Stay with me." I reached out for him. The instant my hand touched his face, his eyes slammed shut, like it burned his skin.

"I can't fight it," he whispered.

"Yes. You can." I drew him closer to me, tipping his forehead against mine, hoping contact with me would help keep him centered. "Remember we do whatever it takes to live and be together. That's the love I want with you. Whatever the outcome. We fight," I said, suddenly reminded of similar lines I said to Ryker in a dream.

He jerked his head up, sucking in air. He blinked, his brows dipping in puzzlement.

Fearful of losing him again, I wrapped my arms around him. "Feel me, Ryker. Remember us. We are more powerful together." My hands drifted over his back, running up and down his body. The scars, open wounds, and dried blood were jagged under the tips of my fingers.

He breathed out, letting his body fall against mine, pressing my back against the wall. In an instant, his hands moved under my top, roughly grazing my skin. His touch was fire to my system. A barely audible groan escaped my mouth.

His touch grew more eager, pulling me into him. Through the thin cloth I could feel him as he brushed against me. Every bit of him. Wanting me. The friction of the fabric as he moved against me sent heat into my stomach, moving lower.

This was not the time or place. *At all*. But I couldn't seem to stop.

His arms went around my ass and pulled me up, my legs wrapping around his torso. He moaned, slamming our bodies back into the wall, his lips crashing down on mine.

Desire exploded in my body. Tuning out the voice warning me to stop, to use this time to get away. But the months of separation, the weeks of pretending to hate him, the guilt of torturing him... it now consumed me, needing an outlet.

He bit down hard on my lip, drawing blood. The pain only triggered more craving for him. I wanted him now. Our breaths became frantic as our mouths moved together with need.

He yanked his head back, his tongue sliding over his bottom lip. He reached to his mouth, blood pooling on his finger. My blood. His gaze went to my mouth. He leaned forward; his tongue slowly licked my broken lip. He watched me as he trailed my mouth. A blaze of need pounded between my legs.

Ryker drew back, swallowing. His eyes glinted, a rumble rolled from his chest, sounding wild and threatening.

It was instant, the shift. The taste of my blood.

"Ryker...?"

A growl flared from his throat. His muscles tightened under me. He pinned my body harder against the wall with his, grabbing my face forcefully. With a snarl, his hands slid down to my neck.

"Ryker. Don't—" My plea cut off as his hands compressed around my neck. A thumb rubbed softly over my vocals. Then his eyes flared, a strangled cry wrenching out of him, full of pain. I saw him fully leave me. The curse battling for dominancy.

And winning.

He grunted. His shoulders grew, expanding with power. The thumb which had caressed my skin was now pushing into my throat. My mouth gaped for fresh air, which would not come. Spots dotted my vision as I fought against his hold. Like a cat put in water, I clawed, kicked, and hissed, but he did not relent.

"A promise is a promise." He drew close to my ear, nipping. "And I never break my promises."

He was going to kill me. It was exactly what I asked him to do, but I was no longer willing to go. Instinct to survive was ingrained deep, and when it came down to the moment, I fought. For myself. For him. For Lexie, Sprig, Croygen, Daniel... for the girl who was still trapped in Duc's warehouse being used as an escort. For all the lives Rapava was destroying or would.

A heaviness gripped my brain, tugging sleepiness into my mind. My sight drifted down a dark ravine into blackness.

The sleeping pills, Zoey! My gut cried at me. But my brain and body were no longer communicating. I tried to fight, to hold on, but I felt my limbs wilt and go limp at my sides. *No!*

I didn't want to go out this way. If I were going to die, I wanted to be far away from DMG, where I knew my loved ones would be safe.

Anger punched my abdomen. All Ryker and I had been through, the love we finally found and let in. Was this how our story was going to end?

It felt life was mocking me again. Daniel's death had been horrible, but this was vindictive and cruel. Memories of Ryker and me flashed in my head, our bodies intertwined, discovering each other. The moment by the creek in Peru where he told me about his past, when I realized I was falling for him. The night he curled up behind me because I had a bad dream. When he kissed me in the rain. The night he snuck into the closet while Amara was across the hall. Putting a birthday candle in the loaf of bread for me.

Every moment played out in my head with the man I fell for.

I held no blame or anger at Ryker as I felt my life slip from me. This was my doing. The only fury I could feel was at myself, for forcing him to do this, something he would have to live with.

I think we all wish for that epic ending, where everything is resolved and our death would have meaning. This was not the case.

A tear slipped down my face. A sorrow for what could have been.

The loss of hope and happiness.

And because my love wasn't strong enough. This time we couldn't fight and win.

I had lost.

Everything.

Not something I was good at.

I heard a strange pop as my life slipped across the divide into nothingness.

**From Burning Ashes
Collector Series #4**

This war is not being played on a battlefield.

Killed by the man she loves, not even death is kind to Zoey. Neither life nor her fae powers will let her go in peace

In this final installment, Zoey's strength, determination, and trust are put to the ultimate test. In the fight to protect the people she loves and stop DMG from experimenting on fae, humans, and animals to create super soldiers, she learns the reality of how far Dr. Rapava will go to achieve his ultimate mission.

Of course, Rapava is not the only one willing to go to extremes. The demon, Vadik, is hunting Ryker, and there is nothing he won't do to get back the property he feels is his: both Ryker and the Stone of Destiny.

To end one evil, Zoey has to make a deal with another. The most powerful demon in the world, the unseelie *King*.

And it might be the deadliest decision of all.

Click here for the final book in the Collector Series:
http://bit.ly/2o29wGH

ACKNOWLEDGMENTS

Seven books in and the only reason I'm still standing is because of my amazing team. I am so lucky for the people helping me along this wonderful and crazy journey! A special thanks to:

- Jordan, your developmental help and editing are crucial to me. You constantly push me to be a better writer while giving me such encouraging positive notes. Thank you. http://jordanrosenfeld.net/
- Hollie, "the editor." Meeting you in person has only made me adore you more. You are incredible. Thank you for your endless support and love. http://www.hollietheeditor.com/.
- Judi at http://www.formatting4u.com/: As usual you have made the anxiety of getting my books out on time so much easier.
- As always to Mom for being there at every turn. There'd be no books without you!
- All the readers who have supported me: My gratitude is for all you do and how much you help indie authors out of the pure love of reading. I bow down. You all are amazing!
- My Street Team for being awesome and so supportive, thank you.
- To all the indie/hybrid authors out there who inspire, challenge, support, and push me to be better: I love you!
- And to anyone who has picked up an indie book and given an unknown author a chance.

THANKS TO ALL!

ABOUT THE AUTHOR

Stacey Marie Brown works by day as an interior/set designer and by night a writer of paranormal fantasy, adventure, and literary fiction. She grew up in Northern California, where she ran around on her family's farm raising animals, riding horses, playing flashlight tag, and turning hay bales into cool forts.

Even before she could write, she was creating stories and making up intricate fantasies. Writing came as easy as breathing. She later turned that passion into acting, living and traveling abroad, and designing.

Though she had never stopped writing, moving back to the States seemed to have brought it back to the forefront and this time it would not be ignored.

When she's not writing, she's out hiking, spending time with friends, traveling, listening to music, or designing.

To learn more about Stacey or her books, visit her at:

Author website & Newsletter: www.staceymariebrown.com

Facebook Author page: www.facebook.com/SMBauthorpage

Pinterest: www.pinterest.com/s.mariebrown

Instagram: www.instagram.com/staceymariebrown/

TikTok: www.tiktok.com/@staceymariebrown

Amazon page: www.amazon.com/Stacey-Marie-Brown/e/B00BFWHB9U

Goodreads:
www.goodreads.com/author/show/6938728.Stacey_Marie_Brown

Her **Facebook** **group:**
www.facebook.com/groups/1648368945376239/

Bookbub: www.bookbub.com/authors/stacey-marie-brown

Made in the USA
Monee, IL
07 February 2023